'I wish to understand...why did you agree to marry me?'

He was so big. And still seething with resentment. What could she say that would appease him? Her eyes lit on the Tudor roses embellishing his gown, and frantically she grasped at the one sure fact she knew about him. His loyalty to the King.

'The King asked it of me.' She risked a glance up at his face. She could feel his breath warm against her frigid cheek. He was looking at her mouth.

'Have you still not decided if I am your friend or your enemy?'

'I d...don't know!' she admitted. 'Part of me wants to trust you...but...'

When she looked up at him with those wide, innocent eyes, he wanted to...hell! She was not innocent! She was playing on her sensuality. 'I will tell you one thing you may depend on.' He straightened up, away from her. 'If you consider me your enemy, you will find me implacable. If our marriage is to be a battleground, there can only be one victor. And it will not be you!'

Dear Reader

I have enjoyed reading historical novels for as long as I can remember. History lessons can teach us the bare facts, but novels help us to imagine what it must have been like for ordinary people to live through the social and political upheavals of their day.

A friend lent me a marvellous story set during the American Civil War. It was called LORENA, by Eileen Townsend, and was published by Mills & Boon. I very soon discovered that they published stories each month that really 'hit the spot' for me, containing exactly the right blend of history, adventure and romance.

It is a dream come true for me to have a novel of my own published by Mills & Boon®, especially in this, their centenary year.

I hope you enjoy travelling back with me to what was a pivotal moment in England's history. Henry VII's accession to the throne brought an end to the Wars of the Roses. Lady Maddy and Sir Geraint are just one young couple trying to rebuild their lives on the rubble left by generations of conflict. It will take a miracle for them to succeed, given that they come from opposite sides of the political divide.

But isn't love the greatest miracle of them all?

Annie

MY LADY INNOCENT

Annie Burrows

MILLS & BOON®
Pure reading pleasure

First published in Great Britain 2007
Harlequin Mills & Boon Limited,
Eton House, 18-24 Paradise Road, Richmond, Surrey TW9 1SR

© Annie Burrows 2007

ISBN: 978 0 263 19783 9

Set in Times Roman 11¾ on 14 pt.
08-1207-85798

Printed and bound in Great Britain
by Antony Rowe Ltd, Chippenham, Wiltshire

Annie Burrows has been making up stories for her own amusement since she first went to school. As soon as she got the hang of using a pencil she began to write them down. Her love of books meant she had to do a degree in English literature. And her love of writing meant she could never take on a job where she didn't have time to jot down notes when inspiration for a new plot struck her. She still wants the heroines of her stories to wear beautiful floaty dresses, and triumph over all that life can throw at them. But when she got married she discovered that finding a hero is an essential ingredient to arriving at 'happy ever after'.

A recent novel by Annie Burrows:

HIS CINDERELLA BRIDE

Abi and Joe:
No mother could be more proud
than I am of you two.

Chapter One

'Hold!'

The man's voice, throbbing with a note of urgency, took Maddy by surprise. She had not thought anyone else from court would have been abroad so early. Looking over her shoulder, past the darkened wake her heavy skirts had trailed through the silvered meadow grasses, she saw a group of horsemen, the heads of their hounds bobbing above the heavy mists that spilled from Tyburn's bank.

And then Piers, sleepy Piers, who had done nothing but yawn and knuckle his eyes in mute protest at being pried from his warm bed before even the sun was properly up, let out a shriek and began to run for the trees. His gangling limbs flapped and his neck bobbed as he ran through the blue-green grasses, putting her in mind very forcibly of some long-legged waterfowl trying to get up enough speed to take flight from a body of water as he streaked past her. If it hadn't been for the persistent, angry shouting coming from the group of riders by the river, she would not have been able to tear her astonished gaze from the phenomenon. As it was, she reluctantly turned to see what all the commotion was about.

The men by the river were milling about in a hubbub of cursing and neighing and baying of hounds, shattering the previously frozen stillness of the dawn. Apparently, the dogs were not very well trained. Else why would the kennel men be having such trouble whipping the pack into some semblance of order?

It couldn't be because they had seen Piers run, and were straining to chase after him, could it? The chill that had so far failed to seep through her dew-drenched skirts now numbed her legs, freezing them to the spot, as she noted the powerful shoulders and blunt-nosed faces of the massive dogs. They couldn't be the King's alaunts, those massive hounds, bred for their aggression, then trained to bait bears, or bulls.

Her breath hitched in her throat as she saw two of the hounds break free from their handlers and bound straight towards her.

She willed her legs to move, to run, but all that happened was that her fingers clenched more tightly round the handle of the gardening trug she was carrying. Her horrified gaze fixed on two sets of open jaws, filled with enormous pointed fangs before she shut her eyes entirely, flinching as she felt two large bodies skimming past her skirts. They had bounded straight past her! They must have had their sights set on the fleeing pageboy!

A whimper escaped her throat as she let out the breath she hadn't realised she had been holding. Then she opened her eyes just a fraction, to see if she had truly survived.

The mist seemed to have grown thicker. She felt as though she were drowning in it, its chill seeping into her very bones. She drew her arms to her chest, instinctively trying to warm herself by wrapping them round her body. Just as she felt her trembling legs crumple beneath her, a third hound came leaping out of the mist at her. The wind was knocked from her lungs as they went down together. The dog's paws ground into her shoulders as its powerful jaws clamped on to the trug, which she'd instinctively used to shield her throat. She didn't need to be a genius to know that once the alaunt had crunched her little wooden shield to matchwood, those fangs would sink into her neck, reducing it to so much mangled pulp.

The life-or-death tug-of-war over the trug went on for what seemed like an eternity, and yet still far too short a time, until there was nothing left of it but its flimsy willow handle. The dog paused before launching its final onslaught. As Maddy stared up, transfixed in horror at a great dollop of drool that was slowly spilling from the beast's quivering red maw, she became chillingly aware that these were her last moments.

She could hear her heart swooshing her life's blood through her ears, feel the frost melting through her cloak and mingling with the sweat of rank fear that beaded her spine. She could smell the alaunt's hot pungent breath. Could almost feel those bared teeth sinking into her throat, severing arteries and tearing muscle. The dog drew back its lips in a menacing growl.

The drool splashed warmly on to her exposed throat.

Then, for Maddy, the darkness fell.

Sir Geraint Davies pulled Caligula's head round savagely, and kicked his heels against his flanks, urging the destrier into the ponderous gait that passed for a gallop, though he knew it was too late to do anything for the girl. He could only thank God it had been over so quickly. She barely had time to register her danger before the hound's massive jaws had closed round her throat. He'd heard tales of the treacherous brutes turning on their own masters, even slaying them, but never had he thought to witness such an appalling sight.

Frobisher had beaten him to the motionless heap of rags, grabbing the alaunt by its thick studded collar and dragging it off its kill before he could even fling himself from his saddle.

He dropped to his knees, reaching down to touch the body that lay in its nest of crushed grasses, though what he thought he could do at this stage… He shook his head, his face grim, recalling the attack in vivid detail. Once he'd brought the girl down, the dog had done what it was trained to do. Fastened its teeth in her throat and shaken her, like a terrier would shake a rat, until all signs of life ceased.

He reached out a hand that was not quite steady to close the girl's eyes, which still stared sightlessly at the sky. She'd had lovely eyes, he thought sadly. Wide and dark, set in a little round face above the tiniest nose. Her lips were bloodless now, but they were exquisite, too. The upper exactly as full as the lower. He traced the outline of

that perfect mouth with his forefinger. What a waste that she had
died before any man had a chance to taste its promise!

He snatched it back with an oath when the lips parted on a rasp
of indrawn breath. Her glazed eyes flickered, then swivelled help-
lessly towards him.

My God! She lived still!

For the first time he forced himself to look directly at the wounds
the dog had inflicted on her, frowning when he saw the brown pulp
covering her throat and upper chest. There did not appear to be much
bleeding. His heartbeat racing, he began to scrape it all away, determined to ascertain the extent of her injuries, and if it were, by
some miraculous means, possible to staunch her wounds…

He straddled her prone body, intent now only on speed, his gaze
fixed on the slender curve of her neck as he scrabbled away the remains
of what appeared to have been something wooden, cursing again, in
heartfelt relief, when he got down to the white, unbroken skin. The neck
of her gown was torn, revealing one plump white shoulder and the
upper curve of her breast, scored with three livid red weals. As he ripped
the fabric further, desperate to assess how much damage the dog's
claws had done her, her hands fluttered up ineffectually against his.

'This is no time for false modesty, you foolish wench!' Anxiety
for her well-being had him slapping her hands aside rather more
forcefully than was necessary. While she lived, if there was any
bleeding at all, if he could only find it and stem it quickly enough…

He shut his ears to her shakily voiced protests, ruthlessly pushing
aside the soft folds of cloth tangled round her arms and upper body.
He could not believe she had managed to escape unscathed from the
ferocious attack he had witnessed. Yet no matter how diligently he
searched, he could find nothing beyond that one set of claw marks
where the dog's heavy paws had torn through her threadbare gown.
He leant forward, his fingers poised to examine those marks,
needing to reassure himself that they had not broken the milky white
skin…only to jerk upright in surprise when the girl delivered a
stinging slap to his face.

'Sto…op!' she croaked. Then rather more coherently, after swallowing convulsively, 'Stop mauling me, you great oaf!'

Sir Geraint froze in disbelief. What did the silly girl think he was about? Assaulting her? Didn't she know how close she'd just come to meeting her Maker? Couldn't she see that his heart had been in his mouth with the shock of thinking he'd just watched one of King Henry's fighting dogs kill an innocent little girl?

His chest heaved with indignation. As he ran his eyes one last time over the claw marks that scored a distinctly womanly breast, his brows knit in a scowl. It was only her diminutive stature that had deceived him into thinking she was a little girl. Probably no innocent either, or she would not have been out here at this hour, making for the seclusion of the forest with that gangling youth. As his lip curled with scorn, the girl's own mouth firmed.

This time, when she went to slap him, he was too quick for her. Seizing both her wrists, he pinned them above her head, glaring with increasing ire as she began to struggle in earnest. Though her back arched off the ground, a testimony to the fact she was exerting all her strength, all he had to do was clamp his powerful thighs more firmly on either side of her hips. It didn't take her long to understand that she would go nowhere until he granted her leave. By the time she stilled beneath him, colour had flooded back to her cheeks. And to her lips, which, pinkly panting, revealed pearly white teeth and the soft moist recesses of the most kissable mouth he had ever clapped eyes on. He would only have to lower his head an inch or so…

For a timeless second, their eyes met and held, his already dark with conflicting emotions, hers widening, softening. Yielding.

As she had been about to yield to that gangling youth in the shelter of the trees, no doubt. Disgust flooded him that at her tender age, she was already so experienced in the art of seduction.

'Oaf, am I?' He pushed himself to his feet, yanking her up with him as he stood.

'Better than being an empty-headed little trollop, I'd say!'

That temptingly kissable mouth dropped open in astonishment in the same moment her rumpled kerchief slipped slightly backwards. Sir Geraint now had to tamp down not only his desire to kiss the girl senseless in full view of all the kennel men, but also the urge to fling the scrap of linen to the ground and run his fingers through the lustrous mass of ebony silk that would tumble round her shoulders. Instead of doing either, he took those shoulders in his hands, giving the girl a little shake as he nodded in the direction of the forest.

'Don't play the innocent with me! Stupid you may be,' he mocked. 'God knows you must be to make the meadow where his Grace's alaunts are exercised your trysting place.'

Trysting place? Did this great bear of a man think she had come down here at dawn to tryst with, of all people, Piers? No wonder he had treated her thus far with such a lack of respect. She looked up past a great expanse of leathern-clad chest to peer into the face of the mountain of muscle that held her in its great rough paws. So far she had been too dazed to take in more than the fact that he was enormous, and angry, and strong. But now she registered a face sporting a russet growth of what looked like several days' growth of beard, and a pair of stormy grey eyes glaring down at her from beneath a shock of shaggy chestnut curls.

When she remained mute, he shook her again. 'Don't you realise how dangerous these dogs are, you foolish wench?'

His gesture put her in mind of the day she'd almost fallen from the top of the watchtower. She'd been leaning over the parapet in an attempt to discern her brother Gregory amongst the cavalcade that was wending its way over the moors and off to do battle with some disloyal noble whose name she'd never learned. William, her next oldest brother, had grabbed her by the scruff of the neck, and shaken her just like this.

'That's why Frobisher exercises them at dawn, in these meadows, where nobody with an ounce of sense would dream of setting foot. Everyone knows how dangerous it is to trespass here!'

'Everyone knows?' she echoed faintly. There was a peculiar

rushing noise in her ears. Piers had surely not known. Or he would not have followed her. He would not have willingly put himself in danger, certainly not on her account. She shook her head. Not that she had told him where she was going, only that she had no intention of going alone, and that if he did not want a particular piece of information which she held from getting back to a certain lady, then he would escort her.

She'd felt ashamed of stooping to that level, but honestly, what choice had she had? If she had just gone to Piers, or any other of the pages who were theoretically there to assist her, and politely asked if he wouldn't mind getting up before dawn and walking to the forest with her, he would have laughed her to scorn. The one thing she'd learned during the few months she'd been living amongst Princess Elizabeth's ladies was that nobody did anything for anyone else, without a substantial motive.

She shuddered. From the first moment she'd entered the dark maze that was the Palace of Westminster, she'd been aware of a creeping sense of malice drifting along its corridors, like noxious miasma rising from some pit of corruption.

It must have finally infected her. In spite of trying to avoid the nobles who'd come pouring into Henry Tudor's new court with their elbows out, jostling for preferment, she had become just like them.

She had just been so excited at the prospect of escaping the stuffy room she shared with five other ladies of good birth to breathe air that did not reek of stale perfume, and listen to sweet birdsong instead of rancid gossip—above all, to be free, for at least an hour, from Lady Lacey's constant sniping—that she'd adopted the same cruel, manipulative behaviour she'd condemned in others.

Well, she had paid for it. But had poor Piers? She tried to turn from the scolding bear's rough grip to look towards the forest. She could see the two great dogs that had decided against breakfasting on her hurling themselves repeatedly against the trunk of a gnarled oak tree. A man with a leashed hound at his side was trotting towards them, clearly intent on calling them off. She supposed Piers must have got safely up the tree.

The bear, who had not slackened his hold on her one whit, shook her again.

'What on earth possessed you? What were you thinking of?'

Maddy blinked. She hadn't stopped to think at all. She'd only wanted to whoop with joy as she'd slipped the bolt on the heavy door that led from the ladies' quarters where she'd been virtually confined since her arrival at court. After all, thanks to Lady Lacey's sudden whim to have a bowl of freshly dug crocuses, she had a legitimate excuse to get outside! It had been all she could do not to skip across the courtyard where Piers had been lounging against the wall, arms folded across his chest. But at sixteen, as Lady Lacey persistently reminded her, she was a lady grown, and, as such, must behave with decorum. So she had forced her feet to behave, and content herself with returning a sweet smile to every one of Piers's scowls.

It had felt wonderful to escape the atmosphere of suspicion that surrounded her. Out here, there was nobody to watch her every move, or question her motives.

But now she came to think of it, why would her cousin have sent her to pick a bunch of crocuses from the forest at dawn? It was almost as if she had deliberately sent her into danger! But that notion was unthinkable! Too horrible to contemplate. Yet if everyone knew about the alaunts…

Sir Geraint swore under his breath as the girl turned white and swayed as though her bones were turning to water, his anger dissipating like the breath that briefly hung in gossamer wisps on the wintry air. She sagged against his chest, her head lolling back. He caught her before she could crumple to the ground, sweeping her up into his arms where she lay limp and unresisting, her brown eyes glazed with shock.

Her kerchief finally lost the battle against the weight of her hair, fluttering to the ground, so that the ebony mass spilled over his arm like a silken banner almost to his knees. Clasped close to his heart, he could feel every feminine curve of her body through her clothes, though she weighed next to nothing. She looked so small and helpless in the cradle of his arms. An unfamiliar desire to shield this delicate, beautiful creature from all the ugliness and brutality that stalked the world began to stir within him.

She moaned softly, her eyes fixed on his face in mute appeal.

'Your clothes are soaked,' he managed to say after several moments of intense silence. 'I should get you back to the palace, so that you can get dry. You do come from the palace, I take it?'

Her eyes filled with tears as she nodded, biting on her lower lip, which was trembling now. Damn it. Now she was going to cry. As if melting and swooning had not been enough, she had to demonstrate that she had tears too in her repertoire to tug at his heartstrings!

He turned abruptly to where Caligula stood, disdainfully ignoring the humans who were milling about him. Flinging her up into the saddle first, and steadying her with one hand in the small of her back, he swung up behind. With an aggressive snort, Caligula turned, snapping his teeth at the unfamiliar feel of skirts flapping against his flank. To his great surprise, the girl laughed as she nimbly tucked her feet up out of the irritated destrier's reach.

'It seems to be my destiny to be bitten by at least one of your creatures this morning, sir!'

Admiration for this brave sally swept his irritation aside, especially since he could feel the tremors racking her compact little body. She had stared death in the face, yet instead of giving way to the hysteria that might be expected of a female, she was valiantly trying to conceal her fear behind a jest!

'You are chilled to the marrow,' he observed, arranging his fur-lined cloak around her and tucking her close into the warmth of his own body. This time she did not protest at his manhandling. On the contrary, as he wrapped one arm about her, she wound both of hers about his waist, clinging tightly as she curled up against him.

'Caligula won't bite you,' he said, yanking on the reins to pull the destrier's head up. 'He's just expressing his displeasure at being mounted by a lady, when he knows he deserves to be ridden only by a knight in full armour.'

'Caligula is a warhorse?' She peeped up at him, all huge brown eyes in a girlishly innocent little face.

One side of his mouth twitched in acknowledgement of her change of tactics. Lying flat on her back beneath him, she had, after a token resistance, acknowledged the attraction that had instantly sparked between them. Now she wanted to place him. If she could ascertain his rank, his wealth, she would then be able to decide whether he would be worth ditching the lanky pageboy for. If he told her he was a knight, he had no doubt she would encourage him to speak about his exploits, so that she could sigh and tell him how brave he was. How grateful she was that he had come to rescue her from the nasty dog. Drop hints that she was willing to express her gratitude at some future date.

He looked away from her, keeping his eyes fixed between Caligula's ears as though he needed to concentrate on the way back to the palace. He did not need to look at her again to ascertain her place in the scheme of things. No well-born woman would be out here at this hour of the morning, leave alone with only the company of a youth who had thought more of saving his own spotty hide than standing to defend his lady love. Besides, he had felt how flimsy her gown was with wear, seen how serviceable the well-worn leather boots that covered her dainty little feet were. But he was damned if he would yield so swiftly to her all-too-transparent attempt to discover if he was a person worth cultivating! If all she cared about was climbing the social ladder, then he would soon find out!

'He was,' he said with what he hoped was an air of complete in-nocence. 'Caligula's fighting days are over.' Let her make of that what she would! He glanced down at her. 'He has served his master well, but now he must adapt to a different lifestyle.'

Would she express chagrin if he let her assume he was just a stable hand, exercising some other gentleman's tired old nag that had been lingering half-forgotten in the stables?

Maddy felt his body tense under her arms, though his face remained impassive. It was as if he was not talking about just the horse. She wondered if the master he referred to had been Richard Duke of Gloucester. There were plenty of men about the court who had once been his followers, who were now seeking to ingratiate themselves with the new King, Henry Tudor.

Frowning, she pushed the thought away. She was in no fit state to try to engage in these courtly word games, where a man said one thing, expecting you to understand that he meant something else entirely. She leaned her head wearily against the man's leather jerkin, listening to the tone of his voice rumbling through his chest. She liked the sound of it. The lilt that was almost musical, now that he wasn't shouting at her any more.

He had scared her, she had to admit, almost as much as that killer dog had, when he'd been so adamant about rummaging beneath her clothes. It had taken her a while to overcome her panic, and realise he must only be trying to find out if the dog had actually managed to bite her anywhere, and simply yield to the indignity of having his hands explore where they would. Yet now his hand upon her back was gentle, running up and down her spine in a way that was incredibly comforting, as well as warming.

She filled her nostrils with the honest scent of his leather jerkin and let her eyes drift shut. The last time she'd been held like this, she had been a very little girl. Her nurse, Marjory, had died, and her father had decreed she must go to live with her mother's cousin, Lady Lacey, for it was unsuitable to raise her in a household of men. And William had done his best to comfort her, rocking her in his arms when she had curled into a ball of misery at the prospect of banishment, even as she was now being rocked by the long gait of this bony old destrier, cradled against this stranger's chest. He had smelled almost exactly like this, too, a mixture of leather, and horse, and sunshine, for he was a man who spent most of his days in the stables and the kennels and the tilting yard.

'What is your name, foolish wench?'

The sting had gone from his voice, though her bear had employed the same insult as before. Her brothers had used a tone like that, she sighed, proclaiming her a nuisance when she trailed after them, though they would never have let any harm come to her.

'Maddy,' she said, surprising herself. She had not been Maddy for so many years. From the moment she set foot in Lacey Manor, she'd been forced to deny everything she had ever thought she was. Firstly, Baron Lacey had declared it was a mistake to name a girl for Margaret, the She-Wolf of Anjou, that strong-willed Queen who had ruled over her husband Henry. He could not comprehend, he had bawled, why her father had permitted her mother to name her, even if she was only a girl. As long as she lived under his roof, she would answer to the name of Lady Agnes, and apply herself to emulating that saint who was the pattern of all the feminine virtues.

She knew, of course, for Marjory had explained to her, that it had cost her father nothing to indulge his wife's dying wishes. She had presented him with four strapping sons, so what did it matter if a mere daughter was saddled with an unfortunate name? It had been her bookish brother Stephen who had come up with a way of addressing her that offended nobody. Taking the initial letters of her full name, Lady Margaret Agnes DelaBoys, he teasingly referred to her as their little MADy, and her other brothers followed suit. She grew up thinking of herself as Maddy. The Lady Agnes was an appellation Baron Lacey had insisted she don, which felt like covering her true self, rather like putting on stiff, uncomfortable clothes for Sunday best.

So why had she confided her true identity, exposed her deepest self, to this stranger? She shivered, and, as she did so, he pulled her tighter into his great warm body. And then she knew. He made her feel as she had not done since she had been a child. The dog's attack had ripped away not only her gown, but all the manners and behaviour that she had painstakingly built up, layer upon layer, to protect herself over the years. Cradled in this man's lap, she now felt both as small and helpless, and yet as secure as she had not done since she had bidden farewell for the last time to her brothers. Though he had scolded and shaken her as they would have done, he had then adopted a teasing manner, demonstrating that his anger had been born of concern. How could she have been anything other than her true self in his arms when he even smelled like her brothers?

'Come, then, Maddy,' he said. 'You must let go of me now.'

She looked up to see that he was grinning down at her, with the sort of wholly masculine superiority that she most detested. It was like being doused with a bucket of icy water, rousing her from that dreamy state where she had wilfully shut out reality. He was not her brother, nor was he to be trusted. He was a stranger. A man whose station in life she was not even sure of, in whose eyes she could now read not brotherly concern, but a smouldering heat.

And then, to set the seal on her humiliation, she became aware that they were standing in the very midst of a busy stable yard. A hammer clanged against an anvil somewhere close by. She could hear grooms shouting, horses whinnying…and when the man she still clasped about the waist saw her confusion, his smile grew even cockier.

Shame flooded her as she realised what a disgraceful figure she was making of herself. She was bareheaded, clasped in the arms of a complete stranger, with her gown all soiled and torn…and worse, not only was this stranger clasping her, but she was clinging to him like a limpet!

'Well, Maddy…' the stranger began, leaning back as though he were about to dismount.

Maddy seized her chance. Without waiting to hear what he had been about to say, she wriggled out of his slackened hold, slithered down from the saddle, and hit the cobbles running.

Chapter Two

Sir Geraint dismounted and handed his reins over to a hovering groom as though there were nothing in the least unusual about having a young woman leap from the back of his horse and flee into the milling throng. Though he couldn't help wondering what had possessed the girl to run from him like that.

Whatever had prompted that mad dash into the crowds, he would stake his last groat it was not any kind of loyalty to that cowardly youth. Though, he rubbed at his unshaven chin pensively, in a way the lad's cowardice had probably saved her from anything worse than a tumble into the wet grass and a nasty gash. The first hounds to break from the pack had enjoyed chasing him too much to bother with her. She had been petrified, thank God and all his angels. If she had run, the pair of alaunts would have split up, pursuing one target each. In skirts, Maddy would have been brought down long before she reached the comparative safety of the trees. A chill slid down his spine. It had been bad enough when the third dog had reached her.

His hand strayed downward, to his neck, though his fingers felt not his own throat, but the soft white skin of a girl who had been lying still as a corpse.

A scurrying stable lad jostled his arm, and he moved from the centre of the yard to lean against one of the massive pillars that supported a covered walkway leading up to the palace proper. He must assume Maddy had run this way, though he could not swear to it. She had just darted into the crowd, and, like some kind of sprite, vanished into the sea of bodies.

His lips curved into a lazy smile as he reached a decision. He was going to track down his little sprite, and persuade her to forget all about the pageboy. He would even confess his rank, if that was what it would take to get her into his bed. He could not now even remember why he had been reluctant to apply that weapon against her, so heated was his blood at the remembered feel of her lithe little body curled up against him on Caligula's back. By heaven, he had never dreamed that a horse ride could be so erotically charged. It was as though she had wanted to burrow right into him. At first he had put down her sensuous little wriggles to the fact she was cold, and, of course, still frightened. But when she'd begun to rub her cheek against his chest like a kitten, breathing him in, it had been all he could do to hold his own body in check. She'd got him so hard by the time they reached the yard that he could scarce dismount, never mind give chase!

He shook his head, his smile growing broader. He had no idea what game Maddy was playing with him, winding him up, then running away, but he no longer cared. Whatever game she was playing was fine by him. He had nothing better to do with his time than chase serving wenches, now that Henry Tudor had become King. Maddy had better watch out!

Maddy wished she had been watching out when, for the second time that day, all the breath was knocked from her lungs, this time upon running full tilt into a tall, velvet-clad male. But the corridor had been so dark after the bustling brightness of the stable yard. Besides, her mind had been preoccupied with the dread of having to give account to Lady Lacey for the torn gown and lost kerchief, never mind what she would say if she ever heard about the brazen way she had come riding back to the palace, with her hair all uncovered, nestled into the arms of a perfect stranger like a—well, even he had called her a trollop!

'Oof!' she gasped, as she bounced off the solid form of a perfumed courtier.

'Watch where you're going, you little—' Then two strong hands closed round her upper arms as she staggered back.

'Lady Agnes?' The harsh voice gentled, but the grip upon her arms remained firm. 'My dear girl…'

Maddy's heart sank as she recognised the voice of Lord Hugo de Vere. Elegant, handsome, witty Lord Hugo. She felt her cheeks heat, and her tongue dry up in agonised self-awareness as he ran his periwinkle-blue gaze over her in that slightly mocking way he had.

'Whatever can have happened to cause you to appear in such… disarray?'

His aristocratic nostrils flared briefly before he added, 'You have been to the stables.'

Oh, why, of all people, did she have to run into him? Lord Hugo, as ever, was immaculately garbed in a doublet of sapphire that both mirrored and enhanced the colour of his eyes. Falling to his knees, the front was pleated to create the currently fashionable bow shape, while the slashed sleeves revealed the sumptuous silk of his pristine white shirt. His lozenge-shaped hat, of the same blue velvet as his doublet, sported a bushy white plume that bobbed jauntily like a squirrel's tail. Whereas she looked as though she had been dragged through a hedge backwards. Her hair straggled all over her face, her gown was wet and grass stained behind, and ripped and liberally sprayed with drying dog drool in front.

'M…my lord, I…I…' She bunched her fists in her cloak as, suddenly horribly conscious of the tear in her gown, she dragged it fast closed about her neck. First, 'Oof!' and now this! She had the undivided attention of one of the wittiest, most charming men to embellish King Henry's court, and all she could do was stammer and blush!

However, he merely held out his arm with a courtly bow, saying, 'Permit me to escort you back to the safety of your gentle guardian's care.'

Feeling thoroughly chastised by both his words and his gesture, she placed her hand on the proffered arm and meekly followed his lead. Her discomfort only increased when a group of nobles caught sight of them, and could not contain their amazement. What could a gaudy peacock like Lord Hugo possibly be doing with a little brown dab of a nonentity like her on his arm?

'You had best hold up your head, my lady,' Lord Hugo said rather sharply, 'else those vulgar gawpers will think you have done something to be ashamed of, whereas…'

He looked down, raising his eyebrows in query, and her heart skipped a beat. He looked so calm and unruffled, his remarks were so studied and mocking, but deep down he was eaten up with curiosity! She, plain, quiet little Lady Agnes, had finally done something that had piqued his interest.

For weeks she had been vainly fighting the feelings this man aroused in her. Knowing he was too popular with the more beautiful, experienced court ladies to ever be likely to look at her romantically she had done all she could to staunch her growing infatuation. She told herself sternly that she would only make a fool of herself if she openly sighed, and gazed after him like a mooncalf.

But even knowing her case was hopeless, she could not quite break free of the fascination he exerted over her. For out of all the court gallants intent on furthering their own ambitions, he was the only one who took time to acknowledge her presence, whenever he sought out Lady Lacey's company, even though openly associating with a traitor's daughter could do his reputation no good at all.

And now, so interested was he in where she had been and what she had been doing that he was actually patting the grubby hand that rested on the rich sapphire velvet of his sleeve. As she looked down at the hand that covered hers, she felt something like a draught of sweet heady wine go surging through her veins.

'I was attacked by a dog,' she sighed.

She felt his arm tense beneath her hand, and looked up. 'In the stables? There is a dangerous dog loose in the stables?'

'N…no. It was in the meadows beyond the palace grounds. On the other side of the Tyburn.'

'Where Frobisher exercises his alaunts?' Lord Hugo frowned. 'May I ask—not that I have any right to question your movements—what you were doing so far from the safety of your quarters, at this hour of the day?'

There was an accusing edge to his voice, now, that made Maddy bristle. The other man, the oaf, he'd assumed that she had been pursuing a flirtation as well. It was the first thing men thought of! She felt so insulted that, for a moment or two, she did not know how to answer him.

She'd always wanted him to think well of her.

But, oh, how dared he jump to such conclusions about her!

She lifted her chin. 'No, you do not have the right to question my movements. Or to assume that I—'

His eyes turned wintry. She went cold. How could she have had the impudence to speak so sharply?

Though she sniffed hard, she could not stop the hot tears that began to flow down her cheeks. Now he would never think of her as anything more than a foolish child. There was nothing for it but to remove her grubby hand from Lord Hugo's expensive sleeve, and swipe them away, while he stood, remote and silent, over her. A sob broke from her throat as she bade farewell to her last hope of ever impressing the most elegant, sophisticated man she had ever met.

To her surprise, as she began to back away before she broke down and disgraced herself completely, he took her by her shoulders, and swung her round into the lee of a stone pillar, screening her from the walkway with his own body.

'Nay…do not weep, my lady. We cannot have that pretty face all blotched with tears, now can we?'

Pretty? Her head flew up to stare at him in stunned disbelief. He could not think her face was pretty. It was decidedly round, to begin with, rather than the oval shape that men classed as beautiful.

He smiled ruefully at her arrested expression. 'And what will become of my reputation? What will be said about this little scene? That Lord Hugo de Vere is the kind of man who reduces ladies to tears in a public place?' He smote his breast theatrically. 'Have mercy on me, my lady!'

Maddy's innate common sense reasserted itself with a vengeance. Of course he did not find her pretty. The only reason he had said that was to tease her out of this bout of crying, which was evidently embarrassing him. Blotting her tears with one of the only dry patches she could find on her cloak, she lifted her chin, and attempted a watery smile.

'Bravo.' He chucked her under the chin. 'I could not possibly return you to the lovely Lady Lacey as you were, and risk having her think I was bullying her ward.'

She heaved a ragged sigh. Why must every act of kindness have an ulterior motive? Why could he not simply want to comfort her?

And how come he had known that those monstrous alaunts exercised in the meadows? She frowned. Everyone knew, that kennel man had said.

Everyone.

No, she breathed, that could not be right. Lady Lacey could not have known, or she would never have sent her there. She may be somewhat short-tempered, occasionally spiteful, but she would never deliberately expose her ward to danger. Why should she? Why should any lady know anything about the daily routine of the kennels? When Lord Hugo, and that oaf who had bundled her on to his horse, said everyone knew, they just meant every man.

Yes! For men had a little world of their own, an existence totally separate from, and deliberately excluding, women. What was common knowledge in their world was not common knowledge to ladies.

'There is no need to weep any more,' he said, raising one of her hands to his mouth and gently pressing his full lips to the back of it. Dazed, she blinked up into his handsome face. His lids drooped fractionally over those compelling blue eyes as he edged a little closer.

'Let me put some heart back into you,' he said, tucking her other hand into his chest as he bent over her.

If she didn't know better, she would think Lord Hugo meant to kiss her! But he couldn't, he wouldn't. So why had he placed his finger under her chin? Why was he tilting her face to such an angle?

Thinking she glimpsed a flash of pity in his eyes, just before his mouth closed over hers, she firmly shut her own eyes against it. She did not want to be reminded that this was just his way of being kind to a poor little creature whose heart fluttered wildly whenever he walked into the room.

Yet a smile spread through her whole being as his mouth gently grazed at her lips, and her breath rushed from her lungs in a rapturous sigh. When he withdrew, all too quickly, she remained standing with her eyes closed, head tilted back, basking in the moment—till she heard Lord Hugo chuckle softly. With a moan of chagrin, she drooped her forehead against his chest. Even though he stroked her hair soothingly, her brief moment of rapture was shattered. Her first kiss, and she had made a fool of herself! Standing there with her eyes closed, and that absurd smile on her face!

When he took her hand and placed it back on his sleeve, she stumbled along beside him, feeling like a complete ninny.

Only when she saw the familiar clutter of baskets of thread, the tables heaped with fine linens waiting to be embroidered, and smelled the clean scent of new cloth, did she come back to reality. This was her domain, amongst the seamstresses who tended Princess Elizabeth's wardrobe. Her hours at court were spent weaving ribbons to decorate clothes the like of which would never grace her own back. But she dared not complain that such a menial position was an insult to one of her birth. When she and Lady Lacey had fled to Elizabeth Woodville's sanctuary at the Abbey of Westminster, penniless, landless, and bereft of male protectors, she had been met with suspicion. Lady Lacey, on the other hand, with her rapier wit, and a late husband who had had his lands seized by King Richard, had quickly secured a position as a lady in waiting to the young

Princess Elizabeth. Now Maddy was simply grateful that she was being housed and fed at all.

Her eyes went automatically to the stool by the ribbon loom that was tucked into an unimportant corner of the light, airy room, well out of everyone's way.

And she gasped at the unprecedented sight of Lady Lacey herself, rising from her stool, her eyes darting angrily from herself to Lord Hugo, whose arm she was still clutching for support.

All the chatter ceased as everyone registered first her bedraggled appearance, then Lord Hugo, lounging in the doorway beside her, then Lady Lacey's furious advance on her cringing ward.

'Lady Lacey,' Lord Hugo said, pushing her before him into the suddenly silent room, 'permit me to return your ward, whom I found without in a somewhat distressed state, after having been attacked by…a large dog.'

Maddy became aware of several things at the same time. One was that most of the other seamstresses did not believe a word he said, judging from the sniggers and knowing looks being cast her way. Another was the feeling that Lord Hugo had sent Lady Lacey a message, hidden in the subtext of the words he had used. And the last, but by far the most unsettling, was recognising the fleeting trace of guilt that swept Lady Lacey's features before she quite managed to mask it with an expression of bewildered concern.

'A dog?' Lady Lacey produced a nervous little laugh. 'How absurd. Lady Agnes is well used to dogs. How can she have been attacked?'

'The dog that attacked my Lady Agnes was one of the King's alaunts.' Lord Hugo's voice was suddenly harsh.

A collective gasp rippled amongst all the other ladies, bar Lady Lacey, whose mouth merely tightened as she kept her eyes fixed on Lord Hugo. Prudence, who had served as seamstress to royalty all her thirty years, made a move towards Maddy, making the clucking noise of the mother hen she considered herself to all those, of whatever rank, who worked alongside her.

Lady Lacey waved her back with an impatient gesture of her elegantly shaped white hand.

'How came you to be wandering so far from the palace, you stupid girl?' she hissed at Maddy.

'B…but you sent me—'

Before Maddy could utter another word, Lady Lacey flew across the room and delivered such a resounding blow to the side of her head that she went reeling backwards, cannoning into a table and sending baskets of seed pearls and rolls of ivory thread spooling across the flagged floor.

'Is there no end to your stupidity?' Lady Lacey wailed. 'Why would I send you out to the meadows beyond the safety of the palace walls? If you must take it into your head to wander off, without telling me where you are going, at least have the intelligence to come up with a better lie than that one!' Her voice had risen so high she was positively screeching, her reddened face thrust angrily forwards as Maddy half-lay across the table, her hand rubbing at her battered ear. 'Do you think of nobody but yourself? While you have been getting into heaven knows what mischief, I have been beside myself with worry at your disappearance. Have I not?' She straightened then, appealing to the other women who had gathered round, their own duties forgotten in the face of such excitement. Most nodded, many of them looking at Maddy with open disapproval.

She hung her head, the hand she held to her ear helping to cover her face. The ringing in her ears now had less to do with the force of the blow Lady Lacey had just administered, than the horrible certainty that what had happened earlier had been no accident. The woman had deliberately exposed her to danger.

She had made sure nobody had been near the previous night to hear the order to leave the palace before first light so that she might reach the forest at the exact time those dogs would be running loose. And she had been pretending to seek her, as though she did not know exactly where she was.

'Oh, it is too much!' Lady Lacey protested. 'You cannot conceive what a burden it is to have to ceaselessly watch over such a foolish girl as this…this lackwit!'

She sank down on to Maddy's stool, weeping most prettily. The blue of her eyes grew lustrous as enormous tears dripped like diamonds on to the backs of her hands that she clasped tragically on her lap. Her nose did not run at all, neither did her cheeks go blotchy. Lord Hugo hastened to her side, dropping to his knees at her feet, dabbing at the jewel-bright tears with a silken handkerchief, which he had produced with a flourish from a hidden pocket of his doublet.

The picture of a beleaguered guardian was complete. She had the sympathy of every person in the room. If Maddy were to stand up now and tell them the truth, they would all assume she was just concocting a wild tale to avoid the punishment her apparently wilful behaviour deserved.

But why should Lady Lacey want to harm her? They were kin!

Though Richard Duke of Gloucester had been both uncle and guardian to the two little princes who had disappeared from the tower. Everyone knew he had callously disposed of them because they stood in his way.

She shook her head. No, that was an entirely different case. A man might commit such a heinous crime as murder to win a throne for himself. But Lady Lacey had nothing to gain from her death. Unless… What if someone else was using her as a tool? It was an unpalatable truth that the noble families of England strove constantly for power, sacrificing smaller pawns in the interests of long-term gain. What if she had somehow become such a pawn in one of these power struggles? Could someone have promised Lady Lacey lands, or financial security, or even a beneficial marriage? For such inducements, the self-centred woman might well agree to dispose of a troublesome ward for whom she had never much cared. Especially if she could do it without dirtying her fair hands.

But why? Why? Who could possibly gain anything from her death? That was what made no sense. She had nothing. Though she lived in the palace, she was virtually a pauper, dependent totally on the young Queen's largesse. Why should some nameless, faceless person…? Her heart began to pound so hard she felt as though it were about to burst through her ribs. She had never felt so alone, so utterly alone, in her life. Not when her nurse had died, not when she had been thrust into the hostile environment of Lacey Manor, not even when she had heard that the last of her brothers and her father had been slain on Bosworth field had she felt as isolated as this. For now she had an enemy. A secret enemy who harboured malice against her, and there was nobody she could turn to, nobody who would even believe it.

She looked wildly about the room. Who here could she count as friend? Which of them might be in league with her secret foe? Menace seemed to hover all round her, waiting to pounce and snuff out her very existence. She felt as though rivers of ice were sluicing through her veins. Wrapping her arms round her waist, Maddy did not know that, in her all-consuming fear, she had begun to rock herself back and forth.

Prudence went to Lady Lacey, suggesting diffidently, 'Young Lady Agnes should perhaps retire to her chamber and change out of her wet clothes before she takes a chill.'

All eyes were drawn to the pathetic figure crouched beside the overturned table, shivering as she rocked herself.

'She just would, too!' Lady Lacey said waspishly as she got to her feet. 'On purpose to add to my worries!'

From nowhere, it seemed to Maddy, as Lady Lacey stalked towards her, a scene from her early childhood sprang to her mind. She had crept to the tiltyard, to watch her father and brothers at their training. Now his voice came to her mind, echoing down the years.

'A skilful warrior,' he had bawled at Henry, her eldest brother, where he lay on his back, pinned to the ground by the sword being held to his throat, 'can still win even when he seems to be over-whelmed by superior strength. His most efficient weapon will always be his brain. Never surrender. Utilise every weapon at your disposal. Think, boy, think!'

And Henry had grabbed a handful of the dirt on which he lay, flinging it into the face of the sergeant at arms who stood over him.

The man had recoiled, swiping at his smarting eyes, and in that split second Henry, lithe as a cat, had leapt to his feet and stabbed at his opponent's back with his wooden practice sword.

She might be alone against an unknown foe, but the plot to destroy her had failed. She yet lived. And now she knew she was a target. She must not squander that advantage!

She saw the pitying faces turned to Lady Lacey, the exasperation directed at her, and knew she had another weapon at her disposal. Lady Lacey berated her for her foolishness ten times a day. In a setting where anyone who was clever enough to do so exerted themselves to attract the notice of the King and Queen, a girl who wanted nothing more than to fade into the background was generally dismissed as a fool.

She lowered her head to hide the militant gleam she could feel burning in her eyes. She was not stupid! She had learnt, in a male-dominated family where the baby girl was out of place, she could draw closer to the action by being unobtrusive than by demanding attention. The habit of assuming a meek demeanour had been reinforced at Lacey Manor. As a lonely little girl, terrified of being beaten yet again for the crime of weeping for her home, it had soon become second nature to fade into the background. And here, where any move she made could be misconstrued as an attempt to avenge her father, whose opposition to the new King was well documented, she had continued to shrink from attracting attention.

Well, let them continue to underestimate her! Schooling her features into a bewildered mask, which was not all that hard considering how bemused she genuinely was by the day's events, she shakily straightened herself up.

'I pray you will forgive me, Eleanor…'

Lady Lacey flinched. There had been a time, just after Baron Lacey had died, freed from the constraints he had imposed, that they had treated each other almost like sisters, using each other's first names. Once they had come to court, the walls of formality had swiftly sprung back up.

'Lady Lacey!' she snapped. 'When will you get it into your head you must address me as Lady Lacey!'

Meekly, Maddy hung her head. 'Yes, of course, I forgot…so stupid of me. P…please do not be angry with me for misunderstanding that conversation we had last night. I did not intend to shirk my duties. I truly thought you wanted some c…crocuses…' For a second or two, she wondered if she had overdone it by raising the back of her hand to her forehead.

But then, 'Oh, that!' Lady Lacey snapped her fingers. 'Is that what sparked off this wild start?' She flicked Maddy's cloak aside, eyeing the rent in her gown, and the livid claw marks on her breast, with distaste.

Looking over her shoulder, Prudence gasped.

'Well, it would seem you have already been punished for your stupidity. Prudence is correct. You must go and change out of these clothes you have ruined. And…and you will stay in your room for the rest of the day! There!' She turned to Lord Hugo. 'Do you think that will be punishment enough?'

He bowed to her. 'You are just and fair as ever. Lady Agnes will surely think twice about venturing beyond the palace walls alone again.'

She had not been alone. Oh, Lord, Piers! For all she knew, he was still up that tree, the two hounds baying at its roots. At the thought, she experienced a wholly inappropriate desire to burst out laughing.

Lowering her head, she backed towards the door. 'Th…thank you, my lord, my lady…'

She only just made it outside before succumbing to a seriously unladylike fit of the giggles. Stumbling along the corridors, her hand to the rough stone walls to support her, Maddy could not understand why she couldn't stop laughing. She had almost died. She had unwittingly put poor Piers in danger. She sobered briefly. Nobody must ever know he had been with her. She did not want him drawn any deeper into the danger that stalked her.

The hysterical laughter that still possessed her began to sound more like sobbing now. And by the time she reached her dorter, she was crying in earnest. Covering her face with her hands, she collapsed on to the wooden frame of the nearest bed, her legs too weak to support her against the weight of terror that was pressing down on her from all sides, as great jagged sobs racked her whole body.

Chapter Three

She didn't know how long she cried for, but what eventually stopped her was the creeping awareness of how cold and wet she was. Stupid, she thought, sitting up and sniffing. 'I'm doing their work for them, sitting here in wet clothes. I shall catch my death of cold, and save them the bother of having to do away with me!'

The ruined wet gown practically fell off her, and once she was completely naked, she pulled the coverlets off all the beds in the dorter, piled them on to her own, and dived in.

Curling into a ball, she rubbed at her icy feet, the vigorous movement gradually warming her entire body. She had warmed much more quickly, she reflected bitterly, curled up in a ball like this against that enormous kennel man's chest. What she wouldn't give for a comforting pair of strong arms to hold her now! A solid chest to lean on. A soothing voice to calm the fear that roiled in her gut.

But it was no use pining for some big strong man on a white charger to come galloping to her rescue. If her own cousin could turn against her, she could trust no one. She was going to have to fight her own battles.

Starting with finding out exactly who wanted her out of the way, and why.

Just how she would go about investigating that mystery was perplexing, though. She barely stirred from her ribbon loom, except to take meals. Not that there would be any meals today, she reflected bitterly. She could expect fasting, as well as banishment to this unheated dorter, to form part of her punishment for her supposed misbehaviour.

She sat up, clutching the furs to her chest, her pale shoulders shivering still in the dank, empty room.

This was the perfect time to find some answers, if she could be bold enough to seize the opportunity. Nobody would expect dull, timid little Lady Agnes to disobey the order to stay put. Flinging the covers aside, she padded naked to the coffer at the foot of her narrow bed, knelt down and pushed open the lid.

Lady Lacey was bound to want to tell her confederates that their plan had gone awry, and get fresh orders. She must follow her, and find out who those confederates were! Once she knew who was behind the plot against her, she might even be able to appeal to someone for protection. Every family had its traditional allies and enemies. She was familiar enough with the various coteries to know who might be inclined to shield her, simply for the sake of thwarting a faction they opposed.

Bolstered by the prospect of gaining some support in her fight for survival, she rummaged through the meagre store of clothing still left to her. She'd hardly grown since her thirteenth birthday, which was the last time her father had sent her anything new. So, whenever she'd asked for a new gown, Lady Lacey had said there was no need for such extravagance, when there was plenty of wear left in what she had. Consequently, everything she owned, even her Sunday best, was patched and altered and well out of fashion. The sort of thing a serving girl would wear, faded to dull shades of brown. Nobody looked twice at servants, she mused, a smile touching her lips as she pulled on a thick pair of stockings. There were scores of them, bustling about the palace. She pulled a fresh chemise over her head. All she had to do was to carry a jug, or a tray, and anybody who might have recognised her would hopefully look straight through her.

Her mouth settled into a grim line of determination as she fastened

a tucking girdle about her hips and adjusted the skirts of her shape-
less gown till they revealed her ankles. It was no use being modest
about her apparel today. If she did not want anyone to look too
closely at her face, then she must give them something else to look
at. Men liked to catch a glimpse of a serving girl's ankles. She
tidied and plaited her hair with trembling fingers, and covered her
head with a demure linen kerchief. As she laid her hand on the door
latch, a steely determination stiffened her spine. She would do what
she must to survive.

Nobody challenged her when she slipped from the room. Nor paid
any heed as she walked swiftly along the edges of the corridors, head
down, like a serving maid, though she was horribly conscious that
her hands were empty. Spying through a half-open door the
remnants of a meal lying upon a table, Maddy darted into the
chamber. There was a tray propped against the table leg. All she had
to do was pick it up, sweep the broken meats and empty cups on to
it, and her disguise would be perfect! Though her heart was
pounding at the audacity of her actions, the two gentlemen hunched
over the charcoal brazier barely looked up as she cleaned away the
debris of their meal. They carried right on with their discussion as
though she was not even there.

It was with a wild rush of exhilaration that she dropped them the
obligatory curtsy before leaving the room, marvelling at the gift of
invisibility that a tray of leftovers had bestowed on her.

And now to catch Lady Lacey!

It felt like ages before she finally tracked her down in the corridor
outside Princess Elizabeth's antechamber. She set off in hot pursuit,
though by now the weight of the tray was making her arms ache.
And her stomach was beginning to protest too, since she had not
broken her fast since rising that morning.

After a while, she began to wonder if she was making a complete
fool of herself. Lady Lacey was not walking like a woman who had
attempted murder on her conscience. She glided along, her satin

skirts swishing as her hips swayed, the rosary beads at her waist tinkling with every step she took. Maddy eyed the way her dress clung lovingly to every curve of her cousin's voluptuous body. And so did the gentlemen they passed. If they were of sufficient rank to merit consideration, she dipped her head, giving them, Maddy knew though she could not see, a coquettish smile. If they were not, her head remained high, her eyes fixed ahead as she froze them out.

Maddy stifled a sigh. She need not have bothered with the tray. As ever, in the shimmeringly vivacious Lady Lacey's wake, she was already invisible.

Then, suddenly, her quarry's demeanour began to alter. She darted several furtive glances over her shoulder, before ducking through a little doorway and into a lesser-used passageway. Maddy peeped round the door frame into the gloom. Though it was going to get harder to follow and remain undetected from now on, her spirits lifted. She was definitely up to something, and Maddy was going to find out what!

She waited until Lady Lacey had rounded a corner, then abandoned the tray on a dusty window ledge, leaving her hands free to hitch up her skirts so she could run to catch up.

She was crossing the courtyard that led into the palace gardens by the time Maddy next spotted her. She waited until she was certain she was not going to double back before running across the courtyard, and through the archway that led outside. Maddy saw a sweeping stretch of empty lawn, bordered by high, neatly trimmed hedges, that were intersected at intervals by gravel paths. Lady Lacey was nowhere in sight. She bit back a wail of frustration. She'd come so close to getting some answers!

There! A flash of blue, on the other side of the hedge! Lady Lacey's gown! It had to be!

Maddy hitched up her skirts and pelted across the lawn, darting into the alley where she had spotted that telltale flash of colour. She kept off the gravel, lest the noise of her footsteps should alert her quarry to her presence. She soon found that keeping to the grass close to the hedge helped her keep Lady Lacey, in her bright clothes, in sight, too, while all she had to do, whenever Lady Lacey looked over her shoulder, was stand completely still. Her drab gown blended in perfectly with the tired colours of winter foliage. She only moved again when Lady Lacey had got well ahead.

There was a short period when she lost sight of her altogether. The maze of hedges was broken by another lawn, across which Maddy dared not go till she was certain Lady Lacey was not going to double back.

Creeping slowly forward, Maddy began to hear the sound of muted voices coming from the other side of the hedge. A man's, and a woman's.

Cautiously, Maddy sought for a gap in the hedge, through which she would be able to spy on the conspirators, and thus identify her enemy. The sight that met her eyes shocked a gasp from her mouth.

Lady Lacey was leaning against the bole of an elm tree that was central to the little arbour this section of hedge enclosed, her bared legs wrapped round the waist of the man who was…well…battering her. Neither of them heard Maddy's gasp above their own little moans and sighs of pleasure.

Maddy immediately began to inch away. She had no desire to witness such an obscene coupling. She knew, of course, that many court ladies took lovers. It should have been no surprise to discover Lady Lacey had one of her own. But knowing it was one thing; coming across them actively engaged in congress was quite another.

Slap, slap, slap, went Lady Lacey's bottom against the rough elm bark, while the man's fingers dug deep into the soft white flesh of her thighs.

And then the man's head flew back, as the grunts and gasps intensified in both volume and pace, and Maddy's jaw dropped.

It was Lord Hugo! Lord Hugo as she had never dreamed he could look, the sinews standing out on his neck, his face red, his lips pulled back from his teeth in a feral snarl. Maddy sank down, stunned, to the springy turf.

Lord, but he didn't look so elegant with his long shanks quivering, his hips jerking frantically. If anything, he put her in mind of the dog she had once, also inadvertently, watched mounting a bitch in Baron Lacey's kennels.

But, faugh, these were people, not animals who had no control over their impulses!

They were both still panting as Lord Hugo, who had disengaged, tucked one of Lady Lacey's exposed breasts back into her bodice.

'I really should be angry with you,' he drawled, making Maddy flinch. Somehow, after she had watched them rutting like beasts in the field, it seemed incongruous to hear either of them converse like rational beings.

'You should take better care of our little pigeon.'

'But she's such a silly little thing, Hugo darling.' Lady Lacey arched her back, inviting her lover to put her other breast away. Maddy, desperate not to witness any more of this, shakily pushed herself up on to her hands and knees.

'How could I possibly guess she would take it into her head to leave her bed at such an ungodly hour and traipse off to the meadows to pick flowers? I was not even awake…'

Maddy froze. They were talking about her. But she need not linger. To judge by Lord Hugo's words, he could not have been the one who had ordered her death. This was just a lover's tryst, nothing more. She was just beginning to inch away when she heard Lord Hugo say, 'She is essential to my plans, and don't you forget it.'

Maddy's head jerked up, and she saw him take hold of Lady Lacey by the chin. Though his voice was quiet, there was an unmistakably lethal edge to it. 'If we lose her, we have nothing!'

'Nothing?' She turned her face into his hand, kissing the fingers that had bitten into her cheek. 'Oh, surely not!'

He laughed, releasing her face. 'Yes, you wanton hussy…we

could still have this, but we would not have her money, would we?'
He spun her round, and began to lace up the back of her gown.

Money? Maddy did not have any money. What could he mean?
They could not be talking about her after all, she must have mis-
understood, she—

'Do we really need Lady Agnes's money, darling? Couldn't we
just get married, and—'

He stepped back and bent to yank up his hose. 'Marry you? What
have I to gain by marrying you?'

As Lady Lacey's shoulders drooped in response to his callous
retort, Lord Hugo seized her and spun her about, so that she had her
back to Maddy.

'But we can continue as we are, my sweeting, once your little
cousin is safely wed to me. And have all her lovely money. Why
shouldn't we have it all?'

'You swear? That we will still be together?'

'Of course. Why not?'

'You might come to care for her…you might put me aside once
you are married. Hugo, I couldn't bear it!'

'Hush, hush, now.' He tilted her face up to his with one elegant
finger under her chin. Maddy knew exactly what impact those compelling blue eyes were having on her guardian right now. Her knees
would be melting, her heart pattering.

'What could I possibly find attractive about a little brown mouse
like that? Compared to your golden radiance?'

As he kissed Lady Lacey with slow deliberation, Maddy felt as
though he had slid a dagger between her ribs. She had always known
how he felt about her, of course she had. But to hear him actually
say it aloud! And she had let him kiss her!

'Although,' he mused, 'I think I could find her tolerably responsive
in bed. The one good thing to come out of the fright she suffered this
morning was that it gave me the opportunity to kiss her, at long last.'

She raised the back of one trembling hand to her mouth, as bile,
thick and bitter, rose in her gorge.

'You…you kissed her?'

'Yes, she was too bemused to object. I thought it went rather well, all things considered. She is not…' a malicious smile slashed across his mocking features '…as frigid as you led me to believe. Under the right circumstances, I have no doubt I could thaw her out.'

Lady Lacey tore herself from his arms and paced towards a bench that was only a foot or so from the hedge behind which Maddy was crouching. The agony in her face was yet one more thing she wished she had not witnessed that day.

'Thaw her?'

Thaw me? Maddy was not sure whether she felt more indignant on her own behalf, or her guardian's.

'Oh, yes,' he smirked. 'She began to melt after only one kiss. She let me hold her in my arms, and run my fingers through her hair. And she liked it.'

'Did she?' Lady Lacey sank down abruptly on to the bench, looking as sick as Maddy felt.

'Oh, yes.' He had finished smoothing the wrinkles out of his hose, and sauntered over, apparently oblivious to the fact he was breaking his lover's heart. 'I think it is time to start courting her in earnest, don't you? Before any of the other impecunious younger sons get wind of exactly what Lady Agnes is worth.'

There he went, talking about money again. But she did not have any. Why did he think she had?

'You know I will always be grateful to you, Eleanor, for giving me the lead in this field. I doubt anyone but you and I know aught of it.'

Maddy frowned. Was Lady Lacey so besotted with him that she had dangled a non-existent fortune under his nose, to make herself more interesting to him? To keep him from turning to another woman? It would be hard to dispute her claim, since Maddy had no other relatives on hand with whom he could check.

'But you must understand that I won't lose sight of my goals. If you stay loyal to me in this, I will see you well rewarded.' He leaned forward, and with an expert hand began to adjust the set of her skewed hennin, tucking the golden curls back into place. 'But if you cross me, or if anything prevents me from closing the trap we have set for her…' His fingers closed round her neck, even as he bent to kiss her lips once again.

Oh, Eleanor, she moaned silently. What have you done? She'd made Lord Hugo believe that if he were to marry her, he would become rich. And Eleanor's reward was going to be keeping her place in his bed! Her fists clenched on her lap. Did they think she was such a spineless creature that she would turn a blind eye to such carryings on?

Memories long buried suddenly rose to the surface of her mind. Servants gossiping about her poor lady mother, who had broken her heart, they said, over her own father's infidelities. Though he had never installed one of his mistresses within his own home. He had even had the decency to send her away before he sank as low as that, though tales of what the atmosphere at Woolton Castle had been like after she left had managed to filter through.

Her brothers had been just as callous in their dealings with women. Though she had worshipped them, she knew how badly they treated the current object of their lust. For she had heard them laughing together, when they thought she could not hear, about their conquests. Boasting about running their current quarry to ground as though it were sport to ruin some hapless maiden who caught their eye.

Then there had been that boy who was brought to the castle shortly before her nurse died, and put to work in the stables. Her father's son, Marjory had clucked disapprovingly. Her lips thinned. If Lord Hugo thought she would see his mistress installed in her home, and expect her to raise a pack of his bastard children, then he had another think coming!

When Lord Hugo commenced this callous, mercenary courtship of his, she would have no trouble in repulsing his advances. The very thought of him smiling at her with those deceitful eyes, kissing her with those lying lips…she shuddered.

He was false, utterly false, and she was glad she had discovered the truth in time. If she had not witnessed this sordid little scene, she would have fallen prey to his wiles. She had already been halfway in love with him, and would no doubt have fallen utterly under his spell.

And would she then have become deranged enough with unrequited love to have considered murdering her rival? Her blood ran cold. Had it been for love of the despicable, faithless Lord Hugo that Lady Lacey had attempted to do away with her? Was there nothing more sinister behind the encounter with the alaunts that morning but Lady Lacey's desire to keep her lover for herself?

Suddenly aware that it had gone quiet within the arbour, she knelt forward, peering through the tangled branches. They had gone. While she had been lost in the maze of her own thoughts, they had crept away.

Something drew her into the enclosed space. She was briefly surprised at how warm it felt within. The thick hedges prevented much movement of air, so that even the pale winter sun made it a comfortable place to sit. Or stand, she grimaced. Truth, ugly though it was, had blossomed here, under that very tree, on this very bench. She sat down on it, wrapping her arms about her waist.

If her suspicion that Lady Lacey was behind her earlier accident was correct, then her life was now safe. Lord Hugo had clearly informed Lady Lacey that he would never consider marrying her, that if anything happened to Maddy, he need not bother with her any more.

She supposed she ought to feel glad.

But she could not get the stricken look on Lady Lacey's face from her mind. She had risked all for a worthless, deceitful man, only to learn that she had no value in his eyes. And if Maddy did not marry him, or if he discovered that there was no money after all, she had no doubt he would be furious with her.

Lady Lacey might be suffering now, but what would he do once he discovered she had misled him?

It made no difference. She could never marry him. So she

would just have to keep him at arm's length, once he began this spurious courtship.

But for how long could she do that? She knew she would have no trouble in behaving in the frigid manner he half-expected of her, but what if he grew impatient, and somehow forced her into a situation where she had no choice? With Lady Lacey as his accomplice, it would be very hard to evade him.

She buried her face in her hands, suddenly feeling utterly overwhelmed by the situation Lady Lacey's obsession with Lord Hugo had put her in. What was she to do? Simply tell him the truth? Reveal her knowledge of his plans? And sacrifice Lady Lacey to his wrath?

She supposed she could. Lady Lacey, after all, had not scrupled to put her in the way of danger, this very morn. *She* would not hesitate to sacrifice a rival in order to achieve her own ambitions.

Hot tears began to slide through her fingers at the thought she might have to resort to such cold, self-serving behaviour. Oh, why did life have to be like this? Why did people have to trample on one another to get what they wanted? Why couldn't people just live in peace? Surely God hadn't meant for his creation to live like this? Every man fighting everyone else.

Yet for generations this was all England had known. The noble houses all seemed to be divided within themselves by personal ambitions. It had led to kings being swept from their thrones, and the whole country being laid waste by warfare.

Bowed from the waist, rocking back and forth, Maddy wept as she accepted that the time had come to bid farewell to any loyalty she felt for Eleanor as a member of her family, and fight for her own survival. So she did not hear the sound of footsteps approaching, or the startled, indrawn breath of the man who halted abruptly under the neatly trimmed arch that led to the secluded arbour.

Sir Geraint had no trouble recognising Maddy, though she was hunched over, her face hidden by her hands as she cried her little heart out. Was not the curve of that soft white neck branded into his memory? Along with every other contour of that delectably dainty little body that had curled so trustingly into his own?

He had almost begun to wonder if he had imagined her. Nobody had recognised the description he had given, or recalled anyone of that name wherever he had searched for her. Though, many had pointed out, the palace was so full of newcomers these days, she might not be a palace servant at all. She might belong to one of the many families that were currently at court to petition the new King for restitution of lands and dues usurped by the grasping Duke Richard.

In an ill humour, convinced he would never find his elusive little sprite again, he had stalked outside to walk off his frustration in the gardens. And had stumbled across her by purest chance.

Well, he was not going to let her slip through his fingers a second time. In two strides he was beside her. She had scarce registered he had joined her on the bench before he had his arms about her.

'Maddy, Maddy,' he murmured, pulling her on to his lap and crushing her to his chest. This was where she belonged. If she stayed here, nothing would make her cry ever again. He would make sure of it. 'Don't cry…'

'Wha…?' For a second, her whole body went rigid. Her hands fell away from her face, revealing eyes that were wide with shock. Then she laid those hands flat against his chest as she began to push him away.

'Oh. It's you.' Recognition of exactly who had scooped her up produced a gratifying lessening to her initial hostility.

For a timeless moment, they gazed into each other's eyes, Sir Geraint struggling to conceal his triumph at having found her. For she was still poised, hands braced against his chest. He sensed that if he made one wrong move now he might lose her for ever.

Maddy's heart was still pounding in shock. For one terrible moment, she had feared it was Lord Hugo, returned to the scene, determined to commence his wooing in a rather more forceful way than she had expected.

To find it was only her tame bear was such a relief she quite forgot she ought to slap his face for his impudence.

Besides, she was distracted by the alteration in his appearance. He had only shaved, that was all. His clothes were all still the same, from the neat little roll-rimmed cap to the serviceable leather jerkin, yet now he looked every inch a man. Not like a bear at all, now that powerful jaw was so smooth. She was not sure how long she sat, studying the contours of his clean-shaven cheeks, but it was quite long enough to put that infuriatingly cocky grin back on his face.

'Y…you ought to let me go.'

She had clearly not put enough conviction in her voice, for his embrace did not slacken one whit.

'I cannot,' he declared. 'Not until I know why you were crying, and what I may do to ease your woes.'

Nothing! A man like this could do nothing to help her! Yet how she wished he could! A surge of self-pity brought fresh tears to her eyes.

He clucked his tongue as he ran his hand the length of her plait, sweeping the kerchief aside. Wrapping the braid round his wrist, he raised the tail of it to his face.

'I have been searching for you all day, my little nut-brown maid,' he crooned, running the soft, unbound end of it across his upper lip. 'I was beginning to fear I might never find you.'

She gaped up at him as he closed his eyes, breathing in deeply as though he were inhaling the scent of her hair. For some inexplicable reason, this huge, musclebound kennel man found her desirable. He had searched for her. After the blow dealt to her self-esteem by hearing Lord Hugo's cold-hearted scheme, it was immensely flattering to think a man could have searched for her. For a moment or two it was all she could do to stop herself from leaning into that rock-hard chest and wallowing in the false comfort she knew from experience she would find there.

But she could not let him hope that anything might come of it. She was a lady, and he was…well, she did not, now she came to reflect on the matter, know exactly what he was, but she did know she ought not to be sitting on his lap, letting him toy with her hair.

Even though it felt so good…

'You must let me go now,' she said in the haughtiest tone she could muster, attempting at the same time to sit up straight.

He smiled down at her ruefully. 'Must I?'

'Yes.' She lifted her chin and tried to look down her nose at him.

He wiped the tears that lingered on her cheeks with the tip of her own plait.

'But what of these?' he persisted, gently. 'How can I ignore these?'

'I've stopped crying now.' But she might start again if she had to speak of her utter isolation, the decision she had just made to fight to the death, if need be, with the last surviving member of her family. Her voice bleak, she added, 'Besides, they are no concern of yours.'

'Oh, but they are,' he argued. 'Did you not know that once a man saves a maid's life, everything about her is his concern?'

'But you did not save my life,' she pointed out. 'That other kennel man got to me first and pulled your dog away. All you did was throw me across your saddle and bring me back.'

'Ah, don't argue with me, my sweet little nut-brown maid. Just let me help you. I promise that whatever it is, you can trust me.'

'Trust you?' she spat. A complete stranger? When she had just discovered she could not even trust the person to whom she was closest? Did he think she was a fool to be taken in by a few honeyed words?

To his concern, her face went from being merely wary, at his close proximity, to utterly furious.

'I don't even know you!'

'Then I must endeavour to rectify that situation,' he replied calmly, placing his hands over the ones she still held braced against his chest. The movement seemed to make up her mind for her. She began to push with all her might, wriggling away from him though he still had her long plait of hair wrapped round his wrist.

'Nay, stop that!' He laughed. 'You will only hurt yourself!' Clamping his hand firmly on her thigh, he hauled her back so that she fetched up against his chest. Ignoring her protests, he tucked her head under his chin, clamped her tightly to him with one hand and began rubbing his other hand up and down her spine. As soon as he felt the stiffness melt from her, he would gentle his hold.

It was not going to be so easy to get her into his bed as he had at first supposed. But if he didn't mistake the matter, she was fighting her own inclinations, as much as him. She would yield in the end. He would make certain of it!

The firm grip of his hand on her thigh suddenly reminded her of Lord Hugo's fingers digging into Lady Lacey's bared flesh, in this very arbour, not half an hour since. A peculiar sensation twisted in the pit of her stomach. She began to tremble.

Looking up into the eyes of the man who held her so firmly, yet was caressing her so gently, she felt warmth seeping from that place in her stomach that had leapt in response to the feel of his hand on her thigh, spreading ever outward…

'Don't fight me, Maddy,' he said reproachfully.

Fight him? What point was there in even trying? He was a great brawny brute of a man, while she was…she was panting, her heart pounding, and she was very, very aware of every feminine contour of her body.

'I mean you no harm.'

Oh, but he did! He wanted the same thing from her that Lord Hugo had wanted from Lady Lacey here in this arbour.

'You're a man, are you not?' she replied bitterly.

So, that was what the tears were about. Some man had bruised her young heart. He supposed he should feel sorrier for her than he did. However, if some fool had cast her aside, well, he was more than willing to comfort her. And to begin with, he would tell her exactly who he was. That would certainly cheer her.

'A man of honour,' he remonstrated. 'The King's man—'

'I don't care whose man you are!' she spat before he could go any further. 'First and foremost you are a man, with all a man's deceitful, animal lusts!'

She had been badly hurt, this one. It would be no use trying to cozen her.

'Aye. I don't deny that.' He deliberately let her see him lower his gaze to her lips. 'You must know how much I want to kiss you.'

She gasped, not at what he was saying, but at her own bewilderingly strong response to his words. Her lips felt fuller, more sensitive to the feel of his breath as it fanned across her face. And somehow naked. She ran her tongue over them, and as soon as she had done so, knew that was not the covering they wanted at all.

'For one kiss from those sweet lips, Maddy, I would grant you whatever you desire.'

His lips looked amazingly soft, considering how hard and masculine the rest of him felt. Incongruous in that rugged face, like a drift of rose petals against a granite buttress.

Her eyes widened. Her lips parted. He could see she was struggling with herself.

'Would you let me go, then?' she begged. 'If I let you kiss me?'

His heart sank. She might let him kiss her, but then she was going to run from him again. And he had learnt nothing about her at all! He racked his brains for a way to prolong this encounter.

'Perhaps you would rather simply tell me why you were crying…then I would let you go. One kiss, or one confidence. Which is it to be, Maddy?'

Chapter Four

Maddy frowned. She should not want to let him kiss her.

'I would settle for even less…' Sir Geraint sighed '…so ardent is my desire for you. Promise to meet me another time, Maddy, and I will let you go for today.'

Something warm and wonderful lit up inside her. He had no idea who she was, but after only one encounter, he wanted her…ardently.

Lord Hugo might think she was drab and prudish, but here was one man at least who found her attractive enough to be worth pursuing. A feeling of reckless defiance swept over her. She would just show Lord Hugo how prudish she really was! Besides, she tossed her head, her freed plait slithering over her shoulder, what choice had this man really given her? She was not going to make an assignation with him. She might be lonely, but not lonely enough to embark on an affair with a servant!

Nor was there any point in telling him why she had been crying. If she confided in anyone about the bizarre plot to seduce her for a non-existent fortune, it would be someone with the ability to rescue her. A powerful noble, who bore a grudge against the DeVere family, for example.

Her defiant mood faltered when he licked the lips she had been contemplating all this while, for all the world like a man about to break a month-long fast on a morsel of tender spring lamb.

Yet what was a kiss after all? She knew now, since Lord Hugo had kissed her, that it would merely be a moment or two of closeness, the mingling of their breath, and then it would be finished.

'I would rather lend you my lips for a few seconds,' she forced herself to say, 'than confide in you.'

'Trust will follow,' he husked, and lowered his head.

In spite of the hunger he had displayed, the first touch of his mouth upon hers was as tentative as a summer breeze, his lips as soft as the rose petals to which she had already likened them. She very quickly found herself basking in a flood of wholly pleasurable sensations. He had begged for this kiss, bartered for it. For the first time in her life, she felt truly wanted.

Without warning, all the years of feeling alone, of striving in vain for approval that never came, surged up within her and, like a dam bursting, broke from her wounded soul in a moan of utter need.

The second her lips parted, he thrust his tongue into her mouth. She was totally unprepared for the intrusion, or for the shocking wave of delight that instantly coursed through her entire body. Or for the overwhelming longings she had never imagined she might experience. Entirely without her volition, her hands reached up to shape the width of his shoulders. Then she discovered she had never felt anything so intriguing as the texture of his freshly shaven jaw. The skin that looked so smooth was bristly. So different from her own. So utterly masculine.

A little mewling sound escaped her throat as her questing fingers delved into the soft curls at the nape of his neck.

And the kiss went on. And on. Oh, he smelt so good! Of sunshine and horses and leather. Good, wholesome, manly smells. Not a bit like the stale scent of shuttered rooms that clung to Lord Hugo's expensive velvet doublet.

She found herself needing to press her breasts against his chest. But that only served to stoke the liquid heat that was pooling between her thighs. She shifted her legs restlessly. There was a heavy, throbbing ache, that needed… Oh, if only he were to shift the great hand that rested on her thigh the slightest bit…or if she were to turn into it, she felt instinctively that it would help.

With a groan, the man broke the kiss.

Dazed, she opened her eyes, to find that his own were still closed. His head was flung back, the muscles of his jaw working as he clenched his teeth. His great chest heaved with each breath he dragged in through flared nostrils.

And, Maddy realised, her own mouth was hanging open, her lips still pulsing from the explosive power of his kiss. That she was panting too, her heart racing as though she had been running.

How could this be? When Lord Hugo had kissed her earlier, for heaven's sake, it had only produced a series of pleasantly confusing thoughts. But this man, this stranger, had effortlessly tapped into a wellspring of longing at the very core of her being.

He opened his eyes and caught the dazed expression on her face. And smiled.

That smug expression of his was like a slap in the face, jolting her out of her passion-clouded haze.

Who did he think he was? How dare he look at her like that, just because she had let him kiss her?

And kissed him back, her conscience whispered. And writhed in his arms, and rubbed herself up against him…

Uttering a little cry of vexation, Maddy twisted off his lap.

Sir Geraint made no attempt to stop her. She might not have confided in him yet, but he had learned a great deal about her. She wanted him almost as much as he wanted her, though she was not yet ready to admit it. And her hands were soft as any lady's. He had been wasting his time looking for her in the kitchens and laundries. It might not be easy, but he would find her again. And kiss her again, too. She couldn't resist him!

That he had kept his word to let her go did not occur to Maddy until she had stumbled out of the arbour and was halfway across the next lawn.

She strode, with her fists clenched, right down the middle of the gravel paths that wound back to the palace. She had behaved like a strumpet! Letting a strange man kiss her…and would have let him do far more if he had not had the decency to break off when he did!

She crossed the cobbled courtyard and slammed through the entry door. She hated men! Every last one of them! They tricked you, and lied to you to get what they wanted, whether it was your money or your body, making you feel one minute as though you were fully alive in the most wonderful way you could ever have imagined, and then dashing you to the ground beneath their arrogant feet with one smug grin. And considered it fine sport!

Well, she must consider this a salutary lesson, she decided as she shut the door of her room against the hateful world outside. Permitting a mere groom to take such liberties with her might have been a mistake, but it had at least taught her not to play with fire. She had not dreamt that a man could wield such power over a woman with a kiss. That was one mistake she would never make again.

Nor would she ever be fooled by Lord Hugo's charming façade again.

Nor ever trust a word Lady Lacey said.

Picking up her rosary beads, she began to tell them through her fingers. And slowly, as the repetitive prayers calmed her down, the outline of a plan began to take shape. She needed earthly assistance to establish her safety, just as much as the heavenly aid she sought for her eternal soul with her prayers. Which meant she would have to venture out of the ladies' quarters more often and search the court for a champion.

Her experience with the groom, regrettable though it had been, had at least given her some confidence in her desirability as a woman. She would have to learn to flirt a little, perhaps. Indicate that she would welcome male attention. A wry smile twisted her lips. She had watched Lady Lacey in action often enough to see how that was done. A coy look, a bold smile…she frowned. And to begin with, she would have to dress a little less modestly than was her habit.

She went to her coffer, and flung back the lid. She had only one gown that would serve. It had been emerald green when new, though now the velvet was faded to muted shades of olive. She drew it out, and gave it a little shake. The seams had all been let out as far as they would go, but the nap was still soft and rich. It might take the rest of the day, but she was sure she could transform this material into the very weapon a lone female would need to cut her way free from the web Lord Hugo and Lady Lacey had spun for her.

All the same, embarrassment was her uppermost feeling when she looked at herself in the mirror the next evening. The velvet of the square-cut bodice, stretched tightly over her bosom, had the effect of thrusting her small breasts together, and upwards, creating that little cleft that she had observed men found so interesting. Well, it was what she wanted, wasn't it? For some man to take notice of her? In fact, she ought to hang some ornament about her neck, something that would nestle in that cleavage, declaring her pride in the creamy mounds of womanly flesh. She frowned. Somebody must have her mother's jewels in safekeeping for her. She had been far too young to have them handed straight to her after she died. And she had never thought to ask for them before, never having wanted to deck herself out like this.

She shrugged. There was no time for that now. She draped a simple leathern girdle about her hips to delineate their roundness in contrast to the narrowness of the waist her straining bodice hugged.

As for her hair…she felt a moment of utter despondency. She did not possess a single fashionable item of headgear. She had covered her head with one of her plain linen kerchiefs, which she had stiffly starched and pressed into a semblance of the gabled shape that was currently coming into vogue. Perhaps…she tugged a single lock from its confines to see what effect that might achieve. Why was it so straight? A teasing little curl over one ear would at least look flirtatious rather than just…well…untidy! With a sigh, she removed her kerchief, brushed her hair back neatly, and tucked it all out of sight. She had achieved as much as she could for her first day of campaign.

She must hope it would be enough. Tomorrow she would begin to see what she could glean from the odds and ends of wire and gauze and velvet left over from the frivolities Margot the tiring woman created for the Princess Elizabeth. Such things were a perquisite of her position, though she had never claimed a share before.

She smiled determinedly back at every single courtier who eyed the contours of her body with surprised appreciation as she entered the Great Hall for supper. If only she knew which one of them would be worth pursuing further! Surely one of them would want to do more than look, after they had got over the shock of seeing her in something other than the drab, formless gowns that had always made her look like a little dumpling on legs.

But to her dismay, it was Lord Hugo who materialised at her side while the servants laid the cloth and began to smooth it out with a rod. By the look of satisfaction on his face, he had clearly decided her sudden attempt to dress better had been for his benefit. The coxcomb! Did he think because she had been fool enough to let him kiss her once, she was ready to fall at his feet?

Yes, clearly, she decided as he pressed her to sit close by him at table, his arrogance led him to believe just that. But he was oh, so wrong! As she averted her face from his, watching the servant setting out her trencher of bread, napkin and spoon, a slow smile came to her face. Wouldn't he be chagrined to know how tepid she had found his kiss in comparison with the scorching experience that lowly groom had given her! Lord Hugo smiled back, serenely unaware of her scorn as he dipped his fingers into the bowl of scented water a kneeling page offered to him.

Perhaps it was better this way, she thought, drying her own fingers on the towel another page lay on the tablecloth. If he thought he was making headway with her, he would not suspect that she was on to him. She dipped her head demurely for the saying of Grace, remembering she was supposed to be a frigid little idiot he needed to coax from her shell and…thaw.

* * *

The first truly awkward moment came during the lull between the first and second course.

'The King and Princess Elizabeth are dining in the privacy of the Royal Apartments tonight,' Lord Hugo said, as though she might not have noticed their absence! Then he went on to explain, 'So I fear there will be no acrobats or tumblers to enliven the evening.'

'I like the music,' she replied, determinedly fixing her gaze on the minstrels, as though she had never seen anyone play the lute and psaltery before. So determined was she to appear intrigued by the musicians that she actually jumped when the fanfare of trumpets announced the second course. Lord Hugo chuckled. He must think she was a complete fool!

Very well, she thought mutinously, she would not disappoint him! Though the King was absent, the cooks had still gone all out to create a feast for all the senses. They had transformed the blandest of ingredients into works of art through dramatic combinations of spices and lavish use of colourings. So it was not hard to convince Lord Hugo that she was enjoying, rather than enduring, his company by exclaiming like a child over everything from the pheasants brought to table dressed in their own plumage, to the raised pies decorated with intricate pastry crusts, via the vibrant colours of jellies and sauces. It was only when the second course was being cleared away, and she felt sure she had lulled him into a state of complacency, that she permitted herself to scan the other occupants of her part of the table.

Directly across from her, Lord Worthing raised his cup to her, a lazy smile lifting one corner of his mouth. She smiled shyly back, before taking a sip of her own clary. He was old enough to be her father. But he was powerful…blushing furiously at the direction her thoughts were taking, she looked away, towards the lower end of the table, where the servants were clearing away the spoons, then any baked meats left over into large voiders. That done, they brought in fruit and cheese, along with delicious little wafers made from batter cooked between iron moulds.

Could she contemplate kissing a man of Lord Worthing's age? Having that great paunch pressed up against her belly while his slack lips slobbered over her face? She took a great gulp from her cup, as though the sweet spiced wine could wash her mouth from the very thought of kissing Lord Worthing. At least Lord Hugo, much though she despised him, was young and handsome.

Lord Hugo leaned towards her to murmur into her ear, 'You do not need to dress in gowns that make you feel exposed to the glance of every lascivious man's eye, my lady, to attract my notice…'

Maddy's cheeks began to burn with indignation! Did his arrogance know no bounds?

'I find your modesty refreshing.' He laid his hands over hers as she twisted them in her lap, evidently mistaking her angry flush as a maidenly token of modesty. 'Your purity shines like a beacon in the squalid atmosphere of this court. I have admired it, from the first moment I met you.'

What balderdash! He did not admire her purity! He laughed at it, despising her for a prude! Wrenching her hands from under his, she reached for her cup, only to be appalled that her action left his hand lying on her thigh beneath the cloth, hidden from the view of other diners.

'Please, my lord, remove your hand,' she hissed through clenched teeth. Yesterday his boldness would have flustered her. Today his audacity made her flesh creep.

'Forgive me, my lady,' he said as he complied with her request. 'My admiration for you has made me too forward.'

She compressed her lips, biting back the retort his insincerity made her want to give. How stupid did he think she was? Fortunately, he took her averted face, her downcast eyes, the stiffening of her spine as further evidence of bashfulness.

'I have no desire to make you uncomfortable…'

No! He wanted her pliant in his hands! Murmuring something inconsequential, she flicked a glance across the board to where Lord Worthing sat idly picking his teeth with the point of his knife. Was it the low cut of her gown that had his eyes glittering so brightly, or was it something about Lord Hugo's attentiveness that had made him sit up and take notice?

Her heart began to beat a little faster. She had often noticed that if one man found something desirable, others wanted to take it from him just to prove themselves the better man. Her spirits lifted. Not that she wanted Lord Worthing to enter the lists on her behalf, but Lord Hugo's very persistence might do more to attract the notice of other men than all her feeble attempts to appear seductive. She might not have to flaunt herself so very much after all!

She heaved a sigh of relief. She had begun to suspect, even after only one feeble attempt to play the flirt, that she did not have what it took to be a seductress. Having men leer at her made her acutely uncomfortable. Lord Worthing's continued attempts to catch her eye were making her feel so queasy that she could only toy with the honeyed wafers she usually regarded as the best part of a meal.

By the time the prayers signalling the end of the meal were said, and the almsgiving organised, she felt completely wrung out. When Lord Hugo bowed over her hand as soon as the musicians struck up a tune, inviting her to partner him in the first dance of the evening, she felt she could not endure another moment of his company without screaming. Dropping a rather stiff curtsy, she began to back away, stammering out a stream of nonsense before finally turning and fleeing as if all the hounds of hell were after her. She did not stop running until she had shut the solid oak door of her chamber, through which no man was permitted to pass, fast behind her.

How long could she keep up this deceptive duel, leading Lord Hugo on, only to parry his advances without letting him know she was determined never to yield?

'Dear Lord, help me!' She sank to her knees beside her spartan cot. 'I'm so alone. And I don't know what to do! I don't want to have to lie and cheat and…intrigue.' She buried her face in her hands. 'If only there were some honourable way to escape this coil!'

Chapter Five

Sir Geraint folded his arms across his chest and scowled at the Bishop of Ely as he swept from the King's apartments with his nose in the air. It irked him to think that men like this surrounded Henry Tudor now. They had fled Richard Duke of York's regime, thinking they would do better for themselves by putting Margaret Beaufort's son on the throne. They had precious little loyalty for Henry himself. One king hadn't given them what they wanted, so they'd just gone out and picked themselves another one!

So now, Henry Tudor had lords to dress him every morning, bishops to advise him, nobles to administer his household accounts. While Sir Geraint had nothing to do all day but kick his heels in antechambers.

One of the yeomen guards beckoned to him, indicating that his King at last required his presence.

Henry looked up from the documents littering his desk, and smiled at him. Sir Geraint smiled back, comforted by the fact that Henry did not smile so broadly all that often, being rather self-conscious about his teeth, which were not all that good. It more than compensated him for the various slights he'd suffered since the impecunious Henry Tudor had shot to prominence.

'Ger, it is good to see you,' said Henry. 'I trust you are fully recovered now?'

Sir Geraint blinked. It had been months since he had taken the sweating sickness that had swept London the previous October.

Since then, he'd begun to wonder if he was being deliberately pushed to the fringes of his King's affairs.

Too weak to rise from his bed and witness Henry's coronation, he had watched with dull acceptance as others were given tasks he knew himself capable of. Surely his own loyalty was beyond doubt?

For he had served Henry Tudor with devotion through all fourteen years of his exile. He had gone hungry with him when funds were low, pretended to be a Breton so that he could stay close to him when all his English servants were banished, and so been in place to effect his rescue when the Duke of Brittany played false and would have turned him over to emissaries from Richard.

But then Henry had appointed Hugh Conway, who had only served as a messenger from Margaret Beaufort during the latter part of Henry's years abroad, the Keeper of the Great Wardrobe for life. Geraint had not even been asked to form part of the yeomen guard.

'I am quite well, your Grace,' he replied, guardedly.

'Excellent!' Leaning back in his chair, King Henry fingered the image of St. George that hung round his neck. 'Because I have a mission for you.'

Thank God! He was not out of favour after all.

'Ale?' Henry enquired. When Sir Geraint nodded, Henry signalled a servant to fill his own cup as well. The King only drank wine in the evenings, and that sparingly. He needed to keep a clear head at all times, Sir Geraint realised, especially surrounded as he was by cunning weasels like that bishop who had just left.

'Come, let us sit.' Henry rose from his chair and sauntered over to a window embrasure, rolling his neck, and rotating his shoulders as he went.

Though his wiry body appeared to be suffering some strain due to the hours spent poring over documents, Sir Geraint could see that Henry Tudor was in his element. He loved all the mental exercise requisite to ruling a vast kingdom, even the skill it took to weave his way unscathed through the tangled web of deception the various factions of the English noble houses spun as a matter of course. In short, his liege lord had never looked so happy. Whereas he...

He stared gloomily around the apartment that was hung with cloth of arras wrought with gold. His backside might be resting on silken cushions, but he could not deny he felt downright uncomfortable. Last night, in the Boar's Head, he had felt at ease among the rough and ready men-at-arms who congregated there. He was spending more and more time in such places, avoiding even taking meals at court. He would rather spend tuppence on three roast thrushes in an alehouse with simple folk who spoke their minds, than take his place at a sumptuous banquet amid nobles who would smile in your face even as they slid a dagger between your ribs.

Dismissing the servants with a peremptory wave of his hand, Henry leaned towards him, saying, 'The mission requires that you leave court, but I have a suspicion that you will not mind all that much, hmm?'

It was uncannily as if his monarch had been privy to his innermost thoughts. Flushing guiltily, he admitted, 'No, your Grace. I do not have the skills a courtier requires. Or the right background.'

'Then I think,' Henry said with a smile, 'you will find I have come up with the most suitable way I could have found to reward all your years of loyal service.'

Sir Geraint shifted in his seat.

'You have rewarded me already, your Grace,' he said gruffly. 'You knighted me.'

'That was only in recognition of the part you played at Bosworth Field. You saved my life...'

'All I did was stick close to you and wave my sword about a bit.' Sir Geraint made a deprecating gesture with his hand.

'It was a great deal more than that, my old friend.'

Henry Tudor's party had become briefly separated from the main force. Duke Richard had seen his chance, galloping down the hill with a small detachment of knights, surrounding Henry and his group of retainers. Sir Geraint would never forget the sound those heavy destriers had made, thundering down the hill towards them. They had all fought for their lives, and he was quite sure they would all have lost them if Lord Stanley, Henry's stepfather, had not finally made up his mind which of the rival claimants to the throne he was going to back, and entered the fray on Henry Tudor's side. Geraint might still have lost his life if not for Caligula, the horse he had bought on the quayside at the last minute from a French knight who had fallen too sick to board. The mean-spirited animal had lashed out with hooves and teeth, just as he had flailed out with whatever he found in his hand.

In the ensuing chaos, King Richard was hacked to death.

Henry Tudor, Earl of Richmond, had become Henry VII, by the grace of God, King of England.

And thus plain Geraint Davies, son of a Welsh wool merchant, had become Sir Geraint.

King Henry got to his feet, and beckoned Sir Geraint over to the desk where he had been sitting before. From among the stacks of documents littering it, King Henry chose one, spreading it out flat and weighing down its top corners with his tankard and a beautifully chased silver inkstand.

'Here.' He pointed to a portion of what appeared to be a map of Britain. 'You know, of course, that Richard of Gloucester's most loyal supporters came from the north of England.'

Sir Geraint nodded. He might not be descended from a noble house, but he kept his eyes and ears open.

'I want you to take Woolton Castle, here—' his finger jabbed at a point close to the north-western coast '—and its surrounding lands.' His hand traced an area north of Lancaster, bounded by the Irish Sea.

'Take?' For a second, Sir Geraint was stunned.

Henry smiled. 'Now you are a knight you should have your own estates to support you. Otherwise you might well end up being my pensioner indefinitely!'

'But this is not…I could not…'

Henry's face grew solemn. 'Jesting aside, Ger, I need to place an ally up there, in the heart of what used to be Richard's power base.'

Sir Geraint sobered immediately. 'Of course, your Grace. You can rely on me.'

Henry cocked his head. 'You don't seem all that pleased, Ger. Don't you realise I've just made you a very wealthy man? The revenues from this estate are substantial. Think how proud your mother would be to see her ambitions for you bear such fruit.'

Geraint's parents, who were wealthy merchants, had helped to fit the ship that had carried him to Brittany after the disastrous defeat at Tewkesbury, sending their own son, Geraint, to act as servant and guard. He'd heard that Henry had already sent them a sum of money, with a letter expressing his thanks for their aid in escaping those who would have sought his life in that, his darkest hour.

Sir Geraint's face reddened. 'I don't really care about the revenues…' He forced himself to stop. The King had just granted him a great honour, and he would be a fool to sound ungrateful. He had not only made him wealthy, but, in granting him land, had elevated him in the social hierarchy beyond anything a man of his humble background could hope to attain.

To his relief, Henry's smile had, if anything, grown broader. 'I know. You would rather stay here and watch over me like some great shaggy guard dog.'

'I cannot deny it, your Grace. These men who swarm round you now, they—'

Henry held up a hand to silence him. 'I need to keep them close, Ger. Why do you think I employ so many of them in my own household? I need to know what they are plotting, and who with. But you…' his eyes seemed to glow a darker blue '…I can trust you to go anywhere and stay true to me.'

Sir Geraint could barely restrain himself from falling to his knees and pledging himself all over again. Henry was not sweeping him aside as an embarrassing reminder of a time in his life he would rather forget now he was King! All he did was say, though rather gruffly, 'I am your man, your Grace. I will hold Woolton for you. When do you wish me to leave? How many soldiers will you be sending with me?'

Henry straightened from the map, his eyes narrowing. 'Ah, now that depends…'

'On what?'

Henry's rather thin lips lifted in a smile that sent ripples of alarm through Sir Geraint. It was a smile that presaged mischief.

'When I told you I wanted you to take the castle, I was not joking, entirely. You see, the DelaBoys family has held Castle Woolton and the surrounding lands since Domesday. The last Baron fell at Bosworth, along with the last of his four sons.'

Sir Geraint frowned. Since Henry had dated his claim to the throne from the day before the Battle of Bosworth, any who had fought against him were legally traitors, and their property forfeit to the King. It meant he could do what he willed with the land. Why did he insist he had to take it, as though by force?

'Only his daughter survives.' Henry's expression sobered. 'As she is a minor, she has become my ward. I can dispose of both her, and her father's land, exactly as I see fit. As an act of clemency, I could restore the land to this daughter, and any heirs she may have, providing she marries a man of whom I approve.'

Sir Geraint sat down rather heavily as the King's cryptic comments became clear.

'You want me to marry this girl.' Now he knew why Henry had warned him that he might have a struggle on his hands. 'She won't have any truck with the likes of me.'

'Oh, come, Ger. I've seen you in action. There's neither a dog nor a woman you cannot have eating out of your hand within five minutes of you turning on your charm.'

'Tavern wenches, maybe…'

'Court ladies too,' Henry grinned.

'Ones that were already married and bored with their husbands, aye. A little bit of sport with a peasant dressed in silks is one thing.

For a high-born maiden to trust a commoner with her entire future is quite another matter.'

Henry's face hardened. 'Have you forgot that some of my own forebears rose through the ranks in part due to most advantageous marriages?'

Sir Geraint flinched. Owen Tudor, Henry's grandfather, had technically been a commoner when he entered into his secret, and illegal, marriage with Katherine de Valois, the widow of Henry V.

'I did not mean to give offence, your Grace.' He spread his hands wide in apology. 'I just…'

But Henry's face had lost all trace of humour. 'She must marry you, Ger. One way or another. As my ward she cannot marry anyone without my permission. I will not give it to any man but you. I need you in Woolton.'

Sir Geraint felt a stab of pity for Henry's ward. He knew it was the way of the nobility to contract strategic marriages. She would have been brought up to expect that. But not to a man of his station. She was bound to feel grossly insulted.

'But…marriage!' He ran his hands through his hair, dislodging his cap as he thrust his fingers through his mane of curls. Life had been too uncertain to contemplate it before. Besides, there had always been, as Henry had reminded him, plenty of females willing to accommodate his need for sexual release. And deep down, he had always assumed that, if he ever did wish to marry, it would be to a girl from a similar background.

'It's not the end of the world, Ger!' Henry chose to find his discomfort amusing, his stern features relaxing into a wry smile. 'In fact, I can heartily recommend the state of marriage.'

'Well, yes, you can, since your wife is just about the most captivating woman we have come across in three royal courts!' Sir Geraint got to his feet hastily, cursing his tongue for running away with him. 'I apologise, your Grace, I—'

Henry shrugged his elegant, narrow shoulders. 'Yes, I have been most fortunate. But you know, if you don't find your own wife so…appealing as I find mine, there is nothing to stop you seeking amusement elsewhere. She has been well brought up. She won't expect fidelity.'

Sir Geraint sat down again, twisting his cap between his hands. If his father had ever dared so much as look sideways at another woman, his mother would have boxed his ears. What was the point of marrying at all if neither partner cared what the other got up to?

Oh, yes…the land. The strategic importance of having a loyal man in a nest of Yorkist vipers. He struck at his knee with his mangled cap.

And if he were honest, plenty of people from his own class married for reasons other than affection. The man with a horse seeking a woman with a plough; the farmer with too many sons looking about for a widow with land.

'Of course I will marry her, your Grace. Though it seems a pity to force her into a marriage she may not want.'

'Yes. It would be better for all concerned if you could persuade her that you are the husband she would choose, if she had a choice at all. By all means, woo her, Ger.'

He would have to abandon his pursuit of his luscious little nut-brown maid, then. He sighed heavily. He could not in all conscience plan to bed her while he was courting another woman to wife.

'Can you tell me…' Sir Geraint turned mournful eyes upon the King '…if she is at all comely?'

King Henry laughed aloud. 'These four nobles all seem to think her land makes her appealing enough to overlook any physical deficiencies she may have.' He picked up four documents from among the piles upon the desktop. 'Since they have all petitioned me for her hand.'

Physical deficiencies. A cold hard knot seemed to form in the middle of Sir Geraint's chest.

'I cannot possibly allow her to marry Lord Worthing.' He dropped one of the petitions to the floor. 'He is a sworn ally of the Percy family. I may have given the Earl of Northumberland a second chance by releasing him from prison and re-instating him as Warden of the north, but if he steps out of line I want to know about it. If you were up there, you could be my eyes and ears. As for these others…' He tossed the remaining petitions aside with a shake of his head.

'I want to show the people I mean to be a just king, one they need not rebel against, by pursuing a policy of forgiveness and reconciliation wherever possible. The people of Woolton will settle better under my rule if I re-instate the girl they will consider the natural successor. And they will be loyal to her children.

'In the meantime, you will have twenty armed men at your back to establish a foothold in what has always been a Yorkist stronghold. You must put aside any squeamishness you may feel about taking the Woolton heiress to wife. With her to hold the people, and you to hold her, I should be able to establish stability in that region.'

Sir Geraint regarded his King with renewed admiration. By brokering this marriage, he had dealt with many issues at a stroke. He had no doubt Henry was going to be one of the greatest Kings England had yet seen.

'I will not fail you in this, your Grace. Whatever I think of this girl, I swear I will persuade her to marry me.'

'For my part, I promise you will not regret it.' Henry strode over to him and clapped him on the shoulder. 'Nor will I leave you to campaign alone. My own wife will introduce the topic of marriage to the girl. We do not know where her political allegiances lie, but I am quite sure we can make her see the advantages of this match. She is, by all accounts, a demure maiden who has been brought up to obey her guardians without question. With the Queen's urgings, coupled with your own…charm…I am sure she will accept her fate with hardly a murmur.'

Sir Geraint's spirits sank in spite of knowing this marriage was for the good of a whole lot of other people.

'Don't you want to know her name?'

Sir Geraint shrugged. 'I suppose I should.'

'It is Agnes.'

Sir Geraint flinched. It just would be. The Woolton heiress was named for the saint whose virtue was so unassailable—probably, he had always suspected, because she was so repellent—that she had even managed to hang on to her virginity when condemned to serve in a Roman brothel.

Apparently oblivious to Sir Geraint's mood, Henry looked up and smiled. 'I will make arrangements for the two of you to meet at the earliest opportunity, so we can proceed apace.'

'Thank you, your Grace.' He was Henry's man, aye, and he would marry this saintly, anaemic child and hold her lands for his king. But he knew himself well enough to know that if he must bid farewell to dreams of Maddy, he could not do so within the palace walls. If he were to run into her again…an ache twisted in his gut as a vision of his beautiful, brave, passionate little sprite flickered tantalisingly across his mind's eye, waving farewell with an impudent grin as she wriggled out of his grasp for the last time. Sir Geraint bowed himself out of the room, his feet already turning to the fastest route to the nearest tavern.

Chapter Six

Maddy smoothed the rumpled linen of her working gown as a smiling waiting woman ushered her into Princess Elizabeth's apartments.

She tried to smile back, but her mouth felt stiff and awkward. She had never had an audience with the young Queen before. She had only glimpsed her from a distance, during the wedding in January. From a vantage point behind a pillar, she had watched the other, gorgeously dressed ladies enjoying the dancing which had followed the wedding feast. That had been the first time she had seen Lord Hugo. He had been dancing with Lady Lacey, and she had felt almost dazzled at the picture they made. He so handsome, she so beautiful, and both so graceful of carriage.

Maddy's feeling of anxiety increased as she caught sight of Lady Lacey, frowning at the plain, workaday gown she had on. On receiving this royal summons, she'd immediately thought of going to change her gown, but the knowledge of what other clothes lay in her coffer promptly had her abandoning that notion. Now she wished she had taken a few minutes to squeeze herself into the olive velvet, though it was so immodest. No wonder Lady Lacey was so insistent on spending any money that came their way on new gowns. Why, if Maddy had to spend her days in a room as luxuriously appointed as this, she would make sure she did not look as out of place as she felt at that minute. Thick, soft carpets covered every inch of

the floor space. All the chairs and couches were piled with satin
cushions in brilliant hues that echoed the vibrant reds and blues of
the tapestries adorning the walls. It was only when she noticed Lady
Lacey jerking her hand meaningfully towards a girl who was looking
back at her with frank amusement, that she took in the significance
of the fact she was the only person in the room seated on a chair.

Colour flooding to her cheeks, Maddy belatedly sank into a deep
curtsy to the woman who would soon be crowned Queen of England,
feeling acutely aware of the ridiculous picture she must have just
made of herself, gawping at the wall hangings.

'Come and sit by me, Lady Agnes,' Princess Elizabeth cooed.

Nervously, Maddy made her way to a little silken footstool beside
her chair, feeling like hedge sparrow come suddenly into a gathering of peacocks.

'We wish to be private with Lady Agnes, and her cousin.'

At the royal edict, the other ladies ranged about the room gathered
up their skirts and swished from sight, though not without casting
curious glances at Maddy on their way out.

'I did not think you would wish others to be privy to this conversation, Lady Agnes,' the Princess smiled.

'No, of course… I mean, yes, that is…what conversation?'

To her utter astonishment, the Princess burst out laughing. Casting
a knowing look at Lady Lacey, she said, 'Oh, I quite see now why
you have taken such pains to shelter her from the hurly burly of
court, Lady Eleanor!'

'Indeed.' Though seconds before Lady Lacey had looked furious,
she now put on a mask of indulgent concern as she said, 'The poor child
is neither quick of speech, nor wit, besides being excessively bashful.'

While Maddy hung her head, to conceal the struggle she was
having to tamp down her outrage at this patronising little speech,
the Princess said, 'Not too bashful to listen to some words of advice
concerning your marriage, I hope?'

'My marriage?' No! Lord Hugo could not have moved this swiftly.

Yet why else would the Princess be interested in the marriage of a lowly ribbon maker? It was only Lady Lacey's audible gasp that made her realise that the subject of this interview was as much of a surprise to her as it was to Maddy. Which might mean that Lord Hugo had nothing to do with it. Though her heart was still pattering with alarm, she managed to lift her eyes hopefully towards her Princess.

'You must have thought about it,' Elizabeth continued. 'Every woman does.'

'N...no...that is...' She knew she could not lie to her Queen. Of late, she had been thinking of little else bar how she was to evade the kind of marriage that Lord Hugo had planned for her. 'I mean, yes.'

To her immense relief, Princess Elizabeth promptly burst into a fit of giggles, her hand flying to her mouth in a gesture so girlish, Maddy remembered she was hardly any older than herself.

'Well, there are five men present at court today who have thought a great deal about marrying you. So much, indeed, that each has petitioned the King for your hand.'

'Five?'

The Princess nodded, clearly highly entertained by Maddy's complete shock.

'Five,' she repeated, bemused. How on earth had five men noticed her enough to want to marry her? She was not pretty. And she tried to attract as little notice as she could. Until...no, surely one outing in a too-tight gown could not have sent five men into a frenzy of lust so hot they had immediately petitioned for her hand!

She gave the Princess a direct look. 'Is this some sort of a jest, your Grace?'

Though Lady Lacey gasped at Maddy's rudeness, the Queen was still disposed to find her gaucheness highly amusing.

'No, oh, no, indeed,' she trilled. 'They are all in deadly earnest. So much, that my lord husband the King has asked me to step in and offer you the benefit of my advice before he permits any of them to besiege you with their attentions. I cannot stress how important it is for you to choose both wisely, and quickly, Lady Agnes. We do not want you to suffer the same fate as poor Elizabeth Greystoke.'

'Well, the situation hardly compares, does it? Elizabeth Greystoke was an heiress.' Not content with receiving a pardon for his part at Bosworth, a certain Lord Dacre had abducted and raped the unfortunate woman, confident that she would then have no option but to marry him, thereby yielding control of her lands and considerable wealth to him.

The Queen shot Lady Lacey a speculative look. 'You have not told her?'

Lady Lacey shook her head. 'I thought it for the best, your Grace. You can see what a simpleton she is. There was no need to trouble her head…or to publish her expectations abroad, rendering her vulnerable to smooth-tongued rogues like Lord Dacre who would covet her wealth.'

Maddy pressed her fists to her temples. 'I am not wealthy! How can you say it? If it was not for your generosity, your Grace, in giving me employment, I would be destitute. My father died a traitor at Bosworth. All his lands forfeit…'

The Princess laid her hand gently on Maddy's arm. 'My lord husband the King has pardoned many who mistakenly fought for Richard of Gloucester, Lady Agnes. All you would have to do is make some gesture of good faith, to demonstrate your loyalty, and he would be willing to restore all that belonged to your family.'

Maddy's head was spinning. 'But I am not a man! I cannot just inherit my father's estates and govern as if I were a man!'

'No, but your husband could manage them on your behalf. You are the last of the DelaBoys. It would please the King to make a gesture of clemency to your family, by permitting you to return to your ancestral home, and, naturally, to restore rights of future revenues to your own coffers.'

'That is…' Maddy gasped '…that is most generous!'

And a shrewd move on Henry Tudor's part. If he simply gave the land to a man of his own choosing, the people might quickly become rebellious. By nominally returning the estate to the last of the DelaBoys he was clearly hoping to ingratiate himself with the local populace.

'Yes…' Elizabeth's eyes narrowed as she studied Maddy's speculative expression '…I am glad you are sensible of how generous a gesture this is. I hope you will be suitably grateful.'

Maddy heard the challenge, and remembered the Princess saying that those who had land restored had done so after making some gesture of loyalty to their new King.

'What is it you wish me to do to express my gratitude, your Grace?'

Princess Elizabeth smiled. 'We wish you to put aside any personal preferences you may have when considering your suitors, Lady Agnes. For a person in your position, there are much more important issues to consider.'

'Yes?' Maddy did her best to look wide-eyed and innocent, though her heart was racing with dread at what the Queen might ask of her next.

'The King considers, and so do I…' she wrinkled her nose '…that certain of these suitors are highly undesirable. They have affiliations that would create an imbalance of power in the north. I am sure you can appreciate the importance of restoring stability to the realm?'

Maddy's face was grim. 'I am quite sure there should be no more fighting, your Grace. I have lost all my brothers, and, I had thought, my home. And for what? I have never been able to understand any one of the causes that provoked my brothers to take up arms. They just seemed to love fighting. If men don't have a cause, it seems to me they will invent one. Lords on their horses with swords, or grooms in the taverns with fists…' she curled her lip in distaste '…they are all the same!'

The Queen positively beamed at her. 'Oh, so you can speak when you are sufficiently roused!'

Maddy shifted uncomfortably on her stool, her face hot.

'No, do not be ashamed of speaking your mind. I think you are a gentle little soul, are you not? Returning to your home, and raising a family will be much more to your liking than the rackety life we live at court, hmm?'

Not if the husband the King wanted her to take was Lord Hugo de Vere!

'I…I'm not sure…that is, I…'

'Oh, you are shy at the prospect of all that entails!'

Maddy tried not to bridle. Princess Elizabeth was scarcely older than she, and here she was taking hold of her hand and patting it as though she were her grandmother!

'But the man the King would have you wed will take the greatest care of you, Lady Agnes. He is an honest and brave man who has proved his loyalty to my husband in a hundred different ways over the years he has served him.'

A huge weight seemed to lift from her shoulders as she heard the description of a man who was the very antithesis of Lord Hugo. He had been one of the many who had been obliged to publicly declare their allegiance to the new King and repent of his former service to the old one.

'He is somewhat older than you…'

Oh, no! Not Lord Worthing! Please, not Lord Worthing!

'About the same age as the King…'

Her fleeting moment of panic subsided. The King was only twenty-eight. Lord Worthing was forty if he was a day.

'But he is not of noble birth.' The Princess caught her lower lip in her teeth as she studied Maddy's downcast head. 'Does that offend you?'

Maddy did not care what her husband was, as long as he was neither Lord Hugo nor Lord Worthing. She was just wondering how to express this in polite terms, when Lady Lacey objected,

'You cannot expect Lady Agnes to wed a commoner!'

The Queen's smile vanished. 'Why not? The Lady Agnes, if we are going to be truthful, is, at this present moment, merely the impoverished daughter of a traitor. He may lack a little polish, but I can assure you he is the very man to hold Lady Agnes's lands for her. Not only did my lord the King knight him for bravery on the battlefield, but he wishes particularly to reward him for all the years of faithful service that went before.'

And she was to be his reward, thought Maddy, bitterly. Or rather, the revenues her land would fetch.

'However, we do not expect Lady Agnes to commit herself today. She must meet him, and permit him to woo her, bearing in mind that he is the King's choice above all others.'

Maddy leapt to her feet, overturning the stool. She paced to the far side of the room, her fists pressed to her temples. What was the point in meeting this knight? He was going to be the means by which she could escape from Lord Hugo. What was more, accepting him would prove her loyalty to the crown. All the stigma of being a traitor's daughter would be swept away. She whirled round.

'I do not need to meet him, your Grace…'

'Lady Agnes!' Lady Lacey's face was pale, the Queen's expression set.

'If it is the King's wish that I wed with this knight,' Maddy continued, lifting her chin, 'then of course I will do so. As soon as you wish!'

There, she had done it. She was free!

The Queen too stood up, clapping her hands together. 'Then we will hold the ceremony of betrothal as soon as you have a suitable gown to wear.' She nodded to Lady Lacey. 'No need to keep her disguised as though she were nothing but a mere servant any longer! And you will want to look as pretty as you can for Sir Geraint, won't you?'

'Sir Geraint?' Maddy's legs turned hollow. Before he had a name, he had been nothing more than a means to an end. Suddenly he seemed alarmingly real.

Was he handsome like Lord Hugo? Or fat like Lord Worthing? Tall, like the King? Or short, like her father? Did he drink heavily and chase serving girls? Would he be kind to her? Or would he beat her? She felt the blood drain from her face.

Why had she been so rash? She had not even heard of this Sir

Geraint before. At least she would have known exactly what to
expect from Lord Hugo.

'You do not need to be afraid.' The Princess was regarding her
with some concern. 'Trust me. And trust in your King. What we have
planned for you is best for all concerned.'

Trust the King? How could she? He neither knew her, nor cared
about her. She was no more than a pawn to him, which he was
moving to further some stratagem he had devised.

But it was too late now. She had agreed to this marriage. The die
was cast. Raising tear-filled eyes to her mistress, Maddy whispered
rather shakily, 'I will try.' She attempted a rather tremulous smile.
'I know how important it is to restore peace to our land, your Grace.'

'How can you be such a simpleton, Agnes?' Lady Lacey had kept
her lips firmly pressed together all the way back to the dorter, but
now she was practically exploding with rage.

'Why on earth did you just tamely agree to marry this…Geraint
fellow? This commoner! How could you do it to me?' She took hold
of both her shoulders, and shook her hard.

'You could have married Lord Hugo!'

'L…Lord Hugo?' Even though Maddy had already glimpsed
something of the obsession the woman had with him, the crazed look
in Lady Lacey's eyes was frightening to behold.

'Yes! He must have been one of the petitioners to the King for
your hand! Why did you not at least ask who they were?'

'Wh…what would have b…been the point?' Maddy jerked out
as her head snapped back and forth under the force of Lady Lacey's
shaking. She was beginning to feel sick, her alarm increasing as
Lady Lacey's hands edged ever closer to her throat.

'The point, you fool,' she wailed, finally flinging her away in
disgust, 'was that you could have made a choice.' Maddy fetched
up against the wall of the sleeping quarters, the back of her skull
cracking against the window ledge.

'I could have persuaded the Queen it would be cruel to force you into a marriage with a man you didn't like!' Lady Lacey appeared not to notice that Maddy was sliding to the floor, half-stunned by the force of the blow. 'That you were so sensitive a creature,' she ranted, pacing up and down between the rows of narrow cots, 'that it would destroy you! But, no! You had to go and agree to a betrothal without showing the faintest glimmer of curiosity about any one of your suitors!'

'I am sorry, my lady,' Maddy sobbed, the tears that began to fall real enough from the pain lancing through her head. 'But what else could I have done, in the end? You heard what the Queen said. The King only grants land back to people who demonstrate their loyalty to him. She was testing me! If I hadn't accepted the King's choice of husband, I would never have been beyond suspicion. Besides, I am his ward. No man may marry me without his permission. He would probably not have granted it to any of the others, if he wants this knight to have my land.'

Lady Lacey sank down on to the nearest bed, shaking her head. 'You could have married Lord Hugo. We could have managed it somehow, if only you had...' She paused. 'I thought you were besotted with him!'

Maddy felt it was better to stick relatively close to the truth. Until her eyes had been opened, she had indeed experienced a foolish, girlish type of adoration for the elegantly attractive young lord. 'Was it so obvious?' She avoided looking her cousin directly in the eye, by brushing the tears from her face with the hem of her gown. 'But the Queen told me to put my personal preferences aside! The King wants me to marry this...Sir something or other, as a declaration of loyalty.'

She struggled to her feet and went to sit beside her cousin. 'We don't know much about this Henry Tudor yet.' She sniffed. 'If I had insisted on marrying the man I really wanted to marry, he might have accounted it treason, executed us both, and simply have given his man the DelaBoys land anyway.' She shrugged, spreading her hands eloquently. 'At least, this way, I will live.'

'But Lord Hugo—'

'He would never have cared for me as much as I cared for him. How could he? He could have any woman he wanted for the crooking of his finger, whereas I am just a plain little dab of a thing. Besides, how can you be sure he ever considered marrying me? He never said anything.'

Lady Lacey's eyes slid away guiltily, then she stalked from the room without saying another word.

Maddy knew she must be furious that her plans had all been scotched, so she was astounded, the next morning, when nobody could have seemed better pleased with Maddy's impending betrothal than Lady Lacey herself. She even spoke of it as if she had been the guiding hand behind the match all along! She breezed into Maddy's workroom, full of plans for the betrothal gown, giving no signs she would leave, even when the cutting and sewing began. In the days that followed, her apparent devotion to her young relative meant she scarcely left her side.

The women with whom Maddy had been working were thrilled to find they had been sheltering an heiress secretly in their midst.

'It's just like something out of a story,' Margot declared through a mouthful of pins as she reverently ran her hand over a length of cloth-of-gold the king himself had sent, as a present to the bride. Although Lady Lacey had talked her into agreeing to wear mulberry and blue for the betrothal, as a symbol of fealty to Princess Elizabeth, whose colours they were, her bridal finery was to be all green and gold, her own family colours.

'It seems almost a shame to set the scissors to it,' Prudence sighed as she spread the costly material on the cutting table.

'Oh, but we must make sure the King sees she is wearing it,' Lady Lacey replied archly. 'She wants the King to know most particularly what a loyal and grateful subject she is.'

Maddy almost breathed a sigh of relief at this acid remark. This was a Lady Lacey she knew how to deal with!

* * *

But when she blithely announced, on the morning of the betrothal ceremony, that she planned to travel to Woolton Castle with her dear Lady Agnes, Maddy could not hide her astonishment.

'Well,' Lady Lacey tittered as Prudence adjusted the long velvet lappet round the genuinely gabled bonnet that perched precariously on Maddy's head, 'you cannot be expected to set so many years of neglect to rights alone! Her father,' she explained as she bent to adjust the material of Maddy's skirts, 'went through one mistress after another during the latter years of his life, but gave none, I dare swear, the rights of a wife. There will have been no chatelaine to oversee the running of the place. The Princess Elizabeth,' she continued airily, 'has already approved of my request to travel with my young cousin, and render her what aid I may. I shall, of course, be returning to my place at court once she feels able to take up the reins of household governance on her own.'

If Maddy hadn't caught the bleak expression in her eyes in the mirror as Lady Lacey adjusted the set of her own headdress, she would almost have believed that leaving court was exactly what the woman wanted most. But suddenly she knew that Lady Lacey was desperately trying to conceal her broken heart. Keeping busy with the wedding preparations gave her the perfect excuse to avoid the confrontation with Lord Hugo she must be dreading. Maddy remembered those steely fingers closing round her neck even as he bent to kiss her, the veiled threats of what he would make her suffer if his plans should go awry. And her heart bled for her cousin's predicament.

Suddenly, she *wanted* Lady Lacey to go to Woolton Castle with her. She needed to escape Lord Hugo just as much as Maddy did. Tentatively she put her hand on her cousin's sleeve.

'Thank you, Eleanor,' she said, 'for standing by me, and…and…'

'Well, you are going to need all the support you can get, aren't you?' She whirled round, her eyes flicking contemptuously over her from head to toe. And suddenly Maddy was aware that though this was the most costly gown she had ever possessed in her life, it did absolutely nothing for her, while this shade of blue suited Lady Lacey particularly well.

'It won't be very pleasant, being married to an ambitious land-hungry peasant. Especially not once he's got you away from the King's watchful eye.' She clicked her tongue, shaking her head in mock-concern.

'He is a knight,' Maddy countered, determined not to show a hint of the nervousness she felt in front of the grand ladies from the Princess's entourage, who had helped her dress for this solemn occasion.

'Lots of landless knights marry heiresses. It doesn't make him a bad man.'

Lady Lacey bestowed a pitying smile on her before turning and walking to the door, leaving Maddy gazing despondently at her lone reflection.

She lifted her chin defiantly. Why should she be afraid? The deal she was about to strike had at least the virtue of being completely honest. The King wanted to reward this knight. The knight wanted her land and her wealth. She wanted a means to escape the court in general and Lord Hugo in particular. They would all get what they wanted. Except…she sighed. There was no escaping her lack of allure. Her huge dark eyes gazed back at her from a round white face. Her very lips lacked colour. No amount of expensive brocade could disguise the fact that she was a pale little dab of nothing.

Stung by the awareness of how little she had to offer any man, she spun away from the cruel mirror, and marched across to the chamber door. Lifting her chin even higher, she set out on the short walk to the King's chapel where her worthy knight was waiting for her. She would be a good wife, in all the practical ways, she would tell him, even if she couldn't do anything about her plain countenance. Lady Lacey had been a good housewife to her exacting husband, and would teach her all the chatelaine of a castle needed to know. And she would be diligent about the welfare of her people, as her mother had been before her.

Yes, she decided, it would be a good thing to run things her own way, for once. It felt as though she had been in other people's houses, dependent on their largesse, for most of her life. At least marrying this man meant she could go home.

Home, she sighed, thinking of Woolton. It had been far too long since she had stood on the battlements and seen the wild moorland blush with purple as the seasons changed, or watched the rough grey tide come roaring over the shimmering sweep of the bay.

Even as the memory of the turbulent sea came into her mind's eye, another image sprang, unbidden and totally inappropriate, into her head. That stranger's eyes had been grey like those stormy seas. He had unleashed a veritable storm within her body when he had kissed her. She felt her cheeks flush guiltily. She must not think of him now. Not ever, except as an object lesson in the power a man could wield over a woman if she once let him take liberties with her person.

Maddy lowered her eyes demurely to the floor, her lips compressing with resolve. She must hope that her husband's kisses did not excite her too much. She had Lady Lacey as a warning of what followed when a woman yearned for a man beyond all reason. And she was not, most definitely not, going to end up like her!

She would take great care never to let her husband into her heart. She would not give any man the power to hurt her.

But this resolve did nothing to calm the agitated beating of her heart.

And, as she set foot inside the chapel, head bowed, trembling hands clasped at her waist, she looked more like the victim being led forth to execution, than a bride on her way to meet her groom.

Chapter Seven

For once, Sir Geraint did not glare back defiantly when the Bishop of Ely looked down his nose at him. He knew he was not a fitting husband for the virtuous paragon of the aristocracy who was so meek she had agreed to this betrothal without even wanting to take a look at him.

Did people of rank really go about things in such a cold-blooded fashion?

Apparently so, for when he'd entered the chapel a short while ago, the King had congratulated him on securing such a biddable woman to wife.

'She will suit you admirably, Ger. Since she's been at court, she's taken as little part in all the amusements on offer as you have. She has kept apart, spending her time at her loom, or studying her psalter.'

Dipping his head, he'd rubbed at a rust spot on the sleeve of the green velvet doublet that had served him for formal occasions in the courts of Brittany and France. He wished he had thought to order a new suit of clothes, but even if he had, King Henry was so impatient to secure Woolton he doubted there would have been time. He'd made do with having this suit brushed and pressed and having his unruly curls severely trimmed. But he still felt distinctly shabby, and totally unworthy of this wealthy baron's daughter.

The sort of woman he ought to marry would be someone like his mother. A plump, bustling woman of great intelligence, a partner without whom his father's prosperity would not have been assured, not a prim bloodless creature who would sit in her room weaving all day. When she wasn't at her prayers!

No wonder so many of the upper ranks took mistresses besides their wives. How long would it be before he too strayed from a cold bed where only duty would hold his saintly wife rigid beneath him while he strove to sire sons to inherit the land the King had entrusted to him? And God, how he pitied his brood already with such a mother!

He gritted his teeth. He would try to be a faithful husband. He had no wish to humiliate his wife when she could not supply his needs. But if ever he stumbled across a delectable creature like that sensuous little nut-brown maid, the temptation might prove too much. He sighed, remembering how Maddy had arched into his caress, mewling like a kitten.

A rustle of skirts, a murmuring of voices in the doorway, broke through his abstraction.

Sir Geraint tried to gain comfort from the way the King and Queen smiled at each other. Theirs had been a marriage made for political expediency. Neither had met the other when they agreed to it. Yet they appeared well content.

He steeled himself to show no emotion as he searched among the women who trailed behind the Princess for the woman who was to be his wife. They were all wearing the Woodville colours of mulberry and blue, with matching little gabled hats. There was nothing to give a clue as to which one of these identically dressed females might be the Lady Agnes.

He found his heart was beating as rapidly as on that one occasion he had gone into battle. Blood surged through his veins just as it had when he had grasped his sword and steeled himself to fight. Though at least then he had known who his enemy was!

Then, for a second, his heart stopped beating altogether, as he saw, lagging slightly behind the rest of the Queen's entourage, his little nut-brown maid!

Maddy! Dressed in sumptuous velvet, with her head bowed, her hands clasped before her…Maddy was one of the Queen's waiting women! Feeling as though he had been punched in the gut, he wrenched his gaze away from her, focusing instead on the plain gold cross that stood on the altar.

Oh, God, he groaned. How was he to make sacred vows to the virtuous Lady Agnes while he was burning with lust for another woman? Even all those hideously coloured layers of velvet could not totally disguise her dainty curves. He clenched and unclenched hands that had once held her close to his body, striving to keep his face impassive. Why did Maddy have to be here, now, as he was in the very act of renouncing her for ever!

Then, as though he was hearing his doom pronounced, he heard the bishop calling the Lady Agnes to come and stand at his side, to make her vows with him in the presence of the assembled witnesses.

He smelt the faint fragrance of roses and felt the warmth of a body beside his. He knew he would have to look at her at some point during the proceedings. But he would not do so until he had managed to erase all trace of his bitter disappointment from his face. Nor would he shame his unwanted bride by sneaking glances at the woman he really desired. He had no wish to wound this poor young woman who had come, in all good faith, to pledge herself to him. With this resolve firmly in place, he turned to look upon his chosen bride for the first time.

And saw Maddy, her head still downbent, her white knuckled hands still clasped at her waist.

For a second he could not understand why she should be standing where his bride should be. But then the Bishop began to say the prayers that would commit them to each other for life.

'Maddy?' he whispered, taking her trembling hand in his.

At the sound of his voice, she started, looking up with eyes wide with shock.

There stood the stranger with the stormy eyes. The man whose kisses still burned in her blood.

'Sir Geraint?' she mouthed. The king was marrying her to the kennel man? No…they said he was a knight. He had been out riding with the hounds, but…he had never said he was a kennel man. She had just assumed it.

And he was going to be her husband! Oh, how wonderful! She need have no more fear. Had she not felt safe with him from the very moment he had swept her into his arms and onto the back of his mean old destrier? She smiled at him in heartfelt relief.

How fortunate that her husband should turn out to be, out of all the men in the court that it might have been, this rugged, handsome man in whose arms she had felt so safe.

That was, until he had kissed her. Shifting a little uncomfortably, she could not help but look at his lips as the Archbishop droned on in the background, remembering the feel of them on her own, her wonder at the magic that they had wrought in comparison with Lord Hugo's tepid embrace. And it struck her now, for the first time, that it was mighty strange that she, who had never thought any man would ever kiss her, should have been kissed by two totally separate men on the very same day.

Her pleasure leached from her like sea foam through shingle. Five suitors, the Princess had said. Lord Hugo was one, Sir Geraint another…and there were three others. It would seem that Lord Hugo and Sir Geraint were simply the two most determined to get at her land. The others had at least gone to the King first, seeking his permission to court her. These two had tried to worm their way into her heart with their false kisses!

Pain sliced through her at the realisation that Sir Geraint's kiss had been as calculated as Lord Hugo's. And far more dangerous to her, because it had affected her much more deeply.

She tore her eyes from his treacherous mouth. She would have done better to marry Lord Hugo. At least she knew exactly what he had planned for her. And she was immune to him! But as for this fellow…suddenly she wanted to free her hand from his, but his grip was too strong. A burst of panic had her looking up at him in dismay.

He held her, now and for ever. Would she end up like Lady Lacey after all? In total thrall to a man? And was it her imagination, or could she detect a hardness creep into his expression, a hint of the very ruthlessness that he must have at his core to have risen from his humble origins to a place this high in the King's esteem?

Sir Geraint watched the expressions flit across Maddy's beautiful little face, from relief, to awareness, as she had looked at his mouth, to the moment when something had driven every last scrap of colour from her cheeks, leaving them as milky pale as when she had first stood at his side.

The brief feeling of euphoria he had known on finding that Maddy and Lady Agnes were one and the selfsame person evaporated. Something was very wrong here. She hadn't agreed to marry him because she knew who he was, and the kiss they had shared had affected her as much as it affected him. She had not known she had agreed to marry the man she had met in the garden at all! Oh, she remembered the kiss well enough. The way she had gazed at his mouth spoke volumes.

But she had not planned on marrying him. Not him. He could not have missed the start of surprise when she had looked up, and recognised him, and mouthed his name in bewilderment.

What was she playing at? Kissing a stranger in the garden, then rushing into marriage with another? He brushed aside the inconsequential fact that he was one and the same man in both cases. From her point of view, it was two entirely different people.

What was she? His mouth twisted into a cynical sneer. Not the virginal little paragon the King had sold him, that was for sure. Nor the cute little kitten he had been dreaming of, either. A sly cat was probably nearer the mark. Deceiving all about her with her skilful wiles.

So deeply was she dyed in deceit, she had even given him a false name.

He glared down at the top of her meekly bent head. Meek! He thought not. She wanted everybody to think she was, aye, while her busy little brain was scheming.

And why? Why would a woman agree to marry a man she had never met? Why would she then look so dismayed when she remembered he had kissed her?

Because he knew how passionate, how wanton she was, that was why. She could not put on her pious virginal little act with him! He knew she had had other lovers…

The reason why she had been crying so bitterly, why she had insisted men were cruel, was obvious now. One of her lovers must have got her with child. And could not, or would not, wed her.

It was the only reason that a woman so wealthy would rush headlong into the first marriage proposal she received, though it was from a commoner.

His rage did not abate until he sat down beside her at table in the banqueting hall and forced himself to look at her again. She sat, hunched and miserable at his side, stirring her spoon in a desultory manner through a bowl of cinnamon soup. Her face was deathly pale. His conscience pricked him. Had he not vowed, as he stood before the altar, that he was going to try to be kind to his wife, even if he was disappointed in her? Just because it was her lack of morals that displeased him, rather than a surfeit of them, was that any excuse to scare her?

And if he was honest with himself, wouldn't he be thrilled to be sitting beside her now, if he had not just become betrothed to her? Was it not illogical for him to be angry, when, before he had known she would be his wife, he would have been perfectly happy to take advantage of her amorous nature?

Why was Sir Geraint so angry with her? Maddy wondered. He had got what he wanted, hadn't he? He had tricked her into this betrothal with his skilful kissing, and the backing of the King.

But now he had her, he did not seem to think he needed to pretend he found her desirable any more. She lifted a slice of duck to her mouth, but the succulent meat might as well have been sawdust. He had extended her the courtesy, for the sake of appearance, of placing this food upon her trencher, but he did not bother to speak to her, so completely did he despise her for the ease with which he had gulled her.

She felt the sting of tears, and blinked them back furiously. She must not let it hurt! Somehow she must find a way to armour her heart against Sir Geraint, or he would break her!

She couldn't help flinching when he laid his hand over hers and gave it a gentle squeeze. What trick was this now? What did he mean by it?

When he raised her hand to his mouth, pressing a kiss to the back of her clenched fist, there was nothing she could do to prevent the very public intimacy. It was a hateful demonstration that he was very much stronger than her. Wounded, furious, helpless, all she could do in her defence was turn her head and glare at him. He might control her body, but he would never control her heart. She would resist him to the last breath she drew!

Whatever her marriage turned out to be like, she would still be the chatelaine of Woolton Castle. Lips pressed tightly in determination, she dipped her spoon into a dish of mint jelly, and began to smear it over her portion of duck.

And, in time, she would have children. Babies. A warm glow thawed a small corner of her frozen heart at the prospect of becoming a mother. Her children would love her. Children could not help loving their mother. And she would lavish her love upon them all, be they boys or girls. Even if her husband never cared for her, or them, he was duty bound to fill his nursery. And she would have what she had been longing for all her life. Her own family.

She barely noticed when a servant came to sweep away the soggy mess she had made of her trencher into a voider, having suddenly become aware that Sir Geraint still held her hand fast in his.

His hand was so large, and though she had felt his strength exerted against her, now his clasp was gentle. He may not ever like her, but the marriage would improve her lot in life a great deal. And anyway, it was too late now. They were betrothed. A betrothal was as legally binding as a marriage. This was her reality now. Her life, pale and fragile as it was, lay within his hands. He could easily crush her. Yet somehow, she could not really believe he would.

Sir Geraint lent in close to her as a group of tumblers burst into the hall. Using the cover of the loud applause their entrance provoked, he murmured, 'The lawyers tell me that our contract is very straightforward. It will not take long to settle all that side of things between us. Do you wish to delay our wedding, perchance, in order that we might get better acquainted?'

Why did she get the feeling he was accusing her of something? Or testing her? Oh, if only she were more practised in the art of glib repartee. Then she could come up with a light reply to turn aside the barb she could detect in his words, though she was at a loss to understand exactly whence it came. Instead, all she could offer him was a plain answer.

'I do not think there is any need.' Putting it off would not make things any easier between them.

'So, you wish the marriage to go ahead as speedily as possible?'

If anything, he looked angrier than ever.

She could only assume he found her so repulsive that he wished to delay the moment when he would have to force himself to consummate their union! Indignantly, she raised her chin.

'Why not?'

For a moment or two he said nothing, but his lip curled as his eyes raked her. She felt her face grow hot as they came to rest on the exposed curve of her breast. The cut of her stiffly boned bodice was so low that it only just concealed her nipples from view. Even as her mind strayed to them, she felt them stiffening, pushing against the fabric as though they wanted to thrust it aside and let him look his fill.

'Why not indeed?'

Her face flooded with guilty heat. He could not possibly know her nipples were proudly displaying their willingness to have him look his fill! He must be speaking of something else. Something that they had been discussing. If only she could remember what it was.

'The King intends to make a progress with his Queen, quite soon.' He slipped his arm across the back of her chair. His breath was warm in her ear, trickling down her neck, setting off a reaction in her spine that had her toes curling within their dainty satin slippers.

'He does?' Her mind seemed to have melted like slush under the first south wind of spring. Vaguely, she registered the acrobats tumbling from the room. A trumpet fanfare heralded the bringing in of the entremets. Everyone applauded the pastry castle that was paraded round the hall before being set on the table before them. Her family's coat of arms was picked out in gold leaf on each wall of the confection that was supposed to represent, she supposed, Woolton, her groom's reward for taking on such an unappetising woman to wife.

'The King would be well pleased if I was in place before he set out.' His lips brushed her ear as he spoke.

'Set out?' Her eyes followed the panter and trenchermen as they set out one of the most spectacular banquets she had ever attended. Why was he remarking on that? She forced her brain to surface from the sensuous haze that pulsed through her from the point where his lips were now brushing against her neck. Oh, yes. The King was going on a progress.

Sir Geraint cut a slice from the showy pastry construction that was stuffed with a sweet mix of dates and spiced apples, holding it on the point of his knife to her lips. Everyone was watching, waiting for her to open her mouth and accept it. When she did so, amidst ribald laughter, he said, 'We could marry tomorrow, or the day after, and set out before the end of the week. Should you like that, my lady?'

There it was. That taunt in his voice. Though she could not get her mind past anything but the nearness of him. Or the conviction that if she were to turn her head the merest fraction, make the slightest move towards him, he would kiss her, here, with her mouth full of pastry and everyone watching.

And she would let him. Would probably not be able to stop herself from responding just like she had the last time. And everyone would know that he had conquered her.

A sense of bitter resentment that he already had such power over her turned the pastry to ashes in her mouth. She only just managed to swallow it, washing it down her throat with a draught of sweet malmsey wine. She was not a toy for him to play with! And she must prove it. To him as well as to herself.

'Like it?' She affected a careless laugh. 'Or like it not. I will obey you in this, as I must obey you in all things from now on.'

'Aye…' his lips twisted into a cynical sneer '…of course you will.'

He reached for his own cup, holding it up as if to toast her. But his eyes were hard and bright, his voice harsh as he said, 'For good or ill, you are mine for the rest of my days.'

He gulped down the wine in one long draught, then held it out to a passing servant for a refill. A feeling of panic fluttered low in her stomach at the expression of cold hard rage on his face. She could feel the antagonism flowing off him towards her in waves. But it was as nothing compared to the effect of the next words he spoke.

'Since there is no escaping our destiny, I find I am of the same mind as you. Let us get the thing over with as quickly as possible, and get out of this warren of corruption you call home.'

She flinched, his words flicking her like a whip. Though he had gone so far as to pretend an attraction he did not feel to make sure he could secure Woolton Castle, coming to the sticking point was clearly harder than he had assumed it would be!

It felt as though he had torn her heart out, leaving a great gaping, throbbing wound in her breast. With a sob, she rose from the table and fled the hall, deaf to the scandalised shouts of her guardian, blind to the scornful looks that followed her headlong rush from his rejection. She did not stop running till she reached her room, where she flung herself face down on her cot, burying her face in the pillow to stifle the sound of her cries.

Chapter Eight

The days leading up to her wedding flew by in a whirl of preparations.

Her travelling coffers overflowed with lengths of wool and silk, gloves and furs and all manner of household items—gifts from people she had never dreamed were even aware of her existence.

Among all her wedding presents, there was only one that meant anything to her. And that was the intricately decorated miniature book of hours she had just received, on this her wedding morn, from Sir Geraint himself. Picking it up, she opened it at random. It was a stunning work of art, the margins and initial letters entwined with vigorous foliage from which gorgeously coloured birds peeped out. It was both a costly and touching gift, making her thoroughly ashamed that she had repeatedly refused his requests to speak with her over the past few days.

She closed the tiny book and tucked it into her wide, fur-trimmed sleeve so that she could keep it with her throughout the day. A beacon of hope, to light her through the ordeal she was about to endure.

She had thought long and hard about her groom, during the hours she had spent sewing the beautiful golden gown she now had on. She had accepted that he had probably obeyed the King's wishes, as she had obeyed the Princess. She had put aside any hope of personal benefit from her marriage, and concentrated on the fact that his presence in the north would be a stabilising influence in the area.

Surreptitiously, she touched the book that was tucked up her sleeve as her attendants tilted the mirror so she could get a look at her appearance. Her dress was beautiful. The golden silk not only looked stunning, but felt wonderful to wear. She ran her palm lovingly over the sensuously soft, yet surprisingly warm fabric, taking a brisk step to one side to admire the way the skirt swirled like liquid sunshine about her legs. The intricately embroidered bodice hugged her delicate form, while the long sleeves, lined with damasked green, flowed from her elbows almost to her knees. It was just such a pity that she did not have the bosom to do the daringly low square-cut bodice justice.

It was a pity, too, that her dark hair fell straight from the green velvet band on her crown, to her waist. No curls, she sighed, no bosom, no colour in her cheeks at all. She should feel grateful that Sir Geraint was loyal enough to his King to go through with a marriage to a female with such little allure.

Lady Lacey came up behind her then, to place the robe of cloth-of-gold over her gown. She winced as one of Lady Lacey's rings snagged in her hair as she arranged the heavy fabric so that it flowed from her shoulders. It could have been an accident, but it was just such accidents as these that convinced her the woman still felt a good deal of spite towards her. She had loved Lord Hugo so much she had been prepared to organise Maddy's death, rather than see him wed her. Now she was marrying Sir Geraint, Lady Lacey had nothing.

Closing her eyes, she offered up a silent prayer of thanks for deliverance from Lord Hugo's plans and Lady Lacey's malice alike. When she opened them, it was to see the woman regarding her with haunted, hollow eyes.

'You look pale, Lady Agnes,' she now said, lifting the heavy mass of her hair from her face. 'Are you afraid?'

Dumbly, she nodded. There was no point in trying to conceal her state of nerves, since she was trembling like a leaf. Not a morsel of food had passed her lips through all the long hours it had taken to prepare for the ceremony, in spite of repeated reminders that she needed to keep her strength up. For she had finally begun to wonder what effect her consistent refusal to see her groom could have had on his already poor opinion of her. He must think she was snubbing him. But it was the very last time she would be able to refuse to do his bidding. She did not belong to him yet!

Deep down, though, she knew this defiance was only making matters worse, and so her fear of facing an angry bridegroom had increased as the hours crept inexorably towards this, her wedding day.

Schooling her features in a mask of concern, for the benefit, Maddy was sure, of the other ladies present, Lady Lacey said, 'Are you quite sure you do not wish to delay our departure from court for a day or so? I know your husband is keen to set out, but you are likely to be quite uncomfortable for some time after your wedding night.'

Maddy felt a tightening in her chest. In all the rush to prepare for this day, in all the time she had spent convincing herself that she had done the right thing in accepting the King's choice, her mind had skirted round the entire issue of what was physically going to happen to her tonight.

'Uncomfortable?' she repeated, bewildered.

'I've heard he is prodigious,' Prudence nodded, frowning.

Margot giggled. 'In size, or in vigour?'

'Margot!' Lady Lacey admonished, as Maddy's face turned scarlet. 'Lady Agnes is hardly more than a child. Such talk will frighten her!'

But you started it, Maddy thought resentfully, as her cousin patted her arm.

''Tis bad enough for a lady to be thrown to a jumped-up peasant at all. But to such a one as this Geraint Davies? A man of breeding would at least know how to go about the business of breaking in a maid with some finesse. But this one, by all accounts, has as much subtlety as a beast rutting in a field!'

It was a pity that these particular words were ones she had already applied to that lady's own wanton behaviour. In her mind's eye, Maddy could see her cousin's head thrown back, Lord Hugo's long shanks quivering as he pushed her up against the tree.

And Lady Lacey had the effrontery to look indignant! 'And only see how frightened our poor chick is to face him. Only remember how his advances at their betrothal banquet terrified her!'

Everyone was watching Maddy's trembling form now, their faces expressing genuine concern. She did not know what to say. This was all such a welter of misunderstanding. She opened her mouth a couple of times, before Prudence, who had never been married, opined, 'You'll soon get used to it.'

'In any event, when I come to you in the morning to collect the proofs of your virginity, and to tend to your wound...'

'Wound?' Maddy gasped. Part of her knew Lady Lacey was deliberately stoking up her nerves, but she could do nothing to stop her words from having the very effect she intended.

'It would be unkind of me not to prepare you for the ordeal you must face tonight, Lady Agnes,' Lady Lacey continued. 'There will be...some pain. It is always so when a man rents his bride's maidenhead asunder. The sheets may well become soaked with your blood. It is what all girls must endure when they become women.'

Maddy's stomach turned over. She had been nervous of many aspects of marriage, but had never dreamed she would have to go through anything as awful as this sounded!

'No, no, do not sit down!' The women rushed to hold her up as her legs almost gave out beneath her. 'You will crease the gown.'

Lady Lacey supported her on one side, and Prudence on the other as her tormentor pressed on. 'Even though you will have to submit to this lout's base urges tonight, in the morning, you must rise from the marriage bed with your head held high, and not give in to the temptation to ease the pain by walking with anything less than your usual grace. You must not allow this serf to strip you of your pride along with your nightgown!'

She had had no idea that marriage entailed pain, and bloodshed, that she would have a wound, afterwards, that would take days to heal. And she could not brush it aside as a tale made up from spite, because the other women had heard every word, and had done nothing to gainsay it. On the contrary, they had offered their unanimous sympathy!

It was all she could do to walk at all after that, but she had to, because it was time to set out to St Stephen's chapel on legs that did not quite feel as though they belonged to her. If she had not had the continued support of the two ladies, one bearing her up on either side, she was sure she would not have made it. There was a swooshing noise in her ears, the same noise she had heard once before, after that dog had savaged her, and Sir Geraint had to catch her in his arms as she almost fainted.

She hoped she would not faint now. Not with so many of the court watching her. Not in front of the King and Queen. And Sir Geraint. It had been bad enough that she had made a complete fool of herself by running out of her betrothal banquet in floods of altogether childish tears. Somehow, she had to pull herself together, and behave with the very dignity Lady Lacey was always telling her she lacked.

She breathed in deeply, the air redolent of incense reminding her that this was a holy place. Touching the little book, that token of…she was not sure what, but it surely meant something, even if it was only that God was looking down on her in this consecrated place.

And suddenly it struck her, as she touched it, that it was after she had prayed with her whole heart for an honourable way out of Lord Hugo's coil that the King had arranged this marriage. Taking a tentative step forward alone as her attendants melted away, she looked towards the altar, and the man who stood on the marble steps, waiting for her.

Was it mere coincidence that the moment she took that step of faith, a bright ray of sunshine pierced the stained glass of one of the high lancet windows, creating a haze of light around Sir Geraint's head and shoulders? She took another step forward. He was no saint, she knew that only too well, but perhaps she could hope that this man was truly God's choice for her. He turned towards her then, briefly, with a look of resolve in those steely grey eyes. Some of that steel flowed into her backbone, and she found herself taking another step. And another, and then another, and then she stood beside him.

Her heart hammering within her breast, she darted a nervous glance up at his stern profile. He looked magnificent in a green doublet that was embroidered with white roses. The longer gown that covered it was of darker green damask trimmed with white satin.

The new clothes had not been able to convince Sir Geraint that he was a suitable consort for this vision of loveliness who stood beside him. His breath had hitched in his throat when he'd turned and seen her gliding up the aisle towards him. Her ebony hair fell to her trim little waist like a cloak. The gold of her gown made her look once more like his little sprite, bathed in sunshine.

But no matter how alluring she looked, he had to remember she was hellbent on deceiving him!

He embraced the anger that licked through him, erasing his own sense of unworthiness. Well, what man would take a pregnant bride with any degree of equanimity!

If only Maddy's baby turned out to be a girl. She would grow up and marry some lord, and become mother to another dynasty. He imagined a little dark-haired sprite, on whom he could lavish all the affection he wished he could feel for the treacherous mother.

Knowing his luck, she would have a boy. A sense of abject defeat washed over him at the prospect of raising another man's son and having to claim him for his own. He did not want the world to know he had taken a whore to wife.

Whoever the father was, the locals were going to accept him because he was Maddy's son. From that point of view, he was irrelevant. He had to remember that. He was gaining wealth and position well beyond the ambitions his mother had had for him when she had sent him into service in the Tudor household.

Whereas Maddy, for her sins, was lowering herself considerably by marrying a man he'd known all along most fine ladies would turn up their noses at. He was gaining far more from the marriage than she.

He wondered if his parents had yet received the letter he had sent them telling them about this match. His mother would be cock-a-hoop! Here was he, marrying a true-born lady, inside a royal chapel, right before the altar, not in the porch of a parish church like his other siblings had done. Nobles and lords would be sharing the mass that would consecrate this union. He wished she was here to see it.

Or perhaps not. His lips tightened. These courtiers would likely snigger down their aristocratic noses at his parents, making them feel out of place. And Lady Agnes might well have been appalled by the homely simplicity of her new in-laws.

The pain in his jaw alerted him to the fact that he was grinding his teeth, and, with an effort, he stopped. Later. He would invite his parents, his brothers and their wives and children to visit Woolton Castle later, once he had gained mastery over his flighty little wife and could be reasonably certain she would treat them with respect.

For he had decided he was going to tell her, before he bedded her, that she could not deceive him into thinking the child she carried was his. Nor would he let her twist him round her finger with hypocritical protestations of virtue. They were not going to base their married life on a foundation of deceit. He had gone into this marriage with his eyes open, and would not tolerate her promiscuity in future. No more sneaking off at dawn for trysts in woods, or kissing chance-met strangers in gardens. Whatever had gone on before, he was her husband now. Her lord.

The Archbishop was speaking to him. Directly to him. With a start, he realised that the final blessing had been pronounced, and they were now man and wife. He had kneeled and stood through the sacred mass, and even spoken his vows through a surreal haze of anger.

Grim-faced, he took his bride by the hand and led her, at right angles from the chapel, into the Great Hall where King Henry, in honour of their wedding, had decreed a great feast was to be held. Garlands of greenery decorated the hall. The floor had been strewn with flowers and green herbs, which released their cleansing fragrance as they were crushed underfoot.

As he handed her into a chair, set in a place of honour, and strewn with cushions, he noted she was trembling from head to toe. She could feel his anger. She would have to be a fool not to! And she was afraid.

He heaved a sigh. Not all of his anger was directed at his wife. Some of his pain had stemmed from the knowledge that this was the reward his King had bestowed, for all his years of loyalty. He had not ennobled him, though he had done as much for men who had done far less than he.

They had been better born to begin with, though. It was the way of things that, at one generation removed from peasants, being married to a noblewoman, and a pregnant noblewoman at that, was all the reward he was entitled to.

His children would carry a title though, Henry had promised him that. Maddy's title. Though it galled him to admit it, as the bastard of some nobleman, it would be more worthy to inherit Woolton than the seed of his own loins would be.

He could not help noticing, though she had not taken the trouble to thank him for it, that she carried the prayer book he had bought her, and several times during the service she had reached into her sleeve to touch it, as though it were a good-luck charm. A judicious mixture of discipline, and reward, that was the way to tame Maddy, he had decided. The same way Frobisher trained his hounds, in fact. Though Frobisher often chanted, 'A woman, a dog and a walnut tree, the more you beat 'em, the better they be', he knew the man never treated his dogs that way. A maltreated hound cringed and cowered, and was no good for anything. He didn't want a wife who cowered from him in fear, either.

He'd watched the fearsome dogs licking Frobisher's hand affectionately, and promptly gone into the city to buy her a gift. The prayer book seemed perfect. She wanted everyone to think she was pious. And his giving it had shown her he could be generous. But after the talking to he planned to give her once they were alone, she would know he could be firm, too!

'Tell me, Lady Agnes...' he slid his arm along the back of her chair as he leaned in to speak with her above the raucous tune the minstrels had struck up '...I wish to understand...why did you agree to marry me?'

He was so big. And still seething with resentment. She tried not to shrink from him, but her whole body automatically clenched at the prospect of just what devastation such a hulking great creature could wreak on her own delicate frame. What could she say that would appease him? Her eyes lit on the Tudor roses embellishing his gown, and frantically she grasped at the one sure fact she knew about him. His loyalty to the King.

'The K...King asked it of me.' She risked a glance up at his face, to see how he had received her response. His face was so close to hers. She could feel his breath warm against her frigid cheek. He was looking at her mouth.

'Have you still not decided if I am your friend or your enemy?'

How could she be so scared of him, yet her body be responding to his closeness? And it was responding. Her lips had parted, yearning to feel the soft brush of his own against them. Her nipples had contracted into tight, needy little peaks. It was so confusing!

'I don't know!' she admitted. 'Part of me wants to trust you, but—'

When she looked up at him with those wide, innocent eyes, he wanted to... Hell! She was not innocent! She was playing on her sensuality, parting her lips and running her tongue over them until he could think of nothing but kissing them. Winding him up to such a pitch he would forget all but the desire to have her horizontal and underneath him! 'I will tell you one thing you may depend on.' He straightened up, away from her as the server ladled a dainty portion of mawmenny on to Maddy's trencher. 'If you consider me your enemy, you will find me implacable. If our marriage is to be a battleground, there can only be one victor. And it will not be you!'

Shaken, Maddy gripped her spoon, staring in perplexity at the golden liquid oozing into the bread. What had she said, or done, now? Nervously, she reached for the little book in her sleeve, praying that she might find some way from making a complete fool of herself. She did not wish to end this banquet in tears, and humiliate not only herself, but also her new husband. She dipped her spoon into the dish of ground capon stiffened with almond milk, which would have looked quite bland without the addition of saffron to render it this vibrant yellow. And her mind went back to the day when she had gone to the forest to seek for the humble British cousins of the exotic flowers that gave such dishes their colour. And how he had come running out of the mist to save her. He had been angry with her then, had handled her quite roughly, but she had sensed a deep vein of concern threaded through his treatment of her.

Taking a deep breath, she lifted her spoon to her mouth, and began to eat. If he was God's choice for her, surely she need not fear him?

Sir Geraint was relieved to see his spurt of anger had not totally robbed her of her appetite. In truth, he did not fully understand why her frank admission had raised such a storm in his breast. Had he not decided to behave with, at the very least, common civility to his wife? Yet every time he got near her, fierce emotion shredded his self-control.

He drained his wine in one draught. At least he had given her fair warning that he would be master in his own household. He would not tolerate being bested by a slip of a girl, though she was far above him by birth!

He pretended an interest in the acrobats that came on during the interval between courses that he did not feel. All that filled his consciousness was the way she sat stiff and silent beside him. Every time he moved, she flinched. If he leaned towards her, she edged away. She could not be acting more differently to that day he had drawn her on to his lap and kissed her till she writhed with passion.

It was as the acrobats departed the scene that he realised it was this that irked him the most. He wanted her to want him as much as she had done before she knew who he was.

It was little consolation to note the way she blushed as the conversation began to veer towards the bawdy. Nobody would have suspected that he had been cheated of his husbandly rights from the way her eyes widened, her cheeks even growing miraculously pale, when the time came for them to leave the table, and retire to the marriage chamber.

Maddy wished her aversion to dancing were not so well known. The dancing that followed this feast would, she knew, go on for hours. She would give anything to have been able to put off the time when she must get into bed with her husband. Her taciturn, sullen husband, who was well on the way to being drunk, since he was not counteracting the copious amounts of wine he had consumed by eating very much food. The ladies who swept her up the stairs to the chamber the King had set aside for their nuptials seemed to find her nerves a cause for great hilarity. They giggled incessantly as they stripped her, washed her, and put her into a scandalously sheer nightgown before crowning her with a chaplet of flowers and leading her to the great bed that dominated the room.

She heard the men who accompanied her husband before she saw them. They burst into the chamber, a crowd of boisterous nobles determined to make the most of the spectacle the bedding of a new bride could offer, along with some minstrels with cymbals and drums, and, bringing up the rear, a priest with the vial of holy water in his hand. Sir Geraint was still fully dressed in all his wedding finery, which only served to make Maddy, standing barefoot beside the bed in her sheath of cobweb fine linen, feel even more horridly exposed and vulnerable.

The atmosphere grew more subdued for the few minutes it took for the priest to say the blessings over the marriage bed, and sprinkle the turned-back sheets with holy water. But as soon as he had departed, the women surrounded her, showering her with seeds, the symbols of fertility. Though she put up her hands to shield her face from the rain of hard little seeds, she could not blot out what was happening on the other side of the room.

Sir Geraint had gone down under a crowd of drunken males intent on stripping him. His boots flew through the air, followed in swift succession by his robe, his hat and his hose. Lord Hugo emerged from the mob, panting. The look he gave her as he took a pace in her direction was enough to have her diving into the bed with a shriek of alarm, and drawing the covers up to her chin.

Suddenly, Sir Geraint surged from the seething mass of males on the floor with a bellow. They scattered, laughing, as he took up position at the foot of the bed. At Lord Hugo's urging, two of the ladies began to tug at the sheet she was clinging to.

'Nay!' Sir Geraint, wearing nothing now but his shirt, strode to the side of the bed, grabbing the pair of them round the waist, and swinging them off their feet, making them squeal in mock-protest. 'You'll not strip my bride before the prying eyes of these drunken rogues!'

Maddy slumped down into the pillows. She had never been so grateful to anyone for anything in her entire life.

There were boos and cries of spoilsport from the drunken rogues in question, though the ladies he had dropped to the floor were already backing off. With another yell, he spread his arms wide, shooing the ladies before him like a flock of geese. But though the men at the door parted to let them through, they stood their ground.

'We have a duty to witness the deed done properly!' Lord Hugo yelled.

Maddy quailed at the malicious excitement she saw in his eyes. Since he could not have her, he was determined to humiliate her by insisting that her deflowering become a degrading public spectacle. She turned to look at her husband. Surely he was not going to go along with this?

Their eyes met for only a brief fraction of a second, for he turned his back on her, to halt the advancing mob. Placing his hands on his hips he said, 'Are you trying to imply I am not up to the task?'

She could see their eyes dropping to the hem of his shirt, sniggering. She knew what they were sniggering at. When he had caught the women up in his arms, his shirt had tented over his manhood, which was quite clearly rampant and ready for action. With that sword of flesh, he would pierce her…somewhere, she was not quite sure where. Where could an appendage of that size go?

He waved his arm in her direction. 'Do you think I cannot manage a slip of a girl like that?'

'We only want to ensure fair play…' Lord Hugo persisted, leering at her where she cowered, the sheet clutched to her heaving breasts.

'You're not seeing any kind of play tonight. I've played often enough to know I can tumble any female, anytime, anywhere!'

The crowd at the door erupted into appreciative laughter at this boast, the atmosphere shifting subtly in his favour.

'Come now, my lords…' He spread his hands wide in appeal. 'You can see my lady wife is shy…'

She wished he had not said that. All those male eyes were turned upon her for a few, searingly humiliating moments. She had pressed her back so hard into the headboard by now, she felt as though it would for ever bear the imprints of the carvings of fruits and grain, the symbols of fertility that decorated their nuptial bed.

Lord Hugo blew her a kiss, one of the others winked at her lasciviously, but they all allowed Sir Geraint to push them through the door with only a few token scuffles. When he had shoved the last of them out, he shut the door behind them and shot the bolt home.

'Oh, th…thank you!' she stuttered through chattering teeth. She did not think she could have borne to go through the painful loss of her virginity with such as Lord Hugo looking on, though it was the practice still, among some families, to establish a bride's purity in this way. And that was one in the eye for Lady Lacey! She had not been married but a few hours, and had already found there was at least one distinct advantage to marrying a man from a less elevated background. He did not care so much for her purity that he could not make allowances for her shyness.

Yet her fleeting feeling of gratitude towards him vanished when he turned to face her. There it was again, his masculinity. She could hardly avoid it. It peeped from beneath his shirt with each step he took towards the bed.

She wondered if she ought not to stare, but he did not seem in the least bothered by displaying his naked flesh as he stalked past her, to a dresser by the window on which a flask of wine and two cups stood in readiness.

He pulled the stopper from the flask and took a deep breath.

From the first moment he had entered their bridal chamber, and he had seen her standing shivering beside the bed, clad only in a flimsy linen shift, her hair crowned with a bridal wreath, he had been aroused. The time of prayer had served only to focus on the bed itself, and when the women had showered seeds over her, he had begun to throb almost painfully, seeing his own seed spilling into her soft young body. He had welcomed the distraction of the traditional horseplay that had ensued between himself and the other young men.

Until he had heard her cry of alarm, and read that mute look of appeal in her great dark eyes. For all that her deceitfulness angered him, he did not wish everyone to know what a fool he had been, in taking a harlot to wife. There would be other ways to get bloodstains on the sheets before morning.

'It was for the best,' he grated.

To give her credit, she had played her part well, with all that cringing and cowering under the sheets. Nobody but he, and the father of her child, would ever have known she was not a terrified virgin, after the performance she had just put on. He supposed he should be grateful, he thought sourly.

Maddy watched him surreptitiously as he stood with his back to her, pouring the wine. Did all men look like that unclothed? She ran her eyes down the backs of his muscular legs. He turned, finally, coming to the bed with the two glasses of the rich spiced wine, his face stern. Though she could not keep her eyes up at that level for long. They kept returning to his…male appendage, jutting from its deep nest of dark curls…

She tried to swallow again, though her mouth was bone dry. Were all men that size? No wonder Lady Lacey had warned her to expect pain.

She took the cup he offered with a feeling of desperation, draining its contents in one sustained effort. She needed to calm her nerves. Perhaps the wine might even help to deaden the pain.

His face was still stern as he took her empty cup. Remembering Lady Lacey's exhortation to meet her fate with dignity, she lifted her chin and looked straight back at him. What did he have to look so sad about? He wanted this, didn't he? His body could not lie. She only had to glance down to see that he was, as he had boasted, ready for action. She felt a spurt of anger. What was his problem?

He reached out and stroked her cheek with one finger, sadly. Defiant to the last, his little Maddy. She was terrified of how he was going to react on discovering she was no true maid, yet she was still too proud to confess and beg for his forgiveness. He sighed, bowing his head. She did not know him, and had already told him she did not trust easily. If she was ever going to confide in him, he would have to prove he was a man worth trusting.

'I accept you are not ready to confess exactly why you agreed to marry me, Lady Agnes,' he began, 'but before we…go any further, there is one thing I must know. Why did you lie to me about your name?'

Chapter Nine

Warmth flooded her veins. It might have been the wine, but she thought it had more to do with the fact that he had not known she was the heiress, Lady Agnes, when he had kissed her. On the contrary, he'd sounded annoyed at the idea she might have deliberately deceived him!

She sat forward, laying one hand tentatively on his sinewy forearm. 'I did not lie to you. Truly. My name is Maddy…at least, it was what my brothers called me. My given name is Margaret Agnes DelaBoys. M. A. D. Do you see? I don't know why I told you I was Maddy that day.' She frowned. 'Perhaps it was because you scolded me, then held me in your arms, like my brothers used to do. And I had been so frightened, and I felt so small…I just forgot I was the Lady Agnes.'

He felt the power of her soft little hand against his naked flesh like a brand. Oh, how convincing she sounded. An innocent little tale to explain why she used a false name when out scouting for potential lovers.

Yet he had wanted Maddy quite desperately. If she were the one here now, and they were not married, he would want her without reserve.

'I liked Maddy,' he finally admitted. Then he frowned into the empty wine cups he still held on his lap. 'Lady Agnes, though…'

He bent forward, placing the cups on the floor beside the bed, then turned to examine her. 'Who are you really, madam wife?' He placed one hand on either side of her head on the headboard, effectively caging her between his arms. 'How long will it be before I really know?'

Maddy was too aware of the massive bulk of him, hovering over her as she pressed herself back into the pillows, to take in what he was saying. His shirt hung open slightly, revealing the pelt that covered the breadth of his chest. Every breath she took smelled of him.

How long, had he said? How long what? Distractedly her mind flew back to the only experience she had ever had of this kind of union between a man and a woman. The time she had caught Lord Hugo with Lady Lacey. That had not taken very long at all. No longer than it had taken her to realise what was going on, quell her shock and disgust, and begin to inch away from the spectacle.

'How long?' she repeated stupidly. He did not smell of horses and sunshine now, she reflected as he leaned closer, and pressed a firm kiss on her forehead. He smelled of…heated male. She closed her eyes. Clean linen. Wine fumes.

He kissed her cheek. 'Whatever went before, we are man and wife now, Maddy.'

Maddy. It was easier, somehow, if he thought of her as Maddy. A wanton she may be, but she was *his* wanton. If he could not reach her in any other way, perhaps he could at least keep her so exercised in his bed that she would have no energy left to stray. His fingers crept to the ties at the neck of her white linen shift.

'Here, in the privacy of our chamber, it is just the two of us.' He tugged the ties open, pulling the gown apart and paused for a moment, just feasting his eyes on the delectable sight of her pert young breasts.

'No falsehood here.' He lowered his head to suckle one coral-tipped peak, while his fingers plucked at the other. He heard her gasp, felt her quiver in response, and smiled to himself. Yes, this was the way to reach her. 'Just us, and what our bodies feel…'

Ah, yes, she liked that! Her nipples were both pebble hard now, and as he murmured his words against her breast, she arched her back, pushing herself deeper into his mouth.

But she had to learn he was the master here. Pulling back, before he lost himself in the delight of her, he looked down with satisfaction into her flushed face. Her eyes flew open. 'Outside this room, though…' he gestured towards the door '…neither of us must ever forget that our union is important to many people besides ourselves.'

Tears of resentment pricked her eyes. Just when she had begun to think it was going to be all right, he had decided to give her a lecture! Couldn't he tell how frightened she was of all this?

His voice took on an edge. 'Yes, I know you think men and women are natural enemies, but I'm telling you now, that you will restrict hostilities to the privacy of our chamber!'

How could he kiss her one second, and talk about being enemies the next?

'I don't understand you, Sir Geraint!' she complained.

'Then understand this. When husband and wife are at open war, the struggle spills over into the household and beyond. Rival factions grow up even within the family. Sons side with mother or father, and the resulting feuds can go on for generations. Do you want our family to be like that? For I do not. I have no wish for our marriage to be the spawning ground for hatred and strife!'

'Well, of course not! Nor do I!' she protested.

'Then you agree? In public, you will appear content with me, and I with you, no matter what we really feel.'

A pang of sorrow smote Maddy to the heart. If he was never going to be able to feel any affection for her at all, then he was predicting a long, cold, lonely future for her. She could not help herself. The tears she had been trying so valiantly to suppress welled up and spilled down her cheeks.

He wiped them from her face gently, almost tenderly. 'Come now, Maddy, it will not be so bad. If we can at least give the appearance of being in perfect amity, we can spread harmony, rather than chaos around us. Won't that be worth something?'

To everyone else, yes, she wanted to wail. But what about me? What is it about me that is so impossible to like?

But he was holding out his hand, and she knew he wanted her to shake on the deal he had just offered her. It was a fair one, she supposed, sniffing back her tears. More than many women who entered arranged marriages could hope for. He had just promised he would always try to treat her with respect. He had not said it in so many words, but it seemed unlikely he would ever humiliate her by parading his mistresses in public, as her own father had done to her mother. Or install them in her home, as Lord Hugo had intended to do. Nor subject her to the kind of treatment Baron Lacey had meted out to her cousin, striking her in the face, even knocking her to the floor once when in his cups and displeased with her, not caring who saw.

Making a huge effort to contain her tears, she took his hand, and shook it. 'I must thank you again, sir.' She raised her eyes to his. 'For my part, I promise I will do my best to be a loyal wife to you…'

'And for my part,' he replied sternly, 'I will try to put everything you have done before this moment from my mind. We start afresh here.'

Taking her other hand too, he raised them both to his mouth. 'And I swear…' he looked into her eyes as he pressed a kiss to the back of each hand in turn '…that whatever passes between us in this chamber, will never be spoken of beyond these doors.'

At her puzzled frown, he expanded, 'If there are harsh words to be said, let us say them in private, where no other can use them as ammunition to spread discord.' He rubbed his thumbs over the backs of her hands as he gazed deep into her eyes, hoping that she would take this opportunity to confess. Had he not promised it would go no further? 'We will be honest with each other, here, in our bed.'

Her response was to tug her hands from his, her face flushing and her brows drawing down in an expression of dread.

Abruptly his patience came to an end. He had given her every opportunity to do so, but she would not own up. With a growl of pure frustration, he mounted fully on to the bed, planting his knees on either side of her legs on top of the coverlet. The time for softly spoken words was over. Now was the time to apply the discipline.

Maddy bit down on her lower lip to prevent herself from crying out in fear. His hands were at her shoulders, tugging the nightgown down her arms till she was bare to the waist. His breathing grew ragged as his darkened eyes fixed on her exposed breasts. She wanted to cover herself from the onslaught of that primitive look, but her arms were pinned to her sides by the material of her nightgown. After one brief attempt to move them, she gave up, with a little moan of despair.

'This is where we will fight our battles,' he growled, raising himself for just long enough to yank the covers off her. 'I give you fair warning, I will fight to win.'

No, it would do no good to struggle. Just look at the size of him! If he wanted, he could snap her in twain like a twig with those massive hands! She was utterly helpless, trapped beneath his powerful great body. Besides, she reminded herself, clenching her fists at her side, this was his right.

'I will be master in my own house. Lord of all the King has entrusted to my care. Do you understand me, woman?'

Oh, lord, yes, she understood now. The fierce look in his eyes, the impatience of his hands as they seized her by the hips and tugged her down the bed so that she lay completely flat beneath him. The years rolled away, and she heard Baron Lacey's voice, bawling that his word was law. And his meaty great hands would bend her over a bench, raising her skirts, and then the pain would explode in her bared buttocks and thighs as he plied the flat of his hand or the birch rod over and over again.

It was her husband's hands that were baring her legs now, thrusting the flimsy material of her nightgown up till it was scrunched round her midriff like a belt.

She squeezed her eyes shut, clenching her teeth in her determination not to cry out, no matter how much he hurt her. Why was it that men needed to establish their lordship over women by hurting them about their nether regions? Whether with a rod of birch, or one of flesh, the intent was the same!

All the same, she let out one frightened whimper when she felt his hands begin to prise her legs apart and he growled, 'Let battle commence.'

His full weight came down on her then, pressing her into the mattress. His mouth was hot and wet on her tightly closed lips, her throat, her breasts. His hands seemed to be everywhere at once, exploring, invading, demonstrating his absolute dominion over her weaker limbs. Was this what Lady Lacey had meant when she had warned he would have no finesse?

Sheer panic almost overwhelmed her when his hard thighs settled between hers, spreading them even further apart, and she felt his manhood begin to prod and probe.

Her fingers clawed into the mattress, fisting up great handfuls of sheeting. She would not cry out! Come what may! All women went through this. And she would survive it with her pride, if nothing else, intact. She had never given Baron Lacey the satisfaction of crying when he beat her. She had always stalked from her punishment with her head held high, though her mute defiance often enraged him to such frenzy that she had to eat standing up, and sleep on her belly for days after. She had survived that; she would survive this!

Men might have superior strength, but she had too much pride to let any one of them break her spirit!

Then, shockingly, his fingers replaced his member. He stroked her there quite gently, albeit intrusively, murmuring, 'Relax, Maddy. I promise you it will be all right.'

His fingers were probing now, introducing his sword of flesh and leaving it there, nestling in a natural hollow place there seemed to be between her legs. This was it then. He was going to pierce her. She braced herself against his imminent invasion. It would soon be over, she told herself, her breath hitching in her throat. Only a few minutes of battering, that was all it had taken Lord Hugo, and it would be over.

He clamped his hand to her hips, and thrust hard. She ground her teeth as his weapon ripped deeply into her. She would not cry out!

But he did.

'Oh, God!' Sir Geraint went still.

As she felt his weight lift from her chest, she drew in a ragged breath. She could feel his whole body quivering as he raised himself on his forearms. She sensed that he was looking down at her, though she could not open her eyes, not while they were slotted together like this. But she started when she felt his hand gently brushing her hair back from her clammy brow.

'Did I hurt you? Maddy?'

It did hurt, but not nearly as much as she had expected. She breathed in again, as her fear began to abate, and out. Now that he was still, the pain was ebbing swiftly. But he was very heavy, and his weight had shifted to the place where they were conjoined when he had raised himself to his elbows. In an effort to ease the discomfort, she shifted a little.

The effect of this subtle movement upon her husband was explosive. Uttering a guttural cry, he plunged more deeply into her, then withdrew, then plunged again, and again, and then she felt a throbbing deep within her, and he collapsed, sweating and panting on top of her.

Spent.

She heaved a sigh of relief. It was over, and it had not been anywhere near so terrible as Lady Lacey had wanted her to believe. In fact, looking back, there had been moments when some of the ways he had touched her would have been pleasant if she had not been too scared to appreciate it.

She felt such a fool. She had known all along that her cousin had been trying to frighten her. Why had she let her? Why had she not remembered that she herself had run to meet her own lover, had suffered him to do exactly this to her, when, since she was not his wife, it was not her duty towards him at all?

'Maddy?' Sir Geraint raised his head and looked down into his wife's strained face with remorse. His little nut-brown maid was a maid indeed.

Though she had bitten down on her cry of pain, he'd hurt her. He had torn into her like some brute beast, forcing his entry into her tensed flesh. What he had just done had been little better than rape.

'Maddy?' he whispered again. When she still made no response, he kissed the frown line between her brows. 'Did I hurt you very much?'

Her eyes flew open, and she smiled at him. 'Not very much, and only for an instant. Now it just feels…strange.'

As she flexed her hips, he realised he was still inside her. That he was still sprawled half over her, and that his weight must be crushing her. With a hiss, he pulled away from her, turning his back to hide the blush of shame that heated his face under the pretext of retrieving the scattered bedclothes.

'I did not mean for it to be like that…' he grated.

What was bothering him now? She reached out and touched his hunched back tentatively.

He tensed. He couldn't remember all the damnfool things he had said in anger before.

Her little hand shaped the contours of his upper arm. He felt her kneel up behind him and lay her head on his shoulder. A feeling of inexpressible relief welled up within him. He could not have gone so far as accusing her of being a whore, else she would not be reaching out to him like this.

'Maddy,' he rasped, catching the hand that rested on his upper arm, and kissing it.

She was a jewel, a treasure. He was the richest man in all of England. His wife was everything he could ever want. Beautiful, proud, and pure, as well as wealthy. And he was the veriest wretch to have treated her so!

He wanted so much to beg her forgiveness for both the verbal, and then the physical, lashing he had dealt her. But the hurt of losing her virginity would be as nothing compared to the damage a full confession would inflict on her proud spirit.

Her heart went out to him at the expression of remorse on his rugged face. With great daring, she seized it in both hands, and planted a kiss on his lips. As he started back in surprise, she let him go, suddenly shocked by her lack of modesty. She was half-naked, in bed, and… Hastily she tugged the nightgown up over her shoulders, bending her head to close the ties and hide her burning cheeks.

'You did not hurt me near so much as I feared.' A wave of curiosity suddenly overcame her. Lady Lacey had lied about so much, and though she felt a little strange, she had been able to kneel up and move about the bed with hardly any discomfort at all. She was almost sure that she would be able to walk as easily as she had ever done. Her lips pressed together in determination, she swung her legs over the side of the bed.

'Maddy? What ails you? Where are you going?'

She looked at him for a moment, weighing her answer. He had insisted he wanted total honesty between them when they were in their chamber. And she had agreed to his terms. She hung her head, her face flaming with heat, but she made herself say, 'You said you wanted me to be honest…so…the thing is, I just wanted to try if I could walk, now that you have…' She faltered, looking up at him with hope and dread in equal measure blazing from her great dark eyes. 'They said—'

'Damn, Maddy!' He pulled her into his arms then, and on to his lap. No wonder she had been terrified, if some malicious woman had been filling her head with tales like that.

'I will never hurt you, I swear!' He kissed the crown of her head as she buried her flaming face into his neck.

'But you were so angry with me. Why were you so angry with me?' She raised her head to search his face for the truth.

With a groan he hugged her to his chest. In spite of demanding she be honest, he dare not confess why he had been angry.

'I have been a fool, Maddy. That is all there is to say. Can we not forget all that went before?'

That was what he had been talking about before. Making this a fresh start. Sliding her arms about his waist, she sighed. She would be only too glad to forget all about Lord Hugo, and his intrigues.

'We will be leaving it all behind tomorrow, won't we?' she mused. 'I am more than ready to make a fresh start, away from the court and all its evils.'

Though he was the one to insist they forget all that had gone before, her oblique reference to her problems roused his curiosity. He would have to find out why she had been out in the forest with that pageboy, and why she had been weeping in the arbour. But not just now.

'That's my brave girl.' He could not resist adding, 'And from now on, no more secrets.'

'Secrets?' She looked into his face then, puzzled. As far as she was aware, she had no secrets from him. Only her doubts and suspicions, and they were too nebulous and paranoid to voice.

'Well, not secrets exactly.' He covered his tracks, knowing he dare not own up to his filthy suspicions. 'I just meant, I want us to be honest with each other. Even as you led the way by admitting that you were worried about whether you could walk…' As she ducked her flaming face into the crook of his shoulder in shyness, he continued, 'I too have a confession to make.'

Reaching behind him to prise her hand from his waist, he laid it in his lap. 'I want you again.'

She gasped, and though her arm went tense, she did not try to pull her hand away from the ridge that was butting against her hand through the cloth of his shirt. After a moment or two, he heard her mutter, 'Of course. You are my husband. It is your right.'

'I don't want it to be about rights, Maddy.' He released her hand, tilting her chin so that she had to look into his eyes.

'When we come together like this, it should be about pleasure. For both of us.'

At her expression of bewilderment, he could not help but lower his head and take advantage of her parted lips. She sighed into his mouth, relaxing into the kiss, even as she had done the very first time he had held her on his lap.

'Yield to me this time,' he urged her. 'Don't fight it. Don't fight me. And I will take you with me to the very gates of paradise.'

Reaching up under her nightgown, he boldly pushed his hand between her legs, sliding one finger inside her before she had time to realise what he was about.

'Does that hurt? Do you feel at all sore?'

All Maddy could do by way of answer was to gasp and close her eyes in shame. Hurt? No, she did not think she had ever felt anything quite so...yes she had, though. That day in the garden, when he had held her on his lap and kissed her. That had been a foretaste of this. She had wanted to feel his hand exactly where it was now, she admitted to herself, doing just this. She uttered a little moan of pleasure as he gently rotated the heel of his hand against the apex of her thighs. Pleasure, hot and sinful, coursed through her entire being. Just as it had that time. But this time, she could yield, wasn't that what he had said? He wanted her to enjoy this. And why shouldn't she? she reasoned, arching into his touch, permitting her body to do what it willed.

'See how good it is to obey your husband,' he teased, lowering his head to suckle at her breasts through the fabric of her nightgown.

She was beyond coherent speech. Though before long, she understood what he was doing. Everywhere that he had kissed or touched before, he kissed and touched again. Only this time, instead of demanding, he was giving. When he finally tumbled her back on to the mattress, and reared up over her, her legs parted willingly. Her hands reached up and clasped him about his neck as he slid slowly inside her, for she wanted to show him she was willing. No, more than that, she wanted to feel her arms holding him in the moment of his possession of her.

This time, the sensation of joining with him was delicious. She should tell him, was the last thought she was aware of before the force of her desire shut down her capacity for anything but feeling. Mindlessly she writhed beneath him, wanting him closer, deeper, and presently, harder.

The sight of her lissom young body given up so entirely to the throes of passion roused him like no other sight had ever done. When she began to shudder, throwing back her head and crying out in shocked delight, he could hold back no longer. Their orgasm rolled between them like thunder echoing across the heavens.

And in the quiet after the storm, when they lay spent, arms and legs entwined, he savoured every little aftershock that thrummed through her, every little moan, each sigh, the slight shifting beneath him that spoke of her complete satiation.

When she began to drift back to reality, she understood what he had meant about knocking on the doors of paradise. She had never imagined that any experience could have translated her out of herself like that. Lady Lacey's lies had been as insubstantial as cobwebs. Her husband's kindness had torn them all to shreds. He was not a brute beast who cared nothing for her pain. He had not been able to help hurting her, that much was true, but he had been sorry for it. And he wanted their marriage to be based on mutual respect.

Sighing with contentment, she curled up beside him and closed her eyes.

But he could not take his eyes off the exquisite little creature who lay beside him as she drifted off to sleep, like a kitten on a sunny windowsill, with that satisfied little smile still curving her delectably kissable mouth.

How could it be, after such a short acquaintance, that he harboured such strong feelings for this woman? If another man had told him that he was prey to such hot jealousy, that his temper had become vile, that his desire for one particular female was so intense that he came to climax almost at the moment of entering her, he would say the poor fool had fallen in love!

For he had truly lost control, twice over. A thing that had not happened to him since his first teenage fumblings, when simply touching a woman's breast had been enough to make him spill his seed on her skirts.

A feeling of intense anxiety knotted his heart. She had not cared who he was when she agreed to marry him. He could have been anyone.

But he wasn't just anyone now. He was her husband.

His face grim with determination, he pulled her unconscious body in close to him, rearranging the position of her limbs to suit his comfort before burying his face in the luxuriant mass of her silky dark hair. She might well have his heart in the palm of her hand, but he would be a fool to let her know as much. Not if he was to have any chance of keeping her in her place. He was her lord!

Chapter Ten

Maddy yawned, and began to stretch her legs in an attempt to ease the leaden stiffness that pervaded her muscles.

And jerked fully awake when what felt like an iron band about her waist tugged her into closer proximity to the source of warmth at her back. A body. A large, naked, male body...

She tried to twist round, but her husband's head was resting on her hair, effectively pinning her own to the pillow.

The sound of a low growl rumbling through his chest was the first sign that he was coming awake too. She froze at this symptom of anger.

He turned her in his arms, hauling her against his chest.

'Nay, do not look at me so. Did I not promise I would not hurt you?' His face was dark with stubble now, reminding her of how he had looked the first time she had ever seen him. She couldn't help reaching out to run her fingers over this most visible evidence of his masculinity.

'Yes,' she sighed. 'I know it, really, but—' Before she could finish, he swallowed her words with a hot, possessive kiss.

Oh, this was a lovely way to start the day! All of her pressed against the entire length of him...held in an embrace that could not lie. Any worries she'd had that he was displeased with her melted in the feel of his manhood prodding urgently at her belly. She arched into it, into his kiss, into him, as the delicious sensations he had aroused so skilfully the night before surged through her anew.

She squeaked out a protest when his mouth abruptly left hers, and he sat up, running his fingers through the riot of his chestnut curls.

What kind of woman would be so eager to pleasure him, after enduring what he had done to her the night before? He knew she was not the wanton he had feared. But if she was not pregnant, then why had she been so desperate to marry him? And why had she been afraid to meet with him before the ceremony? And been so determined to leave court so soon?

He had woken just before dawn, his heart hammering in his chest, with the horrible suspicion that it might be because she wanted to get back to Woolton. At any cost. And King Henry's words about the place being a nest of Yorkist vipers, his uncertainty about her political allegiance, and Northumberland's ambition rang like a warning bell in his mind.

'We cannot start this now,' he grunted, swinging his legs out of bed and bending to retrieve his hose from the floor. 'We have not time.'

Even as he pulled his shirt over his head, she heard someone tapping at the chamber door.

He was right, she thought resentfully. But it was irksome to know that while she had been lost to all but the feelings he was arousing in her, he was calm enough to consider the day's business.

He opened the door to admit the trio of women who were waiting there—Lady Lacey, flanked by two maidservants—and left without so much as a farewell. She pulled the bedclothes to her chin, suddenly conscious that her hair was a tousled mess, and that her nightgown was barely clinging to her upper arms. And, most painfully, that though the previous night had turned her world upside down, she was only one more in a long line of females he'd shared such pleasures with. When she recalled how he'd boasted of his prowess, she felt quite sick.

Oh, but she had been right to decide to guard her heart against such a one! He was far more dangerous to her than Lord Hugo could ever have been, for his kisses reached into the very heart of her.

She dashed a tear from her cheek, but not quickly enough for Lady Lacey to pounce on it.

'Ah, my dear. Was it as bad as that?' she cooed.

That false sympathy was all it took to inject steel into Maddy's spine.

'Not at all.' She lifted her chin, threw back the bedclothes, and set her feet to the floor. 'I feel a little strange, to be sure, but after the first time…' she shrugged nonchalantly as she made for the ewer of warm water the maids had set out for her to wash with.

Lady Lacey was examining the rumpled bedding. 'My poor chick. You mean he tupped you more than once? The lout has no consideration.'

'On the contrary. He made sure that—' She bit down on her lower lip. He'd insisted they keep what passed between them in their chamber completely private. And even though he had also demonstrated she meant little to him as a person, as a wife he wanted her loyalty. Which she had promised to give him.

'I cannot speak of it.' She blushed, as one of the maids helped pull the nightgown over her head.

The other maid was already stripping the sheets that were smeared with the tokens of lost innocence. As were her inner thighs. Her blush deepened as she cleansed the evidence of his possession from her legs.

As she dried herself, she noticed Lady Lacey plucking the broken fragments of her bridal chaplet from the pillows. She had never noticed the moment when she lost that, so completely had her husband filled her consciousness.

She turned away from the sight of her cousin tossing it to the floor with a sneer, holding out her arms for the maid to help her into a clean chemise she had drawn from a trunk that sat by the door. Returning to the same trunk, the girl brought out a gown of heavy, plain gold velvet, lined with brocaded green damask, the sleeves of which were tipped with marten fur.

'Where did that come from?' Maddy asked as she stroked the luxurious nap of the fabric before submitting to having it draped over her head.

'From your husband,' Lady Lacey snapped. 'Where else?'

'But…' She crossed the room to peer into the trunk. Inside she could see another gown of velvet, this one green lined with gold, and beneath it, when she knelt to push it aside, was another one of serviceable wool in a deep shade of russet.

'Oh!' she gasped, running her hands over a fur-lined travelling cloak. Burrowing deeper into the contents, she pulled out a pair of soft doeskin riding gloves. They had long cuffs to protect her forearms, and the backs of each were intricately patterned with beads and embroidery. 'Is this all mine?' She had never had so much finery before. 'But I couldn't wear such things for travelling! It would be a sin to get mud on this fabric…'

'Princess Elizabeth wishes you to make a fine sight when you ride from court,' Lady Lacey said, her voice flat. Maddy noted for the first time that she too was richly dressed in a velvet gown. 'As does the King, no doubt. The two of you have aped what they did, after all. When you ride out, your union will speak to all who watch your progress of the new amity between the houses of York and Lancaster.' She shrugged. 'I only hope that the sacrifice you have made to prove your loyalty to the crown will not be wasted on your husband.'

Maddy sat on a stool to give the maid easier access to her hair. Bowing her head, she reflected with a grimace that she had almost lost sight of her need to prove herself a loyal subject to the new King altogether. It was her husband who filled her thoughts to the exclusion of all else. But Lady Lacey was right. She must not forget, in the pelter of emotions that skittered through her this morning, that she had a duty to fulfil. Whether her husband became fond of her or no, she must never risk the amity he wished to spread by harking on what he could not give her. He was offering her more than enough. He was handsome, in favour with the King, generous to her with both gifts and offers of respect, besides rousing her to heights of pleasure she had never dreamed she could feel.

Maddy utilised every trick she had ever learned during her long lonely years in the Lacey household to mask her true feelings so that, when she walked into the yard where the cavalcade that formed her travelling household was assembling, she reflected that Baron Lacey would have been proud of her. She was calm, she was dignified. She managed to look her new husband in the eye without permitting any emotion to show on her face at all.

Sir Geraint bowed over her hand, his own expression flinty. He too was wearing green and gold, the traditional colours of the DelaBoys family. When they rode out together, the matching outfits would demonstrate the fact that they belonged together, and some of her pleasure in them dimmed. He had not been generous because he felt anything for her. This was all for effect. The effect he had declared he wanted to promote. An amicable union, that would promote peace amongst their dependants.

A man dressed in the sober black gown of a clerk was standing next to her husband. 'This is Lawless, our steward,' Sir Geraint said.

In a daze, Maddy held out her hand, and the man swept off his bejewelled cap, as he bowed over it. She knew the travelling household of a knight would normally number around twenty, so the number of people thronging the yard had not come as too much of a surprise. She had expected, too, that some of the mounted men would be armed in order to protect the baggage carts from wayside robbers. But she had not expected them all to be armed, or for them to look quite so…menacing. If she did not know better, she would have said her husband had hired a band of trained mercenaries to escort them to Lancashire, rather than…

She swallowed. Perhaps that was exactly what he had done. She would have to question his decision to hire a band of cut-throats and inflict them on her tenants at a later time. And why did they need a new steward at Woolton Castle? What had happened to Robbins, the man who had served her father? Or was her husband, she wondered with a spurt of annoyance, going to turn him off, and install a man he knew would be loyal to him?

Taking her arm, Sir Geraint led her across the courtyard to where a young groom was holding a beautiful sorrel palfrey, caparisoned with a harness of green leather, its silky mane plaited with green and gold ribbons.

'We are to ride through the city, side by side,' her husband said. She stiffened.

'I have not ridden for years,' she admitted, then blushed, remembering the ride on Caligula's back. 'That is…not alone.' Suddenly painfully self-conscious of his body beside hers, remembering how she had curled herself up into him, how her body had been his plaything from the very first moment they had touched, she pulled away from him.

Sir Geraint frowned. 'She is a steady mount,' he murmured, 'and I will be beside you all the time. Let me know as soon as you have had enough, and you may rest.' He jerked his head towards a leather-curtained, horse-drawn litter, into which Lady Lacey was climbing.

Finally remembering her manners, Maddy replied, 'Thank you, my lord. She is an exquisite piece of horseflesh.' Then, in a lower voice, she added, 'And I thank you for this beautiful outfit, too. I have never owned anything so lovely.'

Sir Geraint cleared his throat. 'It was all bought with your wealth, my lady.'

Startled, she looked up to see if he mocked her with his talk of wealth. If she was wealthy, why had she been living like a pauper for so many years? But he only looked uncomfortable. Girding her wits about her with her skirts, she stepped up to the mounting block. This was not the time to question him. She had promised. But tonight, oh, tonight, she *would* have some answers!

The groom helped her into the saddle, while he strode away and swung himself on to Caligula's back. The warhorse pawed at the cobblestones, striking sparks from them as Sir Geraint gathered the reins into his left hand. The men, who had looked so menacing only seconds before, scattered like leaves as Caligula rose on his hindquarters, lashing out with hooves the size of buckets. To Maddy's astonishment, Sir Geraint was grinning as though it was fine sport to start his day wrestling for control with such a huge, strong-willed creature.

Not until he'd brought his fearsome mount under control did she tear her attention away, to adjust her heavy skirts and settle her knee over the pommel. Her hands were trembling, she noted. As did the groom.

'Don't fret none about Sir Geraint, my lady,' the lad said. 'Caligula won't unseat him. They're just…testing each other's mood, is all.'

'What is your name?' Maddy asked.

'Rollo, my lady.'

'Then, Rollo, I'm afraid I must confess I am not fretting about Sir Geraint as much as I am about my own ability to stay in the saddle. If that destrier should take it into his head to nip my palfrey…'

The lad's face took on a determined expression. 'I won't let no harm come to you, my lady. On my oath, I won't!'

With her husband to one side of her, Rollo behind, and all her concentration on staying upright as the palfrey lurched into motion, Maddy was oblivious to the stares and cheers of the populace as they rode through London. It wasn't until they had traversed the length of the Strand, and entered the cramped streets of the City proper, that she became aware of the effect their cavalcade was having on the citizens of London. The newly married couple, in matching garments, the baggage carts, even the stern faces of their retainers following behind, sent out a clear message that the King's power was going to reach to the very furthest corners of the land, and subdue it.

'Not much longer now, sweetheart,' she heard her husband murmur.

Dazed, she looked up to where he rode beside her, temporarily loosing the death grip she had on the reins. Leaning down, he gently extricated the reins from her cramped fingers. Knowing that he was leading her mount, that she was no longer responsible for attempting to guide it, was an immense relief.

'You are doing well.' His smile for her was tinged with pride. 'And you look magnificent on horseback.'

'Magnificent?' She frowned over his choice of epithet, shaking her head. He'd looked magnificent, though, earlier, she sighed, as he'd exerted his will over his mount. She could picture him on a battlefield more easily now, his sword in his hand as enemies fled before him. She peeked up at him, suddenly shy of her warrior husband.

'Delightful, then,' he amended, his smile growing broader. 'And once we are beyond the city walls, and out on the road north, you can dismount and ride in the litter with your ladies.'

'Thank you, my lord,' she replied, demurely, fixing her eyes on the city gates, while trying her hardest to conceal the joy his compliment had brought to her trembling heart.

Only to have it wrest from her by Lady Lacey's first words, when she took her place beside her in the horse litter. 'No wonder you can't bring yourself to speak of what that brute put you through last night. I saw how much he enjoyed subjugating his mount. And you so shy, so unworldly!' She flung up her hands in mock-despair as the two maids ran curious eyes over her shrinking form. She carried on in the same vein for several miles, eliciting peals of laughter from the maids, while Maddy's embarrassment mounted to excruciating proportions.

Once she had wrung every last drop of humiliation out of her reticence to discuss the details of her wedding night, she went on to criticise the vulgarity of her husband's taste.

'Everything so expensive,' she sneered, fingering the fur trim of Maddy's cuffs. 'He is really enjoying squandering your money. You will both be paupers before the year is out if he goes on like this.'

At least he was spending her money on her, she thought militantly. When Lady Lacey had charge of her, her own clothes had been altered and mended so often that it was only the patches that held some of her ancient gowns together.

Lady Lacey must have known Maddy was an heiress all along. It probably had not been family loyalty that had prompted her cousin to take her along when she'd sought sanctuary with Elizabeth

Woodville, King Edward's widow, at all! But rather the prospect of still being able to dip her sticky fingers into her coffers!

'And as for this steward, this Lawless that he has foisted on you,' she continued, blithely ignorant of Maddy's mounting anger, 'he is nothing but a spy. Trained up by Reginald Bray, of all people. You should at least protest at having one of Margaret Beaufort's minions installed at Woolton, Lady Agnes.'

But Maddy could well understand why the King would want to have a man trained by Reginald Bray installed in the north country. Rumour had it that under cover of collecting the rents from Margaret Beaufort's widely scattered properties, Reginald Bray had single-handedly sowed enough dissension against Richard of York to pave the way for Henry Tudor's return to England.

Though she had wondered what was to become of her father's old steward.

'I certainly mean to ask my husband if he is going to oust Robbins from his post,' she declared, causing Lady Lacey to lean back against her cushions with a look of satisfaction on her face.

Instantly, Maddy regretted having made any reply whatsoever. The midday stop did not come soon enough for her. Flinging back the leather curtains, she jumped from the litter, and went in search of Sir Geraint. He smiled at her, and was courteous, but it soon became clear to her that he had to see to the wants of his entire retinue. She stood close to him while one after another problems that had cropped up during the morning were brought to his attention. He dealt with each one swiftly and without fuss, and she found herself drawing comfort from his quiet competence without having to broach the matters that disturbed her. He would sort it all out for her, too, she knew, as soon as they found opportunity to be private together. When it was time to set forth again, Maddy asked if she could ride the palfrey for a space.

'I really should practise if I wish to become a good rider,' she announced as Rollo came to help her mount. 'Besides, that horse litter makes me queasy.' Well, it was not a complete lie. It was only that it was one of the occupants, rather than the irregular motion, that sickened her. And she would explain the half-truth to her husband as soon as she got a chance.

When a light rain began to fall, and Sir Geraint dispatched her back to the litter, she raised only the feeblest of protests. She really was not an experienced enough rider to spend very long in the saddle.

A sudden burst of inspiration had her drawing the little psalter that had been her wedding gift from her sleeve. One thing Maddy had learned in the past was that Lady Lacey would not intrude upon her devotions, and, as she had hoped, the woman fell quiet at once. Guiltily, she wondered which of them was the greater sinner, Lady Lacey who masked her malice under a cloak of concern, or she for pretending piety just to get a bit of peace.

There were not so many hours of daylight so early in the year, making the afternoon mercifully short. Sir Geraint explained, as he helped her climb stiffly from the litter, that it would take them near two weeks to reach her home, since they could not cover much distance in any one day.

How on earth was she going to cope with being cooped up in that horse litter with Lady Lacey's malicious tongue for two whole weeks! She saw him frown as she singularly failed to hide her dismay from her face.

'Is the pace I have set today too fast for you? You look weary. Fritz! Captain Fritz is in charge of the men-at arms,' he explained to Maddy as a particularly hard-faced individual with dirty blond hair jerked his head up in response to her husband's summons, before peeling away from the rest of the troops. 'See to it that the ladies have a decent chamber where they may rest and refresh themselves in private.' He gestured towards the tavern outside which they had stopped. He lowered his head after the man had saluted and departed, murmuring, 'I will not trouble you tonight. I will sleep in the common room with the other men.'

Lady Lacey joined them at that moment, preventing her from telling him that was exactly what she did not want him to do. In desperation she shot him a look that she hoped revealed all she wanted to say, but he was already looking past her, to where a scuffle seemed to have broken out among the guard. With a disdainful sniff, Lady Lacey lifted her skirts and stomped into the tavern, the other two women trotting at her heels. Sir Geraint sent her a look that was stern enough to remind her that he did not want her to question any of his orders in public.

Maddy had no opportunity to plead her case until he came to her room after supper.

'I just came to bid you goodnight,' he said, 'and to see that you have everything you need before I retire, ladies.'

'Well, I haven't!' she snapped, her determination to behave herself worn to the bone. Lady Lacey had not stopped sniping since they had set foot in the tavern. She had complained that it was a low place, that the food provided was coarse and the men who were supposed to be guarding them a rabble that would probably murder them all in their beds and make off with their possessions.

'Lady Lacey, you may leave us now, and take the maids with you.' It had come as a shock, when they had begun to prepare themselves for bed, to learn that her new husband had employed these two women for the express purpose of tending to her every need. She had never had a maid before, was not quite sure what to do with them, and, as the day had progressed, had become aware that, subtly egged on by Lady Lacey, they were both beginning to look down their noses at her. Betty and Mary giggled, and darted out the door, though Lady Lacey stood her ground.

'But this is my room…'

'No, it is my room!' Maddy could not hold her tongue a second longer. 'For me to share with my husband!'

Lady Lacey looked outraged. 'Are you implying that I should share the common sleeping room, with the maids?'

'I need to be private with my husband. The matter of where you sleep is quite immaterial to me!' Maddy's heart was pounding. She could not quite believe she had finally stood up to her cousin. For a few seconds, they stood eye to eye, neither flinching. Then Sir Geraint cleared his throat.

'If you will speak to Captain Fritz, he will arrange a suitable room for you,' he said.

'I? Speak to that varlet? Never!' Her lip curled in distaste. 'I shall get one of the maids to do it.'

As she swept from the room, her nose in the air, Maddy flopped down on to the bed, her head in her hands.

'Maddy?' Her husband was kneeling at her side in a heartbeat. 'What is it? What can I do?' He took hold of her hands gently and drew them against his chest. She looked pale and strained, he thought. Ah, poor lamb. She was so tiny and frail. The journey, coming so soon after all the work involved in preparing for a hasty wedding, and the sparse amount of sleep his lustful demands had permitted her the night before, must have worn her out.

'You can answer some questions I have, if you will. You did promise that when we are alone, in our private chamber, we could be completely honest with each other?'

'I did.'

She took a deep breath. 'Then first of all, though I am sure you have good reasons for doing so, I should like to know why you have employed a new steward.'

'Ah.' Sir Geraint kissed her hands, a frown wrinkling his brow as he considered how to answer. He had urged her to be honest with him, thinking she had a dread confession to make. In return he had promised her honesty too. Damn. She really ought not to have to be troubled with some things…

'Do you intend to turn Robbins off?' she persisted. 'He has served our family faithfully for years.'

Now, that was something he could explain. 'Robbins is no longer at Woolton Castle, Maddy. He has not been for some time.'

'Oh?' She frowned down at him. 'Then where is he?'

He took a deep breath. She would find out soon enough, so she might as well hear it from him. 'Nobody knows. Not long after your father's death, he just disappeared.'

'Disappeared? You mean he left?' Mayhap she had been too hasty in blaming Lady Lacey for her state of penury. Any money from the estate that might have come to her would have had to pass through his hands. If he had been dishonest… She pursed her lips. 'Did he make off with a lot of money, by any chance?'

Sir Geraint's face relaxed into an appreciative smile. She was no fool, his little wife. Encouraged by her perspicacity, he rose from his knees and sat beside her on the bed. 'Again, nobody knows. There is nobody left at Woolton who has been able to give a satis-factory answer to that question.' He slipped his arm about her waist. 'That is one reason why the King has made sure we have the assis-tance of one of the finest financial minds he could spare. Things are not…' He paused, searching for the right way to tell her that her home was, by all accounts, in a state approaching chaos.

But she was nodding, her eyes far away. 'With no lord to oversee things, and no steward…that explains the band of cutthroats you have employed.'

'Do not be alarmed,' he said. One good thing about the months he had spent idling about the lowest taverns in the city was that he had got to discover the worth of many of the other men who fre-quented them. 'They look worse than they really are. And Captain Fritz will keep them in line.' Dropping a kiss on the top of her downbent head, he asked, 'Is that all you wanted me for? Shall I call your women back to you now?'

'No!' She had been at Lady Lacey's mercy all day. Without thinking, Maddy wrapped her arms round his waist and clung to him.

'Ah, you little wanton,' Sir Geraint said, hugging her back.

Alarmed that he should have so misinterpreted her action, Maddy raised her face to protest. But he was too quick for her. With a heart-felt groan, he took her mouth in a kiss that was so all-consuming that soon she could not remember what she had been about to say.

Locked together, their mouths fused in a passionate mating, they sank back on to the bed, his hands sweeping the length of her body, hers rising so that she could sink her fingers into the softness of his hair.

'I thought it might be too soon for you,' he panted, raising himself off her to feverishly tug off his jerkin. 'I don't want to hurt you...' his hands were under her skirts now, shoving them out of the way with impatience '...but since you are offering...' With a wicked grin, he found the target he had been seeking.

With a moan, Maddy closed her eyes as his fingers slid into her slick heat. It was useless to protest this was not what she had meant. Though nothing had been further from her mind when she had flung her arms round him, that single kiss had been like a spark falling on to dry tinder. The very idea of him stopping now was unbearable. So, when he moved away from her, to stand at the edge of the bed, her eyes flew open in panic.

'No!' she cried, struggling on to her elbows.

'Trust me,' he husked, parting her legs and tugging her to the edge of the bed.

To her utter astonishment, he then dropped to his knees and fastened his mouth to the place where his fingers had already stoked her to thrumming need.

'No!' she cried in shock as she felt the heat of his breath, the slickness of his tongue gliding. Her hands fastened in his hair as she attempted to push him away, certain this was a wicked, unnatural act...only to relent with a moan as wave after wave of the most intense pleasure she had ever experienced began to surge through her. While her fingers gentled, her hips bucked wildly as sensation swiftly rose to overwhelm her, bringing her to a peak of such intense pleasure that it was almost unbearable. It was only afterward, when she slowly began to come back down to earth again, that shame engulfed her. Painfully aware of her undignified position, her legs splayed wide and her skirts bunched up, she could not bring herself to open her eyes, and look upon the man who had reduced her to a state of such unbridled lust. She just wanted to cover herself up. But as she began to fumble her skirts down, his large hands came down hard upon hers.

'Nay. Maddy.'

His voice was shaking, hoarse, so strange that her eyes flew open in surprise. Afterwards, she was glad that she had seen what was coming, else she did not know how she would have coped with the shock of what he did next. Still standing beside the bed, he tore his hose open with a couple of deft movements, grasped her hips and pulled her forward on to his straining, rigid member. He was pulsing with his own release before she had time to protest against the un-gainliness of her position. And when he was done, he just collapsed forward, somehow tangling her legs up on to the bed beside his, so that they lay panting next to each other on the top of the quilt.

Maddy wondered at the feeling of peace that stole through her, washing away the shame. Her dress was probably ruined. She should get up, and take it off…but then he kissed her hair, and pulled the rumpled covers over them, and she drowsily decided she would worry about all that tomorrow. For now, she didn't want to think about anything but how delightful it was to nestle into the strength of his arms, and know that, while she was here, nothing and no one else could touch her.

Chapter Eleven

Over the next two weeks, Maddy found herself spending more of each day dreaming of the pleasure Sir Geraint had shown her the night before, and anticipating the night to come.

The only cloud on her horizon was Lady Lacey's persistently gloomy predictions for her future.

'Once the novelty has worn off, and he's taken you every way he can think of, or once you begin to grow cumbersome with a child, he'll turn for amusement elsewhere, you mark my words! Then you will remember I tried to warn you,' she said, when Maddy pulled back the curtains to get a glimpse of her husband on horseback.

But Maddy was too busy filling her eyes with the sight of him wrestling Caligula into submission to give her an answer. His skill with the beast reminded her so forcibly of the power he exerted over her own body. There was such strength in those great hands, though he tempered his strength with patience. When the muscles of his thighs bunched as he pressed his knees into the temperamental mount's flanks, she could almost feel the texture of his crisp hair against her own, smoother skin.

'Maddy!' Lady Lacey leaned across her and snapped the curtain of the horse litter shut. 'I hope you are not so foolish as to believe that the fact he is acting like a ravenous beast whenever he gets you alone means he cares about you.'

Maddy sighed, and reached for her prayer book. She had known from the start she ought to guard her heart against this man. But neither her own instinct for self-preservation, nor Lady Lacey's dire warnings, could make any difference now.

She was already lost.

The very night before, she had been on the verge of confessing she would do anything for him, be anything he wanted her to be, if only he would love her a little. The only thing that had held her back had been the knowledge that, loathe as she was to admit it, her cousin was correct. The very way he had positioned her limbs, driving them both mindless with desire, had filled her with the certainty that while she had wished to begin speaking of what was in her heart, all he wanted was to indulge his body. And while she strained to catch glimpses of him during the day, his own attention was always fixed on the welfare of his retinue.

It was quite obvious that while he was fast becoming the focal point of her life, she was still only a means to an end, as far as he was concerned.

'What in heaven?' Lady Lacey remarked, as the litter lurched to a sudden stop. Outside, Maddy could hear the noise of feet pounding towards the back of the cavalcade. Leaning out of the now-stationary litter, she could see that one of the baggage carts had half-slipped off the edge of the road. The horses were straining, their hooves struggling to find purchase in the mud as the weight of the cart pulled them backwards and sideways. At any moment, the vehicle was going to tip over, dragging the poor beasts, the driver who was whipping them on with red-faced urgency, and the entire contents of the cart, off the edge of the road and down the slope to disappear through the curtain of drizzle to who knew what fate.

But the men who had run past her halted its sideways movement, against all the odds, as a forest of arms shored up the side of the cart and shoved, till all four of its wheels were safely back on the highway again. The men were all panting from their exertion, some doubled over, resting their hands on their thighs as sweat dripped from the ends of their noses.

'Faugh!' Lady Lacey spat her disgust at the display of brute strength that had left Maddy open-mouthed with admiration.

'Oh, no!' One of the men had sunk to the ground once the cart was upright, and at first Maddy had not suspected anything might be amiss. But the way the others now began to gather round him, and his sharp cries of distress when anyone tried to touch him, alerted her to his injury. Without thinking, she made to get out of the litter.

'Where do you think you are going?' Lady Lacey put out a hand to detain her.

'One of the men is hurt. I must see if there is anything I can do!'

'Send one of the maids if you must,' she spat, ignoring the way Mary and Betty shrank back, appalled at the very idea.

'Oh, for heaven's sake!' Maddy could not be bothered to argue, not when somebody had been hurt in the attempt to protect her possessions. Without further ado, she ran back to see what she could do to help.

Jan's shoulder had been torn from its moorings, Captain Fritz informed her curtly. From the deft way he'd investigated the man's injury, she could tell he had some experience in field surgery.

'You had better look away, my lady, while I put it back.'

Sir Geraint pulled her face into his chest, preventing her from witnessing whatever procedure produced the blood-curdling yell that issued from the injured man's throat. But when it was over, she was pleased to see that, though pale, he was clearly in a lot less pain than he had been.

'Will he be all right now?' she asked.

Captain Fritz regarded her thoughtfully. 'He will not be able to function efficiently as a soldier for some time.'

'What can be done to help him? Can we find room for him to ride in one of the carts, perhaps?'

Rollo passed Jan a wineskin, from which he drank gratefully. The injured arm hung limp at his side, she noticed, even though he was clearly suffering less pain.

'There is nothing wrong with his legs,' Captain Fritz said. 'He can walk. Though…' he frowned '…his arm might feel better if he kept it in a sling for a day or so…'

Wondering how the Captain could be quite so unfeeling, she leaned over the man who still sat, pale faced and shaking, in the mud, saying, 'I am just going to get something to fashion into a sling to make your arm more comfortable. Don't move.'

A hush fell upon the men as they parted to let her through. By the time she returned, with some strips of linen she had torn from a bolt that had been destined for household use, they had formed a semi-circle around their injured comrade.

'Hold still,' she commanded, kneeling beside him so that she could arrange his arm into a comfortable position, and tie it firmly in place round his neck. 'There,' she pronounced. 'Does that feel better?'

Jan simply gazed at her open-mouthed.

Bemused, she sought her husband's eyes, but his flinty expression gave nothing away. Her heart sank. Oh, heavens. Had she somehow made a fool of herself? She hadn't stopped to think what his reaction might be. She had always strongly believed that one of the duties of a lady was to care for her dependants, and that included tending to their injuries. And with all her brothers being so keen on fighting besides, she had soaked up every bit of knowledge she could that might some day aid them should they return home injured.

Was he annoyed that she had forgotten about the fine clothes he had bought her when she had knelt in the mud? Or did he simply not like her getting so close to one of these men? She had never cared so much what anyone thought of her before. Knowing he was merely indifferent had been bad enough, but the prospect of invoking his displeasure brought a crushing pain to her chest.

At least recriminations would wait until tonight, she reflected as he handed her silently back into the litter. Although, naturally, Lady Lacey felt no such compunction.

'How can you demean yourself so? It is not even as if those men are family retainers! Mercenaries, that is all they are. Scum!'

Maddy's lips twitched in spite of her anxiety about how her

husband viewed her actions. Lady Lacey might profess to despise these men, but over the last few days, she could not help noticing that she had been raising her skirts somewhat higher than was strictly necessary whenever she climbed into or out of the litter. And though she kept her nose in the air whenever she walked past them, she had resumed that hip-swaying walk, the one that was guaranteed to draw every male gaze to her shapely figure. Maddy hadn't even noticed she had stopped walking like that, until the day she'd started again. She might despise these men, but they were males who were openly reassuring her that she was a very alluring female. And if the heated glances that came her way helped her cousin recover from her broken heart, then she could only be glad for her.

Sir Geraint raised his arm, the signal that the cavalcade should set out once more, and set his face sternly to the front. He would not give in to the constant urge he felt to glance back towards the horse litter, hoping for a glimpse of his bewitching young bride.

He shifted uncomfortably in his saddle, hoping his state of arousal was not noticeable to anyone else. He'd had to practically throw her into the litter, so desperate was his desire to crush her to him and cover her darling face with kisses. She was just so damned perfect. The way she had dealt with the injured man at arms, not stopping to care for her finery, had filled him with a deep sense of love and pride... God, but he could hardly wait for the night! Then she cast her modesty aside with her clothing, and revealed a side to her nature that was for his eyes only. She was wild, this little traitor's daughter!

Though everything about her was a delight. She never complained, not like that bitch of a cousin of hers, or the maidservants who took their cue from the older woman. Even when the rigours of the journey, coupled with their nighttime exertions, wore her out, she just curled up and dozed on the cushions of the litter.

His only concern was his certainty she was holding a part of herself back from him. He would be a fool to let her see how much he adored her, until she gave him some sign she felt at least as much for him as he felt for her.

A wry smile tugged at the corner of his mouth as he recalled the expression on Jan's face at the gentle way she had tied the sling round his neck. She had bewitched him, too, that was for sure. Her pleasant manner, and fortitude on the journey thus far, was slowly but surely winning the respect of every single one of the hard-bitten rag-tag of dispossessed wastrels he had rounded up from the taverns with promise of pay, and victuals, and board. She had taken pains to learn each and every man's name. He had known that each man had merit somewhere, deep within, or he would not have hired him, but she was bringing it effortlessly to the surface. Even Barty and Thomas refrained from fighting each other when she was around. The men had agreed to serve him for wages, but he guessed that any one of them would willingly lay down their lives for their lady, out of a visceral loyalty that no amount of money could buy.

Which was a great relief to him. There was no way of knowing what they would encounter when they reached the lands that were nominally his. Or what sort of reception the locals would give him.

A flurry of rain found its way under his collar, making him shiver. Lawless was well aware that he was going to have to steer him through his varied obligations, unobtrusively, in the hopes that nobody would know he had not been trained to such a position, and use his inexperience as an excuse to try to usurp him. His heart had plunged when he had heard exactly what was expected of his new position. It was not just a matter of managing his estates and governing his immediate dependants. As well as hearing minor legal cases in his immediate locality, he was going to have to sit on a Royal commission, alongside other northern nobles and gentry.

Shaking droplets of water from his hair, he lifted his head to peer through the heavy mist that shrouded the landscape. They were less than a day's ride from Woolton Castle now, and the closer they got to Maddy's home, the more the scenery reminded him of the Welsh valleys of his boyhood. In spite of the problems he could foresee in managing the people, he knew he could soon feel at home in such rugged terrain. The very sheep he glimpsed browsing amongst the wind-racked gorse bushes, which Lawless informed him produced the wool from which most of Maddy's wealth derived, reminded him of the sturdy breed that inhabited the Welsh mountains.

He sat a little straighter in the saddle. His own father was a wealthy wool merchant, and two of his brothers had followed him into the business. If he had problems in any aspect of managing his flocks, he could invite any one of them for a visit, and pick their brains under cover of extending his family hospitality. He would not have to depend totally on his steward, or rely on the dubious loyalty of the locals.

'Captain Fritz tells me that we shall soon be crossing the borders into your land, my lord husband,' said Maddy, who had mounted her palfrey and trotted to join him. 'In spite of the weather, I should like to be at your side when we do.'

She looked a little anxious, he noted. Though his first instinct was indeed to tell her she ought not to be on horseback in such weather, her idea to be at his side when they entered her land was a good one. She knew he wanted to promote an image of solidarity between them, and what better way could there be to demonstrate it than to ride, side by side, up to the castle that was only coming to him because of her.

'I wish I had thought of it myself,' he admitted.

Her answering smile sent a shaft of sunshine straight to his heart, warming him through to the core. Ah, Maddy, he mused, tugging Caligula's head round and urging him into forward motion, if only you knew what power you have over me. For a smile like that, I think I would grant you just about any boon you asked of me.

'Do you think we are on DelaBoys land yet?' she asked presently. 'I had hoped I might recognise something, but I was so young when I left…'

He half-turned in the saddle to summon Lawless to his side. The steward had spent hours poring over the maps, learning by heart the area that he was going to teach Sir Geraint how to rule over. He would know exactly where the boundaries lay.

But just as the man began to move his horse out from the protective cover of the column, Maddy urged her own horse forward with a little cry.

He turned in time to see her cantering towards a group of men who seemed to have materialised out of the mists to bar their passage through a narrow pass.

An ambush! The locals had picked a choice spot, here where the road curved between two precipitous slopes. On horseback, his own men could only fight one at a time, whereas their assailants were all on foot, and could scamper like mountain goats over the rocks to hurl missiles down upon them.

And Maddy had cried out in delight, indicating she knew, and was pleased to see these men. Had she known all along they would be waiting at this spot? Was that why she had insisted on taking to horse, at this point in their journey, so that she could flee his own men more easily?

A wave of despair washed over him as she dismounted and flung herself into the arms of the man who was clearly their leader. There was scarcely a pause before the man threw his halberd to the ground, so that he could return her exuberant greeting, swinging her round and off her feet, his ruddy face breaking into an expression of joy at the sound of Maddy's delighted laughter.

She must have been in secret communication with them. This was the reason she had been so keen to get back to her own lands—to join forces with her lover, and the rebels who would resist the lord King Henry had sent to rule over them.

He should sweep down on them now, and cut them to ribbons, his faithless wife along with them! All he would have to do was give the word. The makeshift weapons they carried looked sadly amateurish in comparison with his own men's honed steel. Caligula snorted, sensing his master's tension, pawing once at the ground as though urging him to battle. But did he really want to start his tenure with a show of force? This was exactly what King Henry had hoped to avoid by arranging his marriage to Maddy.

Even as he bit down on the orders he knew he should give, a sense of futility washed over him. Wealth, land, all the honour the King had heaped on him—none of it meant anything if she was false.

She turned then, tugging the leader of the rabble that blocked the road by the hand towards him, her face alight with a joy she had never displayed for him. He wanted to be sick.

'Oh, Ger!' In her excitement, she forgot she was supposed to address him formally when they were in public. He didn't like it, she could see that at once. His face was rigid with displeasure.

'I'm...mean...' She faltered before the icy blast of fury emanating from the lordly man who sat glaring down at her. 'Sir G...Geraint,' she corrected herself, 'this is John, my brother, come to greet us.'

If she thought he was going to swallow a lie of that magnitude, she was in for a rude awakening.

'Your brothers are all dead,' he replied coldly.

Maddy flinched. She had not thought her husband could speak so cruelly.

John disentangled himself from Maddy's clasp, and, sweeping off his knitted cap, he bowed low. 'All her legitimate brothers died nobly on the battlefield, 'tis true. But I am left...a testimony to her father's...indiscretions.'

Sir Geraint took a closer look at the man who claimed kinship with his wife. He supposed he could see some resemblance between them. The man was shorter than average, and of a wiry build. His eyes were brown, like hers, but looked incongruous in conjunction with hair that was fair and curling.

Maddy felt bitterly disappointed. Her legitimate brothers had treated John with scorn, her father with indifference, but she had somehow not suspected her husband would display the same kind of prejudice.

It was all so unfair! What right had her husband to judge John without even knowing him? And what was her life going to be like if she cowered every time he frowned, only acting if she was certain he would not be displeased? She'd abandoned herself to his demands in bed, only to learn from Lady Lacey, a woman who had evidently travelled that road herself, that his apparent delight in her was only a phase all men went through with their latest conquest. With a flare of defiance, she turned to her half-brother, saying, 'You are as dear to me as any of my mother's sons ever were.'

'Aye, you were always kinder to me than any other of my father's children,' he replied thoughtfully. He turned to address the men who followed him. 'If any of us had any doubts about the wisdom of you returning, with this new husband of yours, after being a stranger to us for so long, the way you greeted me now has dispelled them. Isn't that right?'

The men pressed forward to make themselves known to her.

From his vantage point on horseback, Sir Geraint watched her bewitch each one. Within minutes, she had them all eating out of her hand.

'Welcome home, Maddy,' he heard John say. Nobody had the right to call her that, except him! Only iron self-control kept him from riding the impudent wretch down.

Especially since she was smiling up at him, as though he was the only man that existed.

Then, as though recollecting himself, John added, 'Though now you are grown, I suppose I should address you as My Lady Margaret.'

'Oh, no!' Maddy laughed. ''Tis Lady Agnes now, if you please, although...' sensitive to her husband's disapproval, though not entirely willing to appease it, she flung up her chin '...there is no need for such formality between brother and sister. Is there, my lord husband?'

Turning to look at him squarely, she felt her defiance waver under the force of his disapproval. Something inside her clenched. She had promised she would never defy him in public. Now, less than a month after she had made that promise, she had broken it.

And in doing so, she had cut herself off from the man who had come to be more important to her than the air she breathed. In a moment of reckless defiance. Oh, how it hurt!

He saw her resolution waver. And felt his own anger leach away. Maybe she had just been impetuous. Maybe she had not seen any danger in the men who had stationed themselves across the road. Maybe she had only seen her brother.

He shook his head, suddenly unutterably weary of the emotions that surged through him. Maddy wrung him out. He couldn't go on like this much longer, drawn out on the rack of jealousy, suspicion and longing she evoked. He had to put a stop to it. And he would start by asserting his authority over her now. Just because she turned those great brown eyes up at him in appeal, did she think he would tamely grant whatever she asked of him? It was time to show her he was not her lap dog to command.

'That remains to be seen,' he said.

He could almost see the coldness of his words crystallising to ice in Maddy's veins.

But at least his words had the effect of cutting John down to size. He seemed to shrink in stature, from leader of a rebel gang to a humble, slightly muddy servant, bowing before his mounted master in the road.

'Forgive our impetuosity, my lord,' John said, taking a step forward as though to shelter his sister from her lord's ill humour. 'We have not seen each other since we were children.'

Sir Geraint, far from being mollified by the humility in the man's voice, resented the way his words and actions had set him outside the family circle.

'We heard your arrival was imminent…' he waved to the motley crew of his tenants ranged behind him '…and some of us wished to welcome you across the borders to Lady Margaret's…that is, your lands.' He covered the slip with a grin Sir Geraint felt was bordering on the insolent. And the men who'd come with him had not been a welcoming party, on that he would stake his life.

Sir Geraint had never been so glad to have what Maddy termed his band of cutthroats at his back, as he was at that moment. Whatever had prompted John to lead his men to this point, he must have seen straight away that a frontal attack would have ended in slaughter. Though it probably suited him to let it appear that Maddy herself had defused the situation.

John had dropped his eyes now, adopting a subservient posture that didn't fool Sir Geraint for a second. The man resented his presence as clearly as if he had shouted it.

Chapter Twelve

At a peremptory signal from Sir Geraint, Rollo brought the palfrey to where Maddy stood, though it was John who bent, his hands cupped, to boost her into the saddle.

And John who received her grateful smile.

The Woolton men now turned to head the procession that wound its way towards the castle, John striding beside Maddy's palfrey.

'I should warn you that things are in a bit of a state, Mad…I mean, my lady.' John grinned over his shoulder at the slip of the tongue.

'It is as well we have brought a steward with us, then, is it not?' Sir Geraint growled.

John glanced at him sharply. Then nodded, as though he considered his lord's words were welcome. 'It will be a relief to have someone to hand over the reins to, and that's a fact. When old Robbins made off like that…' He shook his head, his brows drawn down. 'Well, I've done my best to hold things together, but I'm not an educated man. It will be a relief to go back to what I know best, the running of the stables.'

'Oh, surely not!' Maddy couldn't help herself. This was her brother. After all he had done, looking after the interests of the people here, surely her husband would not be so base as to relegate him to being a glorified groom, as her father had done? 'My lord?' She turned her eyes upon her husband, imploring him to understand. And came up against a wall of ice.

A shaft of ice struck her own heart. When she had been a little

girl, she had hidden her growing friendship with John, for fear of
displeasing her other brothers, though it had torn her in two, for he
had never pushed her away when she'd sought his company. He'd
always had a smile and a kind word for her. And he'd spent hours
trotting her round on her fat little pony, even taking her beyond the
castle confines over the moors once she'd gained enough confidence. She hadn't been brave enough to stand up for him then, but
she would do so now!

Sir Geraint noticed her lift her chin in that way she had when she
was reining in her temper. And his resolve hardened. She had him so
besotted that he had sat still when threatened with ambush. Such a state
of affairs could not continue. The King had sent him here to do a job!

He eyed John's easy manner with Maddy, and her friendly responses to him. And noted that the Woolton men were looking to
John's demeanour, and taking their cue from him.

They passed through a belt of trees, from which the first Norman
baron to live here had taken his name, and began to mount the
glacis. The earliest wooden fortress had, of course, been replaced
by a series of stone fortifications, intended to hold off the Scots who
had regularly raided the area. The rocky bluff on which it stood in
itself provided a good defence, sloping gently to the woods in the
front, and dropping sheer to the river behind.

Now, here was the place John should have made a stand, he
thought, if he really wanted to prevent him from entering the castle.
Here, at the gatehouse. He looked upwards, shivering, as he passed
through a covered archway, to see the murder holes through which
defenders could drop rocks, or even boiling oil down onto unwel-
come intruders such as he.

Instead, he saw a group of retainers milling about the inner ward
with little apparent sense of purpose.

All that changed when John summoned one of the women from
the crowd.

'Joan!' he cried. 'Come and meet the new lord and lady!'

A pretty, blue-eyed woman glided across and sank into a graceful curtsy at Maddy's feet. As she rose, John gave her a swift hug, which brought heightened colour to her dimpled cheeks.

'Joan has prepared the rooms your mother and father had for you and your husband,' he told Maddy. That meant her own room would be at the top of the north tower, and Sir Geraint's directly below. 'And she has organised a veritable banquet to welcome you home.'

Joan looked at the column of men who were dismounting, and frowned.

'I didn't know you would be bringing so many of your own retainers with you, my lady,' she said, wringing her hands. 'I don't think I've prepared enough beds for everyone.'

Captain Fritz strode across and bowed curtly. 'My men can bed down in the hall, until more appropriate quarters can be organised.'

'Perhaps you would like to inspect the guard house,' John suggested affably. 'My father often housed visiting knights and their men-at-arms there.'

At that moment, Lady Lacey materialised at Maddy's side. She had climbed unaided from the horse litter, and was clearly not enjoying being relegated to the sidelines.

Joan, seeing the frown mar her imperious features, sank immediately into a deferential curtsy.

'Who is that woman?' she said to Maddy, ignoring Joan completely. 'I mean, what is her station here?'

'I don't precisely know,' Maddy hissed, turning away so that Joan could not hear. 'But she has done what she can to prepare the castle for our arrival.' Later, as Joan led them to the guest room she had arranged Lady Lacey should inhabit in the west tower, Maddy whispered, 'I think she must be some sort of housekeeper, or something.'

'You are mistress here now,' Lady Lacey retorted. 'Make her hand over the keys.' She indicated the large bunch hanging at Joan's waist.

'Not tonight,' Maddy declared firmly. Sir Geraint had been ominously quiet on the ride here. She could sense a storm brewing in that quarter, and had no desire to provoke another one. 'I am sure opportunity will arise to settle the question over the next few days.' She wanted to inspect everything, and see how things stood before making any changes.

Her anxiety with regard to her husband's mood abated somewhat when she joined him in the Great Hall later. For he had seated John beside him at the high table on the raised dais, and was deep in discussion with him.

She smiled at him with heartfelt relief as she took her place on his other side. This gesture must mean he had forgiven her momentary lapse into outspokenness. Buoyed up by the hope that he was honouring her half-brother for her sake, she relaxed, and gave herself up to the joy of sitting here, in the place of mistress of her own home, for the first time.

But it wasn't long before she noticed that the festive mood that pervaded the hall did not encompass her husband. Although he was perfectly pleasant to all about him, she could feel the tension riding his shoulders, and, knowing him as she did, saw that his smiles never reached his eyes. By the time she rose from the table, to head for the seclusion of her tower room, she had begun to fear he was still angry with her after all.

It was much later when he joined her, and by then she had forgotten her earlier determination to make a stand.

'Oh, Ger,' she blurted the second the door closed behind him, 'do not be angry with me. I cannot bear it!'

His frown did not abate one whit as he casually drew off his jerkin and tossed it on to the lid of the chest that stood at the foot of her bed.

Taking a few hesitant steps to close the distance between them, she laid a hand tentatively on his chest. Irritably, he brushed her off.

'Tell me about this John, this brother whose existence I knew nothing of until today,' he growled, turning his back on her.

'Well…his mother was the daughter of one of my father's tenants. Very beautiful, by all accounts, though I never saw her. When she died, Father brought John to live at the castle. Everyone knew what he was. But Father never legally recognised him as his son. Instead, he put him to work in the stables.' He could hear the bitterness in her voice. His tender-hearted little wife still felt the sting of injustice against her own flesh and blood so sharply it was all he could do to repress a pang of sympathy for the mistreated lad himself.

'Th…thank you for letting him sit at table with us, and not relegating him to the role of servant again. That would have wounded him so much. After all he has done, holding the place together without the benefit of a steward—'

'We have only his word for that,' Sir Geraint grated, casting his hose and boots aside. 'He claims he has been running the estates in the absence of a steward, but I will suspend judgement until Lawless can examine the books and discover exactly what he has been doing with your revenues.'

Maddy bit her lip, wondering whether she should admit that she had been concerned herself that money had been going astray somewhere. But then wouldn't that only hand her husband more ammunition to use against her brother?

'And I let him stay at table, rather than banish him to the stables, not to please you, my dear…' he drew the shirt over his head, his very nakedness a flagrant challenge '…but because of something the King said to me. When he gave Woolton into my keeping, he advised me to keep the people I trusted least closest to me, so that I can keep a careful eye on what they do.'

If not for the irrational jealousy he felt for John, he might be tempted to take the man into his confidence. He clearly had a great deal of influence with the locals. He claimed he had done what he could to keep the place in some kind of order. Was he going to be able to do any more? He'd come here with no more idea of how to govern such a place than a groom would. If he admitted as much to her half-brother, would he then be admitted into the charmed circle?

Yet he could not discount the veiled hostility of the men who had stood in the road barring their way. That had not just been his own fancy. Captain Fritz had admitted, later, that his hand had been on his sword hilt the entire time. No, he could not admit the fellow into his confidence until he knew more of him. He would have to wait and see how he behaved. And if that offended Maddy, he decided, turning from her and climbing into her bed, then that was too bad.

He was not going to melt in a puddle at her feet in response to one of her bewitching smiles. Though, to give her her due, she did not appear to notice the effect her smile had on her dependants. Though he had. After she'd smiled at him, at supper, all the mercenaries had begun to behave like perfect gentlemen, when each, left to their own devices, would have seized the opportunity to get their hands on the serving women who bustled round the hall. The atmosphere in the hall had grown far less strained. Until that moment, he wouldn't have been a bit surprised to find they all woke up the next morning with their throats cut. The very ale in his cup had taken on a bitter taste to know that *she* was the lady of the manor, and, without her, he would be nothing. He knew he was usurping a place to which he had not been born. But did he really have to rely on his wife's goodwill to govern these people? A man should be lord in his own home!

Holding out his hand, he ordered, 'Come to bed now, madam wife.'

Nervously, Maddy slid into the bed beside him.

'You are my wife,' he growled, grabbing hold of her and ruthlessly stripping away her nightgown.

'Yes,' she panted, torn between excitement and apprehension. For he was still very angry with her.

His mouth devoured her breasts, while his hands shaped her body, relentlessly rousing her almost beyond endurance. Suddenly he reared up over her, his eyes coldly assessing her reaction.

'Oh, Ger,' she moaned. How could he hold himself back like this, at such a moment, when she was going up in flames? 'Oh, please…'

At last, he joined with her fully. But the ardent lover she had known on the journey here had gone. A grim-faced stranger had taken his place.

'Ger…' she whimpered, reaching up to put her arms round his neck and draw him down for a kiss.

'No!' He pulled her hands off his neck, grasping her by the wrists and pinning her hands on the pillow above her head, as though he was determined to keep some distance between them. Even as he skilfully tipped her over the edge, into a swirling maelstrom of hot sensation, she could feel him holding back.

He let her rest for only a few moments, before he began to move again, bringing her masterfully to a second orgasm. Only then did he reach his own release, with a cry that could have come from the throat of a wounded animal. With something like a snarl he rolled to his side, gathering her into the crook of his arm.

At first he felt immeasurably better for having demonstrated his own power over her, sexually. But as his own heartbeat slowed, his mind cleared. He had been a fool to feel jealous of the loyalty she had shown to her own kin. And how could he be angry with her because everyone respected her? He kissed the top of her head, hugging her closer.

'Maddy, I don't want the kind of marriage lords and ladies have,' he murmured into her fragrant silky hair.

She made a muffled sound of acknowledgement, but he knew without having to look at her she was already more than halfway asleep. She made love with such enthusiasm it always exhausted her. He'd tell her later, or better yet, show her what he wanted from their marriage. It had come to him, in the same rapturous second that his seed had spilled into her, and he'd felt her pulsing around him, that many men and women came to this, then got up and went their separate ways. It didn't always mean anything. But two people could be closer than this. Like his parents, who were equal partners in everything.

The King might say he valued his wife, yet he had no qualms about advising Ger to take a mistress. But he did not want things to degenerate to the state he'd gleaned Maddy's parents had. How could her father bring his bastard into the house, openly? Had her mother still been alive then? No wonder the other sons had spurned him, making sure he stayed in the stables. Anything else would have seemed like an act of disloyalty to their mother.

He looked down at Maddy's little round face, sweetly flushed with sleep, and felt his heart contract within him. He wanted not only her loyalty, but her trust, and her affection. He might not win them from her for years. But that was what he had to work towards.

For a start, there would be no more ripping off her clothes and going at her like a stallion. He wasn't reaching her by treating her like a whore. Maybe she felt he didn't respect her, the way he pushed her to accommodate his own dark desires. He frowned. In a way, that was true. For he'd decided on the campaign of inventiveness when he'd mistakenly thought she was already experienced. Had it only been a month ago that he had believed she was a wanton, who had fallen pregnant by one of her myriad lovers, and was using him to cover up her disgrace? Why hadn't he eased up and shown some respect for her modesty when he'd discovered her innocence? Very well, then, he would demonstrate he respected her by showing some consideration for her shyness in the bedroom.

And the only way he would ever be able to lay his suspicions to rest would be by finding out where her political affiliations really lay. Only when there was complete trust between them would they achieve the kind of unity he wanted with all his heart. So he must begin to use the time when they were alone in their bedchamber to talk to her. And really get to know her.

Chapter Thirteen

Maddy was at the end of her tether. Each new day at Woolton only added to her woes, till misery was lodged in her stomach like a lead weight.

Now, the tensions that had always existed between the Woolton staff and her husband's bought men had erupted in a fist fight in the kitchen court.

Barty and Thomas had, naturally, been its instigators, but now two scullions and a groom had waded in, and a crowd was gathering to watch the sport.

'What is going on here?' Lady Lacey's strident voice rose above the hubbub as she strode into the courtyard.

Maddy shrank into the shade of the buttery walls as tears started rolling down her cheeks.

The one thing to be said in Lady Lacey's favour, she sniffed, darting furtively into the overgrown kitchen gardens, was that she would thoroughly enjoy berating everyone involved in this mêlée. She was made for a position of authority, whereas Maddy—she swiped angrily at her tear-streaked face, as she plunged down the path which led through the orchards—was feeling increasingly inadequate.

She paused on the bank of a stream where she had often played as a child. This was what she had dreamed of coming back to, she realised. A place where she had been happy, and loved, and where everything had been simple. It was not Woolton itself, but the carefree childhood she had spent here, that she had longed for.

On the spur of the moment, Maddy sat down, and having glanced over her shoulder to make sure she was unobserved, hastily peeled off her shoes and stockings, hitched up her skirts, and strode down to the water's edge.

Lady Lacey would tell her she was shirking her duties, no doubt. She sighed. She might find her cousin less irksome, if she wasn't always right. Just as she'd predicted, her husband was growing bored with her. He would rather sit and talk, when they were alone in their chamber, than make love to her nowadays.

In frustration, Maddy kicked out at the water, sending a spray of droplets arching over the banks. And soaking the front of her gown.

How typical. Now she would not be able to return to the castle until it was dried. Not that she wanted to go back. They would be tipping rotting herring on to the dung heap this afternoon, and she still hadn't got the stench from her nostrils, from when they had discovered eight barrels of it at the rear of the stores that morning. Lady Lacey, of course, had merely put a handkerchief to her nose, while ordering Barty to begin removing the spoiled fish from the stores, and berating Joan for not rotating the older barrels to the front when new stock came in. Maddy, humiliatingly, had to scramble up the cellar steps, gagging. Just the memory of the stench was making her feel queasy all over again.

Sighing, she turned up towards the headland, hoping the tramp across the heather would blow all the shadows from her soul. She was out of breath by the time she reached the vantage point from where she had watched the tide come racing in across the bay, so many times as a child.

She supposed she was not the first wife to love a husband who cared little for her. Her own mother must have felt just as she did, when her father conducted his affaires.

Please God, let Geraint not be unfaithful. She shivered. Though for all she knew, he could have come across someone else already.

He rode out every day, taking John, and the steward, and a comple-ment of his men, ostensibly to view his estates, coming back later and later. Wrapping her arms about her waist, she bit down on her lower lip, furiously blinking back tears as the wind whipped her hair across her face.

She nearly jumped out of her skin at the feel of a large hand de-scending on her shoulder. Whirling about, her heart leaped in her breast when she saw it was Sir Geraint.

'Ger!' She couldn't help smiling at the sight of him. She knew Lady Lacey would say she ought not to reveal her pleasure at his presence, lest it increase his advantage over her, but she had never been any good at disguising her feelings. She loved him, for better or worse, and she was always glad to be near him.

Sir Geraint felt some of the anxiety he had been carrying on his shoulders for days roll away. For Maddy seemed genuinely pleased to see him for once.

Ever since they had arrived at Woolton she had been growing more and more reserved towards him. It seemed the harder he tried to reach her, the further she withdrew. She did not seem to want to open her heart to him. Whatever he chose to talk about, she would frown, and return monosyllabic replies.

He guessed that part of her grudge against him stemmed from his inability to take her half-brother's claims at face value. The more he observed him, the deeper his suspicions grew. Lawless was already muttering about bringing a charge of theft against him. But he had warned the man not to make a move until he had a cast-iron case, reminding him that the man who had collected the disputed rents in the absence of an officially appointed steward was his wife's brother. 'I suppose,' Lawless had conceded, 'that his lack of educa-tion may have caused him to make genuine errors.'

But then again, given the way his father and half-brothers had treated him in the past, he would not be a bit surprised to find he had taken advantage of the position he'd found himself in, to help himself to what he probably considered was rightfully his. He felt as though he walked a knife edge where that plausible rogue was concerned. If John was found guilty of stealing, and it became necessary to punish him, would Maddy understand that, as lord, he had to mete out justice to every wrongdoer, no matter who his sister might be? And, given her blind partiality, would she ever be able to forgive him?

Yet that worry paled into insignificance beside the fear that had gripped him when he'd seen her sneaking out of the castle yard, just as he had been walking into it, having returned somewhat earlier than planned. Her furtive flight through the kitchen garden had resurrected all the suspicions he'd had when first they wed. It was like being stabbed in the heart to witness her creeping into the orchard, at a point in their relationship when he had deliberately withdrawn sexually. He strode after her, jealousy and mistrust roiling poisonously through his brain. To picture his Maddy, in some other man's arms! Or worse, plotting treason against his King!

He'd watched in disbelief as she bared her legs, and waded into the water. And began to play, splashing about in the stream like a child.

And even now, even though she had smiled at him, he couldn't quite let go of his suspicion.

'All alone, Maddy?'

She heard the accusation in his voice, and leapt to the defensive. She supposed he thought she should be back in the castle, about her dreary tasks among the rust-spotted linen and the rotting herring all day. Lifting her chin, she glared at him.

'Sometimes I feel the need to be alone!'

He felt as though his soul was drowning in those deep brown eyes. She wanted him gone, and it was killing him. 'Shall I leave you to your solitude, then, madam wife?' Very well, he would go, but not so far that he could not see who she had been waiting for all this time.

'No!' As he turned to leave, Maddy flung her arms round his waist and buried her face in his chest, breathing him in. Even if he did find her boring, and was already thinking about taking a mistress, at least he was here now. And he could not have come up here, to this isolated spot, by accident. He must have been seeking her out!

'Tell me what is troubling you, Maddy,' he murmured, wrapping his arms about her waist. She leaned into her husband's strength, as his body warmed her. What more could any woman want than her husband's strength and support? She had more, so much more than many women ever knew. Why could she not stop herself craving what she could never have?

And what could she tell him? That she feared she had fallen in love with him and he was going to break her heart? How would that help?

'I just felt hot and tired...' she sighed '...and remembered the stream, that was all. I used to love it there as a child. And this bay always fascinated me, too. I always loved watching the sea race in, as though it was in a hurry to devour as much land as it could while it had the chance.'

For a few moments they stood quite still, just watching the waves tumbling endlessly over each other.

'For some reason it always made me feel peaceful. And I needed to find a bit of calm. There is none within the castle today.' Her voice became querulous. 'Barty and Thomas have been fighting again. I cannot get Betty or Mary to do a stroke of real work. Lady Lacey is never happier than when she is finding fault with something. And I couldn't get the smell of herring out of my nostrils.'

'I could never understand why you wanted that witch to come with you on your bride trip.' He cuddled her closer, his lips a balm to the curve of her neck where he breathed his words.

'She is my kinswoman. I have no other.' Maddy sighed, angling her head so that his lips had better access to that sweet spot. 'When she leaves, may I have Joan to my companion? Until I came back, she had a position as near to being chatelaine as made no difference, and now I am here, she must feel slighted, and, Ger, I do like her! Sometimes when Lady Lacey's tongue is at its most cutting, she has a way of rolling her eyes that makes me feel as though she is on my side, even against those other two that came with us…'

'Maddy, the household is yours to run. You may do whatever you wish with your women, you know that.'

'Truly?' She turned in his arms, catching a burning look in his eyes that took her breath away. For timeless moments, she just gazed at him, hearing nothing but the pounding of her heart within her breast, echoing the soughing of the waves on the shore. Then he was kissing her, with an urgency he had not displayed since the first night they had slept in Woolton Castle. Dizzy with relief, she kissed him back, her hungry hands desperately seeking entry to his clothes so she could feel naked skin. His breath hissed from between his clenched teeth as she found a gap under his shirt, and her hand slid from his waist to his spine, ruthlessly bunching material out of her way.

Then, suddenly, he was tumbling her to the ground, his own hands roaming beneath her skirts, seemingly as needy to feel bare flesh as she was.

Rolling on to his back, he hitched her over so that she lay pressed to his heart. Without breaking his kiss, he pulled her skirts up, then unlaced his hose, pushing them aside so that there was no barrier between them.

Startled, she broke away, trying to wriggle free. She got no further than a position where she was sitting astride him, her hands braced on the broad expanse of his chest, when his hands clamped down on her hips, rocking her against him.

'Ger…' she protested feebly when he let her go long enough to slide a hand between them. 'You must not,' she moaned as his fingers nipped and stroked, leaving her in no doubt of what he wanted. But he ignored her protest, his wickedly skilled fingers inciting and inflaming her until she was rocking against him.

'Ah, Maddy,' he groaned, 'I want to take you every way there is!'

Though his words sent a chill of foreboding through her, she was powerless to resist him. And when he finally guided himself into her in one slow, sure thrust, her moan was one of pure pleasure. His hand remained beneath her skirts even as he bucked into her, building her excitement until she was riding him, head thrown back, oblivious to anything but her own sweet pleasure as it built and burst like a dam, drowning her in wave upon wave of molten ecstasy.

Only then did she come back to a sense of where they were, and how shamelessly he had caused her to behave.

'I cannot believe I just did that!' she gasped as he rolled her on to her side.

'Nor I.' He chuckled, hauling her close when she would have wriggled away.

'Outdoors,' she groaned, covering her face with her hands. And she had no certainty that this meant anything more to her husband than Lord Hugo's illicit tryst with Lady Lacey had meant to him. Though…she gulped at a sudden feeling of audacity…at least it had excited her husband. If she could keep on providing him with the variety he seemed to crave, perhaps she could prevent him from seeking it elsewhere. With a feeling of sick shame, she let her hands drop from her face and gazed mournfully up at him. She knew she would do whatever it took to keep him from leaving her. She could not bear to think of him thus intimate with any other woman.

'Forgive me, Maddy,' he whispered, full of remorse at the expression on her face. 'I should not have tumbled you here, in the open air, where any man might spy on us!'

Frowning, he pulled her skirts back down, sitting up and turning his back to her, running his fingers through his hair.

'Oh, Ger,' she whispered, rising to her knees behind him and laying her cheek upon his broad back. 'It's all right. We are quite alone here, and not like to be disturbed. Did I not tell you that was one of the reasons I came here?'

With a puzzled frown, he turned to look at her. She had surprised him yet again. When he had been braced for recriminations at his unbridled lechery, tears, protests even, he sensed she was trying to soothe him.

'This is just about the only spot within five miles of the castle that cannot be overlooked from one of the watchtowers. The sea itself is a firm defence against this part of the coastline.' She smiled. 'So you see, we can stay a while, without fear of having our privacy invaded, if it would please you.'

'Would you like to linger with me, sweeting?' He sought her face diligently for signs that she was merely humouring him, but the sweet smile that lit her face at his endearment swept aside any doubts he might have that she would rather be anywhere else but here.

She took hold of his hand, and, with a sigh of contentment, lay back down onto the bed of springy heather. He lay beside her, gazing up into the sky. For a while neither spoke, content to just be.

Beside him, Maddy finally stirred, clearing her throat.

'Ger?'

'Hmm?'

'If you say you want me so much, then why are you…that is, why have you been so…cold towards me since we arrived at Woolton? I had begun to fear I had displeased you.'

'Oh, Maddy, no,' he groaned, rolling on to his side and propping himself up on one elbow. Was that why she had seemed to withdraw? 'You have not displeased me at all. But we do need to talk to each other when we are alone in our chamber. Our marriage is about so much more than just you and I. We must not lose sight of that. We must not get distracted by personal feelings.'

'Am I a distraction to you, then?' Hurt gleamed in her eyes as her brow puckered in distress.

'Yes, you are a distraction.' He grinned, kissing the frown away. 'Of the most delightful kind. Shall I tell you something that will shock you? Last night, at supper, while I was endeavouring to engage in a serious conversation with Lawless, I couldn't help wondering what you would do if I was to run my hand up your skirts under cover of the table.'

Her eyes went round with shock, and a blush suffused her cheeks.

But for all that, he could not mistake the gleam of very feminine satisfaction that shone from her eyes.

'What would you have done, madam wife, had I begun to seduce you at table?'

'I…well, I don't know.' Her brow puckered in innocent confusion. In some distress, she added, 'Do you really wish to do things like that?' She sat up quickly, her cheeks fiery red now. 'I mean, if that is what you wish, then of course I would not prevent you, but—'

'Oh, Maddy, sweet Maddy.' He chuckled. 'Have I not sworn I would always treat you with respect when we are being observed?'

He got to his feet, drawing her up after him. Making a great production of brushing little bits of broken heather from her gown, she grumbled, 'Yes, but you could perhaps smile at me once in a while. Or mayhap give me a kiss. A very chaste one.'

'Like this, perhaps?' He laid his hand upon her shoulders, and saluted her cheek.

'Yes,' she agreed. 'That would not be disrespectful.'

'How about this?' he asked, sliding his hands down to her waist, and applying his closed lips softly to hers for a second. A hot chill slid down her back. She gave a little shuddering gasp.

'N…no, I don't think you should kiss me like that…'

'It was perfectly chaste.'

'Yes, but it made me feel altogether…' She blushed in delightful confusion, turning her face away from his penetrating gaze.

'I will not tease you any more, sweet wife,' Sir Geraint vowed, laying an arm about her shoulders and hugging her as he turned them both back towards the castle, and their responsibilities. 'But I don't believe there can be any such thing as a chaste kiss, between us two. We are like flint and steel, needing only to brush against each other for sparks to flare. It would never do to start a conflagration that would set the castle in an uproar.'

She nodded, understanding dawning as they began the descent towards the orchard. The first time he had kissed her, she had been astounded at the heat his lips had unleashed within her. And just now, he had only grazed his lips against her neck, and she had been ready for him to take her. But at least he had admitted he was just as susceptible to this wanting as she was. Glancing up at him, gathering her courage from she knew not where, she said, 'Should you like to return to this headland sometimes, Ger? I can promise you, nobody will disturb us here.' The thought of luring her husband to this secluded spot, in order to…light his fires, and thus keep him enthralled with her, was making her heart hammer with excitement.

He cleared his throat. 'You mentioned that before, but how could we be sure? That is,' he amended, his own cheeks flushing dull red now, she observed to her delight, 'shouldn't I set some guards to watch such an isolated spot? Is it not a weak point in our land's defences?'

'Oh, no,' she assured him. 'The bluff on which we lay together forms a natural barrier. It sweeps up to that point, then drops sheer to the beach. The cliff would be very hard to scale, even if there was anywhere below for ships to land. Which, of course, there is not.'

'But there is a beach, with a jetty…'

'Only the ruins of a jetty. It collapsed years ago. Only a few of the upright timbers remain. And the only safe way on and off the beach now is at the far end of the bay. The sands up at this end are treacherous.'

'Treacherous? How so?'

'On account of the quicksand.' She frowned. 'Did you not know? I had thought you had been all over Woolton land, learning all about its many vagaries.'

'John seems not to have got round to telling me about the beach just yet,' he replied drily, while the hairs on the back of his neck began to prickle with unease. They had ridden across the sands not two days previously, and the man had said nothing about any danger then. On the contrary, he had led him quite close to this very bluff, on the pretext of visiting a fisherman's widow who lived in a ramshackle dwelling tucked between the dunes. He had remarked, for something to say to his tenant, upon the unusual craft she kept tied to the wall of her pigsty. A coracle, the woman had called the circular, shallow-drafted vessel.

'For when the tide is comin' in,' the windswept woman had explained in exasperation, as though he were an imbecile.

'Is the quicksand dangerous all the time?' he asked in a tone that he hoped showed nothing more than mild curiosity.

'Well, no, that's the funny thing. Pockets of quicksand only form when the tide is coming in, and not always in the same place twice. There is a sort of pattern to them, I believe, which varies according to the tides and phases of the moon, and so forth. But unless you spend a great deal of time making a study of them, it is safer to assume that this whole end of the beach is just not safe to venture upon.'

A cold hand clamped about Sir Geraint's heart. John must have led him right through the maze of danger, knowing that one foot placed wrongly could have led to his doom. A frown gathering on his brow, he reflected that the man must, at the very least, have been mocking his ignorance.

'Ger?' Her little voice cut into his growing suspicions, but he could not recapture the light-hearted mood their spontaneous lovemaking had engendered.

'Thank you for telling me about the danger, Maddy. I must go and warn all my men never to venture on to the beach.'

She shivered at the grim set of his face as he turned and strode away from her the minute they entered the outer ward. In spite of what he had said, she was convinced he somehow held John's oversight against him. And it was so unfair! The knowledge of such hazards was so ingrained, locals forgot strangers needed to be told.

He did not seem to be able to let go of the fear that her people might mean him harm. Couldn't he see that all they wanted was the right to grow their crops, sell their produce at market, and raise their children in peace?

How long would it take, she mused, before he could let go of his fears that he had walked into a hotbed of Yorkist rebels, and simply settle down to being the lord of tenants who craved the very stability and prosperity he wanted to bring them?

Chapter Fourteen

'Where have you been?' Lady Lacey accosted Maddy the moment she set foot in the Great Hall.

'Just for a walk, on the headland…I felt in need of some fresh air.'

Suddenly resentful that she felt obliged to account for her where-abouts to her cousin, Maddy added rather sharply, 'And now I need to wash and change before supper. I am going to my room.'

Lady Lacey kept pace with her as she crossed the chamber.

'You were with that great lummox of a husband of yours, weren't you?'

'What of it?'

Pausing only to push Maddy before her into her room, where Joan was laying out a fresh gown for the evening, she hissed, 'It is not fresh air that has put that sparkle in your eyes, nor the roses in your cheeks, nor the stains upon your gown! You let him tumble you, in broad daylight!'

'Eleanor, he is my husband,' Maddy protested. 'Are you suggest-ing I should gainsay him?'

Lady Lacey's eyes narrowed. 'No, I suppose not.' She twitched a sprig of heather from the back of Maddy's gown, twirling it between her fingers with a speculative look, before remarking, 'In fact, it may have been an astute move on your part.' As Joan began to unlace Maddy's gown, she perched herself on the edge of the bed.

'If you are willing to accommodate him whenever the urge takes him, he may be less likely to stray.'

'It was not like that!' Maddy cringed to hear her cousin voice the very thought that had crossed her own mind.

'Oh, no?' Lady Lacey reclined across the counterpane, a sultry smile spreading across her face. 'Are you trying to tell me that *you* wanted to see what it would be like to lift your skirts out of doors?'

'Eleanor, really!' Maddy exclaimed, so embarrassed she didn't know where to look.

''Tis only natural,' Joan interjected as she poured water from the ewer into a washbasin. 'Them being newly-weds and all.'

'Who gave you permission to speak?' Lady Lacey spat at the serving woman, before rounding on Maddy. 'As for you, Agnes, let me tell you something. Letting him treat you like a whore won't do you any good in the long run. When he does stray, you will be left feeling far more humiliated than if you had preserved some distance!' She flounced out of the room.

Joan shook her head, her lips pursed. 'Not all men stray, my lady, and don't you think it just because that one has had a run of bad luck with her men.'

Before Maddy had a chance to ask how she could possibly know anything of Lady Lacey's history, the woman continued, 'Me and my John have been together now for seven years, and he's never looked at another woman.'

Maddy smiled wryly at her. 'Why should he, Joan? You are very beautiful.'

It was true. Maddy had never seen a woman with more appeal, not even in the court where women used all kinds of artifice to make themselves attractive to men. She had a pretty face, a graceful carriage, and a manner that made her easy to get along with.

'And so are you, my lady,' Joan replied. 'Besides which, there is a type that will take mistresses, and a type that don't. Your husband, to my way of thinking, is the type that don't.'

'How can you tell?' For a moment, Maddy's heart soared in hope, only to plummet back to earth as she reasoned that the woman was merely trying to soothe her mistress's ruffled feathers. 'You hardly know him,' she said, her voice flat.

'I see the way he looks at you. And I noticed you seemed to have had a bit of a falling-out…'

'Oh, no, hardly that!' Maddy argued.

'Well, a bit of a hiccup, like,' Joan said.

'Yes, I suppose…'

'And he made sure he put it all to rights with you, didn't he? Up on the headland. Because he's the type who cares about such things. And the type who puts himself out to make sure things are right with his wife isn't the type to stir up a nest of hornets in his marriage by taking another woman, you mark my words.'

That was not the first time that Joan's words had acted like an antidote to Lady Lacey's venom. She found herself able to believe what he had said about the importance of spending time simply talking, instead of fearing that it was a symptom of his dissatisfaction with her as a wife, so that she began to look forward to the time when, alone in their chamber, they did just that. To her delight, she found they were, more often than not, in complete agreement over how to tackle the neglect they were uncovering all over their estates.

'I don't want to be the kind of lord that the ordinary people resent for being unnecessarily harsh,' he mused one evening, when they had been considering what action to take over an illegal fish trap John had found on the beck.

'But you must not let them think they can take advantage, either.' She had smiled, settling back amidst the pillows.

His eyes had followed the curve of her leg, only dimly hidden by the diaphanous material of her gown. 'I was not above a little poaching myself, as a lad,' he admitted, joining her on the bed.

'Really?' She was intrigued.

His hand had pushed the garment aside, his hand sending tingles up her leg as it stroked her calf.

'After sowing…' he sighed in mock repentance '…we all did it. The pigeons from his lordship's dovecote would come in great flocks and ruin the crops if we let them. There was no point in just shooing them off. And they tasted so good, boiled up with onions and served with salad greens from the hedgerows.'

It made her feel much closer to him, to hear him finally speak of his childhood. She had always known his early years would have been very different from what was standard for noblemen, who were normally fostered out to another great household from the age of seven or so, trained as pages, then squires, before being knighted almost as a matter of course. It made her heart swell with pride to think he had risen from such ordinary beginnings, and gained his knighthood for bravery on the battlefield.

And then, rising on his elbow, he had confessed, 'Sweeting, I know so little of being a lord. I was not born to it. Every day, I am feeling my way.'

'You certainly are,' she had giggled, as his hand caressed her knee.

The conversation had ceased for some considerable time, but afterwards, for the first time, Maddy felt as though they had been of one mind, as well as one flesh.

This morning he had ridden out to dismantle that fish trap, taking enough men with him to send out the message that he would not tolerate that level of poaching in future. But, to her delight, he had said that since she was in agreement, he would not pursue the culprit too diligently, no matter how much Lawless grumbled.

'Did you hear me, Lady Agnes?' Lady Lacey was saying with some asperity. 'Heavens, are you daydreaming about that husband of yours again?' she mocked.

'Certainly not,' Maddy lied guiltily.

'Then it must be that he is not letting you get enough sleep.' With a lift of her eyebrow that was the most lascivious gesture Maddy thought she had ever seen, she purred, 'Do tell, Agnes—is he really as prodigious as the gossips said?'

'The sun is giving me the headache, if you must know,' Maddy
lied. The time she spent alone with her husband was growing so
precious, the prospect of revealing one word of what they shared
would have felt like casting pearls before swine, even if she hadn't
already promised him to keep it all secret.

Tucking the shuttle between the threads to pin her pattern cards
firmly in place, she rose from her stool, remarking, 'I think I will
go to the still room to get a remedy for my head.'

'Send one of the maids,' Lady Lacey reproved her. 'That is what
they are for.'

But even she could see that for once, the two were working in-
dustriously, making good a pile of household linen.

'The walk alone may help to alleviate the pain,' she retorted, desperate to escape the woman's presence. 'The sun today is unsea-
sonably hot. It has made the solar quite stuffy. The still room will
be much cooler.'

But as she descended to the ground floor, the nagging worry that
Lady Lacey might pursue her to the still room, in order to continue
prying into her private married life, had her darting across the courtyard, towards the stables.

With so many of the men gone, it was likely to be the quietest
place she would likely find this afternoon. Making sure nobody
was watching, she climbed swiftly up into the hayloft. At last, she
sighed, settling on to a pile of hay, peace and quiet. Just for a while
she need not watch every move she made, or weigh every word she
spoke. Shifting until she found a comfortable position, Maddy lay
back and watched the motes drifting in the sunbeams that pierced
the roof wherever the boards had warped with age. Another task to
report to Lawless, she mused, her eyelids growing heavy. With so
much work to do, she ought not to be shirking here...

How long she slept, she did not know, but the commotion that was
coming from the stable yard would have woken the dead.

Flushed and dishevelled, Maddy slid down the ladder from the hayloft, rubbing her eyes as she stumbled into the yard to see what was going on.

The yard was full of riderless horses, since most of the men were streaming into the armoury. As she dodged between the milling beasts, she noted blood upon the saddles of at least two of them. A chill struck her to the core when she saw Caligula's flanks, too, were smeared with blood.

Her heart hammering, she broke into a run, pushing her way through the men-at-arms who were thronging the doorway.

Her eyes sought, and found, the form of her husband, who was leaning, ashen-faced, against the far wall. There was blood upon his surcoat.

'My lord!' she gasped. 'You are hurt! Let me see!' She ran to him, her hands fluttering over his chest as she stretched on tiptoe in order to try and assess the extent of his wound.

'This is nothing!' he growled. 'A mere scratch. It is Christophe that needs your attention.'

Following the direction of his gaze, she registered the hapless man who lay on the table, groaning, an arrow shaft protruding from his thigh.

'If you are sure?' Maddy could not help checking one last time that her husband was truly not in any danger before going to the injured man's side. Captain Fritz drew out a hunting knife, and began to cut away the hose from around the portion of thigh from which the arrow was sticking, while Jan came over with a bottle of wine.

'We are going to get the arrow out, Christophe,' she said gently. 'You will be fine.' Out of the corner of her eye she could see Barty applying the bellows to the brazier with vigour. Moving her position so that she blocked the patient's view, she took the wine skin from Jan and held it to the suffering man's lips herself.

'Dammit!' Captain Fritz swore. 'There is no arrow spoon in the armoury.'

Maddy knew that pulling an arrow out could cause far more damage that it had wrought going in without such a device to cover the barbs. 'You could use goose quills,' she said, just as Betty and Mary came in to see what all the commotion was about. 'Betty, run and fetch several goose quills from the lord's day room, as fast as you can!'

While the woman dithered in the doorway, Thomas pushed past her with an oath and sprinted off to carry out her order himself.

'Aught I can do to help, my lady?'

Maddy smiled with relief as the ever-practical Joan materialised at her side. 'You know which healing herbs we have in the still room,' she murmured, one eye on Christophe, who was lying much quieter with a belly full of alcohol. 'You will need to mix up whatever you can find with honey to pack the wound after it has been cauterised.'

Joan bustled off, leaving Maddy feeling grateful she had at least one level-headed woman she could rely on in such an emergency.

'What is going on here?' Lady Lacey's imperious tones rang across the crowded little room, just as Thomas barged past her with a fist full of goose quills.

'Can you do it?' Captain Fritz asked Maddy as Thomas thrust the quills into her hands. 'Your fingers are like to be more sensitive than mine.'

'Do what? What has happened?' Lady Lacey demanded, as everyone continued to ignore her.

'I have to slide the quill down the arrow shaft until I can feel it cover the arrow barb, Eleanor,' she explained, shifting so that the woman could see Christophe splayed out on the table, the arrow sticking from his bloodstained, naked thigh. The Captain laid his hand on the shaft even as Maddy tentatively began to insert the quill into the fresh wound. 'Is the cauterising iron ready?'

Barty partially pulled the iron from the coals to inspect it. It glowed red hot.

Hearing another commotion at the foot of the staircase, Maddy briefly lifted her head and saw John drop the brace of plover he'd had in his hand, to catch Lady Lacey, who had fainted clean away.

It was only when Christophe had been carried, now completely unconscious, from the armoury, and Maddy sank to a joint stool, regarding her trembling, bloodied hands, that she became aware that Sir Geraint was standing completely still, watching her with an inscrutable expression on his face.

'We need to talk, madam wife.'

'Perhaps we should retire to my chamber,' she agreed, rising unsteadily to her feet. 'I need to wash my hands and change my gown.' She looked down at her skirts, which were liberally smeared with blood, and suddenly her head began to swim.

When she next opened her eyes, it was to find herself lying supine upon her own bed, clad only in her loose fitting chemise, and Sir Geraint standing over her with a goblet of wine clenched between white knuckled fingers.

'What happened?'

'You fainted,' he growled, holding the goblet to her lips. 'Though at least *you* had the decency to wait until after tending to my man's injury.'

'No,' she countered, between sips of the restorative liquid, 'I mean today, to you and the men. Oh!' She sat up suddenly, her face draining of what little colour the wine had restored to her cheeks. 'There was another man, laid upon the floor…' She had forgotten until then that other form, swathed in cloaks, lying ominously still.

'He was taken care of,' he replied, his voice harsh. 'I put Mary and Betty to that task. Your cousin—' his lip curled '—was too distressed by events to rise from her own bed and see to it. But I saw no reason why she needed two women to wait upon her, when you…' His mouth compressed into a grim line. 'Forgive me for speaking ill of your kin, Maddy, but the more I know of the woman, the less respect I can feel for her.'

'Has nobody tended your wound yet?' The blood on his surcoat was dried now, she noted with relief. Kneeling up on the bed, she reached for the neckline of his shirt, shakily pushing it aside to see how badly he had been hurt. There was a rent in the shoulder of his doublet.

'You will not be able to rest until you have seen with your own eyes that it is naught but a scratch, will you?' Some of the sternness left his face as he brushed her hands aside, remembering how his heart had pulsed with love and pride as he had watched her calmly take charge of the chaos in the armoury.

'Lie down and rest, while I get my things off, and I will tell you what happened. When you have some colour back in your face, I will let you tend me, or have Joan apply some salve. We were taking the cut through the lower slopes of the forest down to the beck, when suddenly we were hit by a shower of arrows.' He paused in the re-counting, as he remembered that the arrows had come from only one side of the track. They had not been surrounded, which was the im-pression he had first taken, due, he supposed to the panic that had ensued. Caligula had snorted and plunged, wheeling round and round, disorientating him…and possibly saving his life. 'One of the arrows tore through the material at my shoulder when Caligula shied. It ended up piercing Lawless through the neck.'

Maddy gave a little whimper. 'The man who died, that was Lawless?' She felt terrible. She had been so concerned about the scratch on Sir Geraint's shoulder she had not bothered to ask about the identity of the dead man.

'Aye. Then, after Christophe was hit in the leg, Captain Fritz managed to restore sufficient order to send several men into the undergrowth where the assailants were hiding, and give chase.'

'Are they still giving chase? Or did you…?'

'They may have returned to the castle by now. I should really go below and find out if they have anything to report. I felt my main priority was to get the wounded back home for treatment.'

Home. He stilled as the word left his lips. It had not occurred to him before that wherever *she* was, he now considered his home.

'But someone…tried to kill you…' Her face bleaching, she sank back into the pillows. If she lost him now, her own life would have no meaning. She might as well be dead herself. With a little sob, she shut her eyes on the devastating truth. She loved him with an intensity that frightened her.

She felt the edge of the mattress depress as her husband sat down, put his arm about her shoulders, and made her drain the goblet to the dregs.

'They did not succeed. Whoever they were,' he growled. 'But from now on, I will have to exercise greater vigilance. And just when I had begun to think my suspicions were unfounded.' He shook his head ruefully. He wished he had thought to take down the names of each of the men who had stood behind John, barring the road to Woolton when he had come to take up his lordship. One, or more of them, had laid another ambush today. And this time, without Maddy to defuse the situation, they had given vent to their resentment at having a Lancastrian overlord thrust upon them.

Maddy was swamped with guilt for having discounted his fears before, especially since she knew exactly how harrowing it felt to be marked down for murder. Suddenly she was back in the ladies' dorter at Westminster palace, naked and shivering, with the terrible sense of being completely alone, as a faceless foe lurked somewhere, intent on doing her harm.

'I had begun to think the people were resigned to having me here…' He paused, frowning. Maddy's face was averted from his, just as though she felt guilty about something. He went cold, as the memory of her tumbling into the armoury, her face flushed, and her clothing dishevelled, pierced him like an arrow.

'Where were you, when I came home?' he asked, trying to sound casual.

For a second his heart contracted as she blushed scarlet. 'You are going to think this sounds completely ridiculous,' she said nervously. 'But the truth is, I had dozed off in the stables. I was trying to find somewhere to get a bit of peace and quiet, and…' She spread her hands in exasperation. 'If I had gone to my room, I would have had to explain to Lady Lacey that I needed a nap, in the middle of the day, and then bear her lewd comments about what you and I do during the night when we should be sleeping.' Her face was beetroot-red now.

And it was then that she recalled how long it had taken her cousin to arrive in the Great Hall. Why had it taken her so long to come down the stairs from the solar? She had been right across the court-yard, in the stables, and had still managed to get there first. Even the slothful maids had managed to get there before her.

Could she have had something to do with the ambush? Maddy couldn't help recalling the numerous times her cousin had warned her not to get too fond of her husband. Or her constant opposition to the match. Nor the lengths she had gone to once before, to arrange an 'accident' to take place far away from the castle. Though she did not have the stomach to fire the arrow herself, she had several of the men panting after her. She could have twisted any one of them round her little finger, especially since they were mercenaries, with no tradition of loyalty to her husband they would find hard to abandon.

Maddy twirled the wine goblet round and round in her hands as her mind raced with possibilities. If Sir Geraint died, how would that be of advantage to Lady Lacey? Well, the King would not permit her to remain a widow for long. He would want a strong man to take charge of the demesne. Lord Hugo could well have supporters within the court who could persuade the King that he was the very man to take Sir Geraint's place. And if he had somehow managed to contact Lady Lacey secretly, and convince her that their relationship could be resumed if only she could get Sir Geraint out of the way…

'Maddy?' Sir Geraint had watched her thoughts flit across her expressive little face. It was quite clear she had some suspicions about who could be behind this fatal attack. 'Is there something you want to tell me?'

She gazed at him, her eyes widening with horror. Could she really confess she suspected her cousin? Just because it had taken her such a long time to get to the Great Hall?

The woman might be somewhat shrewish, she was fairly certain she'd once tried to harm her, but was that enough to accuse her of conspiring with some unknown person to commit murder?

'No,' Maddy croaked, her eyes sliding guiltily from his. She refused to believe it. 'No…' It was just too dreadful to contemplate.

She could not expose her foolish, unhappy cousin to the risk of being hanged, on the basis of a few such tenuous suspicions.

Her expression hardened. She needed evidence.

Cut to the quick, Sir Geraint got up from the bed and strode from the chamber to go to fetch a clean shirt. She knew something, or suspected something, he could see it in her face. But she had decided not to share her suspicions with him. Whoever it was she suspected must be very dear to her heart.

Like her half-brother, for instance. He grimaced with pain as he reached into the chest that sat at the foot of his bed for fresh linen. She might have come to care for him to some extent, but she had deeper, older loyalties, and, at the first test, she was clearly torn as to which held the greatest priority.

They lay, stiff and silent beside each other, in their bed that night. For the first time since they had married, there were neither words, nor caresses. He could not believe how much it hurt to know that she could keep silent when his life had been threatened. And for her part, Maddy was too sickened by the thought she might lose him to notice how withdrawn he was.

Should she warn her cousin that she was on to her, admit that she had even known about Lord Hugo's earlier plot? Or just watch her like a hawk until she left, as she claimed she intended to do, at Easter? If she could just keep Ger safe until then, all might be well. She reached for the reassuring mass of his body beside her in the bed. He did not move. She sighed. He must be deeply asleep. She was glad he could rest, for he would need to be on his guard every moment of his waking day. She did not think anyone would make an attempt on his life while they slept. There was too much risk of being caught. Anyway, whoever wanted him dead would need time to lay another trap for her husband. They would have a breathing space, most likely. Comforted by that thought, she succumbed to the exhaustion that had dogged her from the moment she had taken up the reins as chatelaine of Woolton Castle.

Beside her, Sir Geraint shifted uneasily. He should have responded when she reached for him in the dark, instead of letting her think he slept. She might have been ready to talk to him, to share the suspicions he could see were tearing her apart. But what if all she wanted was to use sex to bedazzle him into forgetting those telltale signs of guilt? He couldn't bear to contemplate it.

He was gone when she woke the next morning, feeling decidedly groggy. The events of the previous day, followed by that nearly sleepless night, had really taken a toll on her. When she got out of bed, she went so light-headed that she had to clutch at the bedpost for a few seconds. She would probably feel better once she had got some food inside her.

No maid was close to attend her. She assumed they must be busy attending to the sick man, or the dead one. She dressed hastily in a gown of moss-green linen, deciding it was time to put aside the woollen gowns she had been wearing to date. They were too warm, now that spring was so well advanced, too constricting and cumbersome.

'Sir Geraint has already eaten,' Joan informed her as she took her place at the table. 'He is huddled with that Captain Fritz, and the band he sent scouring the countryside for the outlaws who attacked him yesterday.'

'Outlaws?'

'Well, it must have been outlaws, mustn't it, my lady? Who else would do such a wicked thing? Not one of our own people, that's for sure. Why would they?'

'Yes, why indeed?' She wondered, with some alarm, where Lady Lacey was this morning.

'Yes, right glad we are that arrow missed its target and only ended up in that Lawless fellow.' She wrinkled her nose. 'Not a likeable man, he wasn't. Never saw such a pompous, sneering fellow... The way he spoke to my John, well, it fair made my blood boil, and so I tell you. Not that I wish to speak ill of the dead, and I dare say he felt he was only doing his duty—' She broke off as the door burst

open. The man who strode into the Great Hall, unchallenged, Maddy
noted with anxiety, was undoubtedly a soldier, by the metal breastplate and helmet he wore.

Maddy rose to her feet, unsure how to greet the man who scowled
about the Hall. He could not be come against them, not one man on
his own, armoured though he was. But could he be somehow connected to the disturbance of the day before? If there were other
soldiers in the area, then they might be responsible for the ambush.
Some of her anxiety began to lift. She might not have to worry about
finding a culprit among the tenants of Woolton at all.

'I seek Sir Geraint Davies,' the man declared, his attention drawn
to her, as she rose to greet him, silently proclaiming herself the lady
of the manor. 'I have urgent tidings from the Duke of Bedford.'

'My husband is in consultation with the captain of our garrison.
I will send for him, while you sit and refresh yourself.' She gestured
to a place at the table, which he took with unfeigned gratitude. As
Joan poured ale into a beaker, and set it before him, he collected his
wits, removing his helmet.

'I have ridden hard,' he admitted with a rueful grin. 'Your hospitality is most welcome.'

'Not at all, sir,' Maddy replied, wondering what kind of urgent
tidings the Duke of Bedford could have for her husband.

But before she could glean any further information from him, her
husband came bursting through the door, closely followed by
Captain Fritz and half a dozen of the men-at-arms.

'What news?' he said, his attention focused on the stranger. Maddy
tried not to mind that he had not so much as glanced in her direction.

The stranger got to his feet, his face grim.

'The worst, Sir Geraint. Treason. Sir Francis Lovell and
Humphrey Stafford have left their sanctuary at Colchester, and are
even now raising an army of rebels.'

With a groan, Maddy collapsed on to her chair again. A few short
months of peace, that was all England had known. And now they
were to be plunged into another conflict. Her husband would leave

her to fight for his King, of that she was certain. She clenched her fists in mute fury in her lap. If some sneaking rascal failed to murder him on his own land, he would just cheerily ride off to die on some battlefield instead.

'My lord the Duke of Bedford is charged by his Grace King Henry to raise an army of loyal subjects to come to his aid.'

'Where is the King?'

Sir Geraint's face was white. His own problems paled into insignificance before this latest threat to his King. Henry Tudor had known nothing but treachery and conflict throughout his life. He knew he should never have left his side!

'The royal party had just reached Lincoln when news of the rebellion came,' the messenger replied. 'But my orders are to send you to intercept Lovell's force, which is gathering at York.'

'I will ride before the day is out, with the twenty trained men of my garrison.'

'My lord the Duke will welcome your contingent, Sir Geraint. On his behalf, I thank you. And if it is possible—'

'Anything!'

'I have need of a fresh horse, and provisions, if you can spare them. There are others I need to contact, and…'

'Yes, of course. Fritz! See to it that this man has the swiftest horse the stables can provide, provisions for his journey, and anything else he requests.'

Maddy gazed after her husband as he strode from the hall, his men tumbling after him like a pack of hounds scenting their quarry. She might as well have ceased to exist, for all he cared. She'd been in a fool's paradise these last few days, mistaking his continuing lust for her body for real affection, she reflected bitterly. And it struck her then, with a force that crushed the breath from her chest, that while he was her whole life, she was only a very small part of his.

Chapter Fifteen

Morosely, Maddy trailed back to her chamber. She had not been there more than a few minutes, struggling to come to terms with her insignificance in her husband's life, when Lady Lacey rushed into the room in a whirl of velvet and lavender.

'You must speak to your husband for me, Agnes!' she said, dropping to her knees beside the bed and gripping Maddy's hand.

'If he is leaving today, I must go with him!'

'Go with him?' Maddy's heart began to beat wildly. Was her cousin so determined to see him dead, she would follow him to the very battlefield?

'You cannot go with him! He won't want a woman trailing behind him while he's quashing this rebellion!' From counting the days until Lady Lacey should leave, Maddy was now racking her brains to think of reasons to prevent her.

'Agnes, please,' Lady Lacey pleaded. 'This is my chance to get away from here!'

'Get away? I though you were enjoying yourself here.'

'Enjoying myself!' she echoed with incredulity. 'I am going out of my mind with boredom. I need someone witty to talk to, and flirt with. I want the chance to wear pretty dresses for a man who is worth making the effort for! You know I always planned to return to court once I'd got you settled in. I can travel with Sir Geraint to York, and await Princess Elizabeth's arrival there. I can get lodgings with, oh, one of any of a half-dozen good families I know.'

Maddy regarded her cousin with a set, white face. 'My husband is going out to fight rebels, Eleanor. He is in a hurry to join the King's army. It will be a forced march, and he won't want you holding him up.'

'I won't, I won't!' she breathed, her eyes glowing. 'It won't take me any more time to throw my belongings back into my trunks than it will for him to organise his own retinue, I promise you! For if he leaves without me, who knows how long I will have to moulder away here, waiting for another chance of getting an escort to rejoin the court!' Giving Maddy a swift hug, she swirled from the room and pounded along the corridor to her own rooms.

The woman was unstoppable. Still, would she really be able to do Ger any harm en route to York, while he was surrounded by the most hardened band of cutthroats he had been able to round up from the lowest taverns in London? Even if she somehow managed to get a message to Lord Hugo, it would be well-nigh impossible to arrange another ambush, and she was too squeamish to attempt anything on her own…

Though it wouldn't do any harm to put Captain Fritz on the alert. Maddy set off to find him.

'Lady Lacey will be travelling with your band, to York,' she informed him as he emerged from the stables. As his face set in the prelude to what she knew would be his objections to having a woman slowing them down, she added, 'But that is not what I really wanted to talk to you about.' Twisting her hands nervously, she ventured, 'Somebody tried to kill my husband yesterday, within our own lands. Do you think they may make another attempt, during the journey?'

His eyes narrowed. 'What are you trying to tell me?'

'W…well,' she stammered, suddenly conscious how stupid it sounded to ask him to protect her husband from her cousin. She took a deep breath. 'All morning, all sorts of unlikely people have been flooding into the castle, saying they want to follow my husband to fight *for* the same King they followed my late father to fight *against*.'

By this time, the outer ward was beginning to resemble the market square on a feast day. Tenants from even the furthest reaches of her estates were coming in answer to Sir Geraint's call to arms.

'He was…touched by the unlooked-for display of loyalty…' his face twisted into a sneer '…and has announced that he will welcome any who wish to follow him.'

'Oh, dear.' Their eyes met. His softened fractionally.

'My lady, these are simple folk who may not even realise they have appeared to change allegiance. They have never seen King Henry, but they have seen Sir Geraint. In their minds, yesterday's outrage has merged with the threat posed by Lovell's rebellion. Following your husband into whatever fight he deems…appropriate, is a demonstration of their loyalty to the lord of Woolton.'

She drew herself up, and looked him squarely in the eyes. 'It occurred to me this morning, as soon as the Duke of Bedford's man entered my hall, that yesterday's events may have been caused by outsiders.'

'So that is why you came running to me, to beg me to keep him safe from everyone who travels with him.' His face took on a mocking cast.

She hung her head. 'I know you must think me extremely foolish. All I can ask, I suppose, is that you be watchful.'

She heard him sigh. 'I cannot promise he will not suffer any injury in battle. That is beyond my power. But I can assure you I will never let him die by an assassin's hands.'

Looking up, she caught an expression in his eyes so fierce that it made her feel heartily sorry for anyone who would dare cross his path. This man killed for a living, because, she suddenly realised, that was exactly what he wished to do.

'But who,' he continued, 'will guard you, while we are all absent?'

'Me?' she gasped. 'Why should anyone need to guard me? If I should die, then all…' Lady Lacey's ambitions to rekindle her relationship with Lord Hugo would come to naught. But she dared not speak her suspicions aloud. Blushing, she stammered, 'That is, I am far too unimportant to be a target for an assassin.'

'On the contrary, my lady, you are…' He ground to a halt, a faint line of colour staining his cheeks.

'W…what?'

His eyes grew fiercer still, as he snapped, 'Sir Geraint would hardly be pleased to return from battle to find that his lovely bride had suffered a mishap, would he? I would be remiss in my duties to leave you unprotected.'

He half-turned from her at the sound of a booted foot on the cobbles. John emerged from the stall where his own brown cob was stabled, his face lit by a guileless, open smile.

'I apologise, but I could hardly help overhearing. You need not fear to leave my sister here, Captain Fritz. I will take care of her. And not all able-bodied men from the estate wish to follow Sir Geraint to fight for Henry Tudor. Only the—how shall I put it?—' he shrugged, spreading his hands '—those young enough and hot-blooded enough to want a little adventure.'

Captain Fritz grunted his understanding. For a peasant, bound to his lord and the land, his only chance to travel anywhere further than the nearest market town would be on such an expedition as this.

'The men who will remain are loyal to the DelaBoys family, and will protect their lady with their lives. I guarantee it.'

Though his words reassured the captain, for some reason Maddy experienced a *frisson* of unease. To hear her brother emphasise the loyalty of the locals to the DelaBoys family only seemed to throw her husband's position as an outsider into stark relief. Perhaps her husband was correct. Perhaps it was a local man, displeased to have an overlord thrust upon him, who had tried to dispose of him. Rubbing her aching forehead with her fingers, she made her excuses and left the two men alone in the courtyard. She had done what she could to ensure that no harm should befall her husband, from whatever quarter it might come.

* * *

For the rest of the morning, she concentrated on doing her best to ensure Sir Geraint would lack no comfort on his journey. It was the only way she could think of to express her love for a man who was so focused on doing his duty, he had not spared time for one word with his wife.

At last, she took a seat beside Sir Geraint in the refectory, where the castle staff were serving all the men who'd gathered to follow her husband to fight the rebels. It was a substantial, if simple meal, that ensured all who were about to march away would do so on full stomachs.

But she couldn't bring herself to look at him. She knew that if she did, the knowledge that this might be the last time she saw him alive would fill her with terrible anguish. She scarce knew how to keep from flinging her arms round him and begging him not to leave her as it was. But he would only be angry, perhaps even accuse her of treason if she were to point out that while the King had plenty of men to defend him, she only had one husband! If she lost him… She bit back a sob. And stiffened her spine. He would not thank her for making a public spectacle by weeping into her pottage.

But at last the meal ended, and the volunteers, full of ale and visions of glory, began to swagger into the yard, where Captain Fritz made a valiant attempt to establish some kind of order over them. She couldn't help worrying over the dearth of real weapons, or even rudimentary armour supplied to this hastily assembled army. Would any of them survive? She felt Sir Geraint come and stand beside her. And take hold of her hand.

'Before I take my leave, madam wife,' he said, 'I would ask one thing of you.'

Fighting the grief that was threatening to tear her apart, she managed to raise her face only so far as his chest. He had donned a breastplate of tanned leather, she mutely noted. Would it stop an arrow, or a sword, from piercing his flesh? She shuddered.

'Tell me who you suspect of murdering our steward.'

She gasped, glancing up at his stony features. This was the one thing he wanted to say before he left her, perhaps for ever? She hadn't expected professions of love, but couldn't he have said he would miss her? No, she shook her head. No, for he was not going to miss her. His expression was quite cold.

And then she couldn't hold back the tears any longer. 'Oh, Ger, don't look at me like that! I don't know what I will do if you don't come back to me,' she sobbed, pulling her hands from his, to swipe angrily at the evidence of her weakness.

She could say no more, since Lady Lacey and the two maids were approaching.

'Go, bid your kinswoman farewell,' Sir Geraint grated, stepping back and bowing to her in a horribly formal fashion. Then he turned on his heel and strode out into the courtyard.

Damn Maddy for her determination to keep him at arm's length! And for turning on the tears, and making that melodramatic and totally insincere statement, in order to divert him from her double dealing. She had not made any attempt to seek a private moment during that morning, to bid him farewell as a fond wife would have done. No, instead she had busied herself making sure his leavetaking could take place at the earliest opportunity! She had lain in bed beside him the night before, oblivious to his torment, and at dinner, it was as if she had retreated behind a wall of ice, so cold were her responses.

'Betty and Mary are returning to court with me,' said Lady Lacey brightly.

Yes, thought Maddy with annoyance. Everyone would rather leave than stay here with me!

'I can almost understand what you see in Sir Geraint,' Lady Lacey murmured into Maddy's ear. 'Dressed like that, mounted on that great warhorse.' Her eyes ran over his muscular frame appreciatively as he swung up into the saddle, and began the customary struggle for control that mounting Caligula entailed. 'He is certainly quite a muscular specimen of manhood.'

'Eleanor…' Desperately, Maddy made one last attempt to sway

her cousin from the course she was almost certain the woman intended to take. 'I beg you, please leave him alone. You see, I know about you and Lord Hugo…'

'Oh, do you?' Lady Lacey turned on her then, her face paling. 'Are you telling me that you have known, all this time, what your marriage to that great…peasant cost me! And you have said nothing!' Her eyes narrowed with fury. 'You sly little cat. You deliberately came between me and the man I loved!'

'Eleanor, no, it wasn't like that…'

'Why should you have it all, when I have been left with nothing? Nothing!' Her voice lowered to a hiss. 'To think, all this time, I had your welfare at heart…well, let me tell you this!' She drew herself to her full height and glared down at her smaller cousin. 'Your husband does not love you any more than Lord Hugo loved me. All either of them care about is this benighted place!' She made a dismissive gesture towards the curtain wall. 'I'll prove it to you, shall I?' She bent down, pressing her face closer to Maddy's, her voice dropping to the merest whisper. 'I will bed your precious husband before we reach York. I have lain alone in a cold bed long enough, because of you. And do you know what? Once he's had me, nothing you can do will ever be able to restore his interest in you. If he ever does attempt to bed you again, he will have to keep his eyes closed and imagine he's with me!'

Maddy reeled back, stunned by the virulence of her cousin's spite. And the helpless knowledge that nothing could stop the woman now. She was beautiful, and she had always had the knack of making men lust after her. And once she had taken her revenge on Maddy, by seducing her husband, once his guard was down, it would be ridiculously easy for her to dispose of him. Oh, why hadn't she thought of it before? She might faint at the sight of blood, but she could easily poison him!

Gathering up her skirts, she fled to the yard, her eyes searching frantically for Captain Fritz.

'Captain, Captain!' she cried in desperation when she could not immediately spot him.

'What is it, my lady?' Alerted by the urgency in her voice, he at once left off his attempt to marshal the volunteers into some kind of marching order to attend to her.

Grabbing hold of his arm, she whimpered, 'Lady Lacey.'

'What of her?' The captain, sensing her need for discretion, bent down, so that she could speak into his ear.

'I have not time to explain it all now, but I believe she is intent on revenge for…an incident that occurred between us at court. I believe she may have had something to do with that ambush, too. I am certain she will harm my husband if she can!'

She felt him grin against her cheek. 'I know just how to neutralise her sort, don't you worry.'

She recoiled, recalling her insight into the cruelty of his nature. She didn't want to be the instigator of yet more violence. 'You won't hurt her? I might be wrong. She might be completely innocent!'

'Innocent is not the word I should apply to the likes of her. But, no, I will not hurt her. Not unless she wants me to.'

'Wants you to?' she echoed, perplexed. 'Why should she want you to hurt her?'

He straightened up, his face growing red. 'Pay no heed to my illchosen words, my lady. I have her measure, that is all you need to know.'

From Caligula's back, Sir Geraint watched the conversation with a sinking heart. He could have sworn he could trust Captain Fritz. Then again, he had badly wanted to trust his wife, too. And there they stood, in full view, bidding each other a fond farewell as though they were lovers! All he'd got was obstinacy and tears. Leaning forward to conceal the grimace of pain he could not control, he clapped the destrier on the neck, provoking the beast to snort and toss his proud head. This rebellion had clearly come at just the right moment so far as she was concerned, he decided, pulling Caligula round to face the drawbridge. If he fell in battle, it would save her the bother of getting her assassin to do away with him!

Amidst the mass of excited humanity that swirled round the courtyard, Maddy felt like an island of rock-solid misery. Her husband, the pivotal point of her existence, had turned and left without so much as a glance in her direction. As soon as his King had been mentioned, he had forgotten all about his drab little wife. And once Lady Lacey turned her charm in his direction, he would forget all about his marriage vows, too. She had lost him.

But then, he had never really been hers.

She clasped her hands round her waist, hugging herself against the nausea that welled at the thought of him lying with her cousin. It was no consolation to know that he would pay for his betrayal by being betrayed in his turn by a woman without scruples. He would be doubly lost to her.

She could not bear it!

Choking back a sob, she turned and ran from the courtyard as the ragged procession set forth. Without conscious guidance, her feet carried her through the guard house and up the stairs that led to the watchtower. From here, she could not see into the outer ward itself, but she could still hear the sounds of men and weapons, rumbling cart wheels and clop of horses' hooves. And soon, by dint of leaning over the edge of the parapet, she saw the head of the cavalcade rounding the first bend in the road that wound down towards the forest and thence out on to the road that would take them, eventually, to York. Every so often, the contours of the land swallowed the snaking procession, only to disgorge it, some minutes later, diminished by distance, until they looked like a column of ants. And still her eyes strained after them as they gained the lower slopes of the distant moors, tears blurring her vision as she recalled the other time she had come to this spot, to watch someone dear to her heart riding away, his head full of glory, and not one thought for her.

He had never come back.

'Oh, God,' she groaned, sinking to her knees, her forehead grinding against the rough, unforgiving stone of the watchtower, 'not my husband too!' But how could she dare hope she would ever see him again? If Lady Lacey did not succeed in poisoning him on the journey, then he was bound to fall in battle.

'Oh, please,' she moaned, twisting her hands together in prayer. 'I don't care if he betrays me, so long as Lady Lacey does not succeed in betraying him. I would rather endure the knowledge that he *has* lain in another woman's bed, than see him lying for ever in the cold dark earth. Couldn't you somehow turn her heart to draw back from murder? Wouldn't she,' she prayed in earnest, 'still have revenge on me by seducing him, and sending him back to me, knowing I could not hope to compare?'

And then, clear as the matins bell ringing sharp on a cold, frosty morning, certain of her cousin's words pushed through the muddled fears that swirled through her brain.

Lady Lacey had said part of her revenge would be in knowing Maddy could never compete in terms of bedworthiness. She straightened up, turning to lean her back against the rough stone of the tower. She had also said she was bored out of her mind buried in the country, and wanted only to get back to the gaiety of court life. That might have been a lie, of course. But what if she really no longer wished to fall in with Lord Hugo's initial plan that she should live in Woolton as his mistress? Not now that she had tasted what life in such a far-flung outpost entailed.

Dropping her head back against the rough stone, she closed her eyes, wondering if she was just clutching at straws in regard to Ger's safety. Of one thing she could be certain. Lady Lacey's pride would not permit her to play second fiddle to a woman she considered so inferior in every respect. There was no doubt she would enjoy seducing Sir Geraint, of playing with him as a cat would play with a mouse, then returning him to her drab little cousin reeking of her perfume.

She wanted to humiliate Maddy. But his infidelity would do much more than that. It would devastate her.

'My lady!' From the door which gave on to the battlements, Maddy heard Joan calling to her. Wiping her face one last time with the sleeves of her gown, she pushed herself to her feet.

'I am here, Joan!'

Pausing to recover her breath, Joan eyed her with concern. 'Yes, John said as how he remembered you running up here to watch when one of your brothers rode away to war,' she panted, 'and that you'd want some time to yourself. But you've been up here hours, and that wind is cold. So he sent me up to make sure you had a warm cloak, at least.' John had sent Joan to comfort her. She was not completely alone. As Joan draped the cloak over her shoulders, she embraced the warmth both of the garment, and the thoughtfulness that went in its provision.

'Lord,' Joan grumbled, tying the ribbons with brisk fingers, 'I should have thought you would have had more sense than to come running up all them stairs and standing about in this weather in your condition.'

'My condition?' Maddy sniffed. 'What mean you?'

Joan cocked her head to one side. 'Well, you are with child, aren't you, my lady?'

'With child?' Maddy gasped. 'Whatever gives you that idea?'

Joan frowned. 'Well, I have looked after your linen ever since the day you arrived, and you have not had your courses, for one thing. And then fainting away, and being off your food, not to mention putting an extra inch on the waist and bodice of all the gowns you have been sewing for the warmer weather…'

Maddy's hand went to her stomach. A child? Was it possible? Of course, one of the reasons for marrying was to provide an heir for Woolton…

'Hadn't you guessed?'

Maddy shook her head, her eyes round with astonishment. 'All those things you mentioned, the missing of courses, the sickness— they are signs I might be with child?'

'Lord bless you, my lady, hasn't anyone ever told you about such things?'

Maddy shook her head again. Lady Lacey, as her closest female relative, should have done so, yet her only words on the subject of marriage had been intended to frighten her. Now she had to rely on a servant to explain how her own body worked.

'If I thought about it at all, I was just relieved my courses had ceased.'

'How many have you missed?'

'Two, I think.' Maddy frowned. The moon was on the wane again. 'My next time should be in a day or so.'

Her eyes flew to the last remaining stragglers of the column as it disappeared over the crest of moorland. This was dreadful! He might die, never knowing that he was to become a father! Or that she loved him!

Oh, what did it matter what he thought of her? She loved him, and she was going to bear his child. There would always be a part of him, living on in this world, no matter what the outcome of the battle.

Eyes filled with wonder, she turned to Joan. 'I am going to have a child.'

'Yes, let us hope so, my lady. I think you are almost in the safe time, now, but you really should take more care of yourself. Especially with this being the first. Running up all these stairs and letting yourself get so cold!' she grumbled, chafing Maddy's chilled hands between her work-roughened ones. At her words, the chill struck her forcibly in her mid-section.

'What do you mean?'

Joan sighed, shaking her head. 'It is naught for you to worry about now, I am sure. But if you ever get pregnant again, you should know how delicate babies are in the early days. Almost anything a mother does can make a pregnancy slip. Riding, catching a chill…even being too boisterous in the marriage bed can do it, for some women,' she said grimly.

She could lose the baby too? Because she had been so ignorant? Oh, why hadn't Lady Lacey warned her about how delicate a babe could be? But then, why should she? Her triumph would be complete if she lost both her husband and his child in one blow. She swayed into Joan's arms, as her legs threatened to give way beneath her.

'You mustn't go getting yourself all worked up like this. You have to think of the baby. Come, now.' Joan supported her towards the stairwell. 'Let's get you out of this cold wind and into your nice warm room.'

The stairs. Her legs were too wobbly to carry her down the stairs. What would happen if she fell? Her heart began to race.

'Go down first, Joan, if you please,' she begged. If she did stumble, Joan's body would prevent her from falling far.

'You mentioned something about a safe time before, Joan. What did you mean by that?'

As they wound their way down the turret stairs, Joan's matter-of-fact answers to Maddy's questions went a long way towards steadying her trembling limbs. She explained that if a woman was going to lose her baby, it nearly always happened very early on. Once a woman had missed her courses three times, the babe was not like to make its appearance until it was grown to full size.

'Then, in another week or so, I could write to my husband and tell him…' Maddy's heart began to flutter with hope. He could surely not be unfaithful to her if he knew she was in this delicate condition! He must know that causing her any distress would be dangerous to his heir.

'Why, my lady, if you are sure it is best…only, won't it be hard on him, to tell him in such a way? Won't it distract him?' Finally, they reached the foot of the winding staircase. 'He will want all his wits about him in battle, and thinking of you with child…well…' She shrugged her shoulders expressively.

Maddy blinked in the gloom. For a moment she had thought more of her own pride than his safety. Writing to him might well keep him from Lady Lacey's bed. But Joan was right. It might get him killed as well. She wanted nothing to be on his mind during the battle he was to fight in except staying alive.

And he had to stay alive and come back to her. Whether he had been faithful or no.

Chapter Sixteen

The great feather bed felt so empty. She missed the weight of Ger's arm over her waist, his hot breath on the back of her neck. She even missed the discomfort he invariably caused her when he had used to manoeuvre her against his side as he slept, sliding his hair-roughened thigh between hers, and tugging her close.

Now the luxury of being able to move as freely as she wished felt achingly lonely. Worse was the dread that his bed, wherever it was, was not likely to be as lonely as hers. Hot tears soaked her pillow as, night after night, she pictured him lying entwined in her cousin's sinuous golden beauty.

She stumbled from her bed, bleary-eyed each morning, sick at heart, as well as sick in her stomach, to climb up to the watchtower. Each passing day saw her growing more pale and lethargic as her appetite waned. How could she eat, when, for aught she knew, he might already be dead? Or in the act of betraying her?

'My lady,' Joan scolded one morning, after Sir Geraint had been gone for about a week, 'you cannot go on like this. You must think of the baby.'

'The baby,' Maddy repeated woodenly, her hand going to a stomach that was still flat. It felt hard to believe that she could really be with child, though her courses had failed to come again. According to Joan, that was a sure sign.

'Look…' Joan placed a hand on her shoulder, giving her a comforting squeeze '…it is clear that you are worried your husband may come to some harm, but that is no reason to put your baby in danger too. You must eat. If not for yourself, then for the babe. If you grow ill, you may become too weak to sustain that life, or even give birth when the time comes, should your lord not return at all.'

Fear pierced her like an arrow. If Ger did not come back… She shivered. What would become of her then? The King would not permit a widow to govern alone. He could send anyone to replace Ger. Her next husband could be a brute beast like the Baron Lacey, or a scheming philanderer like Lord Hugo de Vere. Neither type of man would be willing to take on another man's child. They would want fruit of their own loins to inherit. If she had a boy, he would be in danger from the minute he was born.

'What am I to do?' she said aloud, though she had not expected anyone to provide an answer.

'Eat your porridge,' came the prosaic reply, startling her into the realisation that Joan was in the room with her. 'And try to build your strength up. I will go and tend to Christophe again today. He is mending nicely.'

Someone knocked on the door.

'Are you talking about Christophe?' John poked his head round the door. 'How strange! It was of him I wished to consult you. May I come in?'

'Of course,' Maddy declared, clutching the porridge bowl a little tighter. How could she have forgotten all about Christophe! She should have been checking on his injury every day. Besides, he was the only one of the mercenaries left behind, and must feel wretchedly abandoned.

'He is well enough for light duties now,' John said, closing the door behind him. 'Why not set him to patrol the watchtower? If he spies a messenger approaching the castle, the news can be brought to you, wherever you are, whatever you are doing.'

When she frowned, he went on hurriedly, 'You ought not to spend so much time prowling alone up there, especially when the weather is so inclement. And he needs something constructive to do.'

At a meaningful nod from John, Joan left the room. He drew up a joint stool to the side of the bed, and sat down.

'Maddy, you have got to stop worrying about your husband so much. He is in no more danger away from home than he was here, not really. Death takes who he will, when he will. And whether he lives, or whether he dies, it is you the people look to for guidance. You are your father's heir, not him. Life here will go on just as it has always done. You will still have me to support you. And Joan.'

She shook her head, tears welling in her eyes. 'I thank you for your kind words, but you are quite wrong. If Sir Geraint does not return, the King will send someone else to rule here. I will have to marry again, if I am to remain in my own home, for he will not permit a woman alone to garrison and defend a castle. And he may choose a man I cannot love.'

'You love Sir Geraint?' John's eyes registered surprise. 'I was not aware of this.'

'I have tried not to show it,' she admitted woefully. 'For he does not love me, and I feared revealing how much power he has to hurt me.'

John rose and paced across to the window, bracing both hands on the window ledge as he gazed out. It was a while before he turned, a sad smile upon his face.

'If I could spare you pain, you know I would.'

'I know it, John. You have been a great comfort to me, both you and Joan.'

His smile faded. 'Nevertheless, Maddy, you must try to rally. If you continue to mope like this, everyone will know you are in love with your husband, and you will have no dignity to hide behind if…I mean, when he returns.'

That was true. Pride would be all she would have to cling to if her cousin had been successful in seducing him. But her conversation with her half-brother had clarified some points in her mind. She would rather Sir Geraint came back to her with a dozen mistresses in tow, than submit to another arranged marriage with any other man.

And even if he never loved her, he was the only man she could trust to protect this baby she carried. The only one who would really want to raise it to adulthood. Her hand went once more to her still-flat stomach. She would be able to love this child unconditionally, and it would love her.

She was going to be a mother. She really was!

Laying aside her half-eaten porridge, she got out of bed. She did not know what the future held, but, as John had reminded her, life was uncertain. Sir Geraint could well have died during that ambush. But he had not.

But if he did die, she would have to be strong, courageous and alert in order to protect his child. She *would* eat, and exercise, and go about her duties, and trust in her loyal supporters to keep her and her baby safe, should her husband not return. She was fortunate to have John, she reflected. Whatever her future held, she would always be able to rely on him. And upon Joan, who was so much easier to get on with than her cousin had ever been.

And gradually she discovered that, now her cousin had gone, now she wasn't being admonished twenty times a day for her many failings, she was truly filling the position of lady of the manor, at last. Everybody, without fail, treated her with a kind of deference that set her apart.

It made her feel even lonelier than ever.

So lonely, that at times she almost missed Lady Lacey. She supposed it must be because their lives had been bound up in each other's for so many years, that her removal felt as though some clinging creeper had been stripped from a wall, leaving the bricks and mortar of her life strangely exposed.

If she had been here, she would have reproved her for moping about without her absent husband. She could almost hear her scathing voice, urging her to start up a flirtation of her own, if she thought that great lummox was inclined to stray. A wry smile touched Maddy's lips. In spite of everything, she hoped Eleanor would be able to find happiness one day. She was so beautiful, so full of fire and life. It was so sad that she'd never found what she most wanted—a man who truly loved her.

Eventually, she decided she would write to her. Aside from the fact that the woman was the only relative she had left, apart from John, she couldn't stay in this agony of suspense any longer. If Ger had been unfaithful, she needed to know. The very fact he had made no attempt to communicate with her made her more convinced of his guilt with each passing day. But she could not write and ask him what he had been up to! Eleanor, however, would be only too pleased to crow over her, if indeed she had triumphed.

She went up to her day room, where she could now sit all day in the very solitude she had craved when Lady Lacey and her maids had filled it with gossip.

For a while, she sat at her writing desk, chewing on the end of a quill. Once words were set down on parchment with ink, anyone could take them up and read them.

It took the best part of the morning to come up with something that was not so blunt that anyone reading it would know she suspected her husband of infidelity, yet made it plain to Eleanor she wanted to know the truth.

Flinging down the quill as she strove to think of some way to end the missive that would not sound pathetically like begging, she got to her feet.

The voluminous skirts of her newest gown swished round her legs as she paced up and down the sun-dappled room. She paused for a minute before the mirror, examining her reflection critically. This was the first of several gowns she and Joan had designed to cope with the expected changes to her body. It incorporated yards of soft linen pleated over her torso, which could be let out as she expanded. Her breasts were already much fuller. For the first time in her life, she did not feel ashamed of their size. Soon, she and Joan would finish another dress, to the same pattern as this, but made from a shimmering sea-green satin, the neckline embroidered with a delicate tracery of leaves from which tiny daisies, picked in beading, peeped out.

'You will want to have something beautiful to wear when your lord returns,' she had said. 'yet still comfortable enough to wear for special occasions right up till your confinement.'

She cocked her head to one side. Would Ger think she looked beautiful, when she was swollen with his child? Or would he just think she looked fat and ungainly? What she needed was someone like Lady Lacey to teach her how to make the best of what assets she had. Her breasts, for example…no man ever objected to a woman having larger breasts. Perhaps if she wore some jewellery, to draw his eyes to her cleavage, he might not notice how cumbersome the rest of her was.

She whirled away from the mirror in exasperation. She was growing as vain as her cousin, wanting to dress herself up in satin and jewels. Anyway, she didn't have any jewellery. With a shake of her head, she ended her letter. *The castle seems very quiet since you have left. I hope that you will reply, for I am alone here, and full of anxieties.*

It was only after she had sealed the letter, and handed it to John, that she had second thoughts. Reaching out her hand, she stayed her brother from leaving her sitting room.

'I am not sure if I wish to send that letter just yet,' she admitted, looking at the missive that lay in his capable, work-roughened hands. Raising her face at last to his, when he remained silent, she asked, 'Do you think I am being very weak, to forgive her so readily?'

'Forgive her what, Maddy?' Without being asked, John drew a stool up to her chair and sat down. Feeling an overwhelming gratitude that someone, at least, was entirely ready to listen to her worries, she decided to unburden herself.

'Oh, John…' she sighed, bewildered tears springing to her eyes '…I don't know how I managed to earn her enmity. I never wished for it. She just took an instant dislike to me, I suppose.'

'When you were sent to her for fostering, after your nurse died.'

'Yes. At times, I felt as though we were becoming closer, and then…' Her voice dwindled away as she recalled the years of trying to earn affection from a woman who showed very little sign of ever wishing to reciprocate. Was writing this letter just another such attempt to gain her favour? Should she perhaps rather threaten retribution for the attempt she had made on her life, and on her husband's life? Or at the very least, call her to account for the way she had administered her funds while she had been playing the role of guardian? All those years when she had altered and mended her own clothing, while Lady Lacey flitted about in her finery. And now she came to think of it, she had never discovered what had become of her mother's jewels.

She took the letter back.

'I am not going to send this letter, John.' She ripped the parchment in half, and the halves across again. 'She wronged me, and she will only think me a weak fool if she thinks I am so ready to forgive her.'

'Whatever did she do to raise your ire, Maddy? I have never seen you so determined to nurture anger against anyone.'

'She…she…' Maddy pressed her hand to her temples, which were suddenly throbbing. The trouble was she had no proof of what her cousin had done. She knew what her intentions were regarding her husband, but she had no confirmation that she had succeeded yet, either.

'I have no proof.' Her mind suddenly cleared. She could not prove that she had set the dogs on her. She was unlikely to ever be able to prove that she had plotted with Lord Hugo de Vere, unless, for some reason of his own, he chose to confess. People would think her a fool if she made a great fuss over her husband's adultery, if she ever found out that it had indeed taken place, for theirs was an arranged marriage. Infidelity was almost expected of a husband in such cases.

But the jewels were objects that could be traced. If she could have nothing else, she could have them restored to her.

'John,' she said, leaning forward in her urgency to reclaim something out of the wasteland Lady Lacey seemed determined to make of her marriage, 'do you perchance have any idea what became of my mother's jewels when she died? If they were put away in the strong box, then they should have been handed over to me when I arrived, along with all the rest of its contents. But they were not there.'

He blinked in surprise. 'I am sorry, Maddy, I did not work indoors at that time, as you know.'

'No, of course not.' She frowned. 'But since that time, you have gained a great deal of responsibility. You must know who to ask what my father did with them.'

Frowning, he ventured, 'Well, the most obvious person to ask would have been Robbins.'

'But we cannot, since he has disappeared.'

'And since the jewels seem to have disappeared as well…' He spread his hands, attempting a wry smile.

Maddy sighed. 'Yes, he could well have stolen them, along with all the rest of the estate money that appears to have gone missing.'

'You think estate money is missing?' John looked concerned. 'What makes you say that?'

'Lawless spotted discrepancies in the accounting practically the first day he arrived. He was still trying to make sense of where so much ready coin could have gone when he—' She gulped. She still could not bear to dwell too much on how closely her own husband had come to the same fate that dreadful day.

'But if Robbins absconded with it all, that explains it. Except…'

'Except?'

'Well, I have always wondered if my father might not have sent the jewels to me, at some stage. Perhaps for one of my birthdays, or on the anniversary of my mother's death. Even just her pearls, for a keepsake.' She frowned, pondering his absence of communication of any sort, save through the Baron and Lady Lacey. It was a depressing thought that as soon as she had left his castle, he seemed to have forgotten all about her.

'Although that is not very likely,' she sighed, suddenly feeling despondent. Her father had forgotten her, she had been nothing but a burden to her cousin, and now even her husband did not care enough to write and let her know whether he was alive or dead. She shook her head at her last absurd thought. He could not write at all if he was dead! She was such a fool. No wonder she was so unable to inspire admiration from anyone who knew her. 'I expect your explanation is the correct one,' she said, her voice grown dull with acceptance. 'He locked the jewels away, and Robbins stole them.'

John reached forward and patted her knee. 'I think you have to accept that. After all this time, there is no way to find out what became of them.'

She got to her feet, angry suddenly that she could not even call her cousin to account over this small matter. Tears of frustration sprang to her eyes as she paced the room back and forth, like a caged animal.

'Maddy…' John had got to his feet when she did, out of courtesy, but now he was watching her with growing alarm. 'I had no idea these jewels meant so much to you.'

'It would make no difference if they did.' It was not that the jewels meant a great deal to her, it was that she did not seem to matter a great deal to anyone. She paused, mid-stride, her fists clenching and unclenching as she tried to gain control over her unruly emotions sufficiently to make John understand, without sounding as though she were wallowing in self-pity. 'She has taken, or tried to take everything. If only I could be sure Robbins stole them, then at least I would have the satisfaction of knowing she hasn't got them.'

'Maddy, you are making no sense. Who do you suspect of stealing the jewels, if not Robbins?'

'I don't know,' she murmured, sinking back onto her chair, suddenly feeling drained and shaky. 'It doesn't matter anyway. Take no notice of my humour. Perhaps the truth is that, since I have discovered I am with child, I have lost my ability to reason as I used. I have fainted, which I never used to do, and I feel like crying almost all of the time. And I feel trapped, and alone…'

'You are with child?' he gasped. 'Why did you not tell me before?'

'Even my own husband does not know yet. And I suppose he ought to know before anyone—that is, if he lives.' Tears began to run down her cheeks again. 'Oh, I told you I cannot seem to stop crying. Everything seems so hopeless!' she wailed.

'Poor Maddy,' he said in a rather stilted tone. 'I…I do wish things could be different for you. I am very fond of you, you know. But in the end I fear it is a woman's lot to weep.' He backed away from her awkwardly, and left hastily.

After that outburst, he appeared a little uncomfortable with her, causing Maddy to regret having let herself go as she had done. John's slight distancing, after that scene, was a reminder that, as the lady of the manor, she had a position to maintain, no matter how she felt. She often found herself wondering if her mother had felt this same sense of crushing isolation. Her husband was absent. She had no friend to confide in. Her only companions were servants.

Suddenly, it seemed more important than ever to discover what had become of her mother's jewels. She had borne her faithless father four fine boys, and only then the despised little girl. But she was certain, from the fact the nursery was situated right next to her chamber, when it was often the practice to install a wet nurse and a nursery maid in rooms far enough away that a crying child would not disturb a lady's sleep, that she had gained comfort from all her babes. If she could find her jewels, she would at least have a tangible link with the woman she felt sure would have loved her, as strongly as she loved her own child.

She began by making a thorough search of her mother's rooms. Maybe she had a hiding place, that only she had known of?

'We have assumed, because the jewels vanished, that they were taken from the castle,' she said to John, one morning when he found her standing in the hearth of the nursery, peering up the chimney. 'But has a thorough search ever been made? Either my father or Robbins could have hidden them in some secret place only they knew of. In a castle this size, there could be any number of secret recesses, built into the walls, or hidden behind tapestries. I have gone over my mother's rooms and have not found anything, so next, while the stewards' rooms are vacant, I will make a thorough search there.'

'Nay, Maddy,' John protested, his face puckered with concern. 'You should not be wearing yourself out on such a fruitless occupation. Think of your baby.' He smiled. 'You need to rest, and take care of yourself.'

'I do not think I will be able to rest, while this mystery is plaguing me.'

'Then let me take care of it for you,' he suggested. 'Before you make yourself ill tearing the castle apart on what is probably a pointless exercise. I promise, I will search diligently…'

'Under the floorboards,' she interrupted. 'Robbins was the type of man who might have had a secret compartment fashioned under the boards of his room.'

'Very likely,' John agreed. 'I would get a couple of men to help me pry them up, but with so many gone with your husband to quell this rebellion…' He shrugged. 'It will take me longer, on my own, but whenever I have a moment, I promise I will conduct a thorough search, if you will promise to rest.'

'Very well,' she agreed, grateful that she could leave the matter in her brother's capable hands. 'I do have much work to do, to prepare for the baby,' she admitted.

'Then do you go about your sewing, while I conduct the search.'

It was late one morn, a couple of weeks later, as she was folding some of these baby clothes into a cedar chest, that John burst in, saying, 'It's him! At least, we are almost sure it is him!'

'Ger?' Maddy leaped to her feet. John had to catch her in his arms and lower her gently to a low window embrasure when she went dizzy for a moment.

'Christophe has reported a column of men breasting the moorland. They carry your husband's banner, and though they are still too far away to pick out individual riders, one of the horses is quite definitely Caligula.'

Nobody else was quite strong enough, or pigheaded enough, to try to ride that bad-tempered brute. Why Ger insisted on doing so, when he could quite easily have picked a more comfortable mount, had often bewildered her. But now she could only be glad of this eccentricity. The man riding Caligula back to Woolton could only be her husband.

'Get my horse saddled!' She leapt to her feet. She could not sit quietly here and wait! She had to ride out and meet him. But not in this gown. She glanced down at the comfortably soft, but rather drab linen dress that she had been in the habit of pulling on in the mornings. 'While I run and get changed!' Thank goodness she had finished the sea-green satin! She could just picture all those yards of material flowing across her palfrey's back. 'And tell the groom to use the green harness with the golden bells.' Ger had said he thought she had looked magnificent riding from London, dressed in like finery, with her horse so elaborately caparisoned. And she so wanted to make a good first impression on his return. Whatever came later, she wanted admiration to be the first expression she saw on his face when he caught sight of her.

'Oh, and I must get Joan to prepare a suitable feast for his homecoming. She can handle it, can't she? Only I cannot stay here, while he is so close!'

'Maddy?' John caught at her arm as she hastened towards the door. 'Do you mind if I make a suggestion?'

'Not if you do so quickly!' She laughed.

He smiled. 'So eager to greet your husband?'

'Yes! Yes! Oh, I have missed him so much!'

'Then, would you not wish your first greeting to be…how shall I put this? Would you not wish for some moments alone?'

'Oh.' Her husband did not like her public displays of emotion. Her face fell when she considered exactly how constrained she would have to be when she came face to face with him. She wanted to be able to hug him, and tell him she loved him, and was carrying his child. She would not be able to do that while she sat on her horse, and he towered over her on Caligula, with the entire cavalcade gawping.

And if he had been unfaithful, she might be able to see it written on his face. Surely, if he had spent the last month enjoying her own cousin's favours, he would not be able to look her straight in the eye?

Or perhaps he would. Perhaps it would be nothing to him. She worried at her lower lip. She must not forget that they had parted on such bad terms that he had not even bothered to write letting her know that he had come through the battle unscathed. If he was so indifferent to her, and had been unfaithful to boot, well, she was not at all sure she wanted anyone to witness her humiliation when she went riding out full of hope, to fling herself at him, like the love-lorn fool she was, only to be greeted with cool disdain.

'W…what do you think I should do? Wait here? In my chamber, and bid him come to me? Won't that look rather cold?'

'Yes, it would, Maddy!' John said. 'That wasn't what I was going to suggest at all. No, I was going to suggest sending a messenger requesting he meet you alone, on the headland. I believe it is a special place for you?'

When Maddy's jaw dropped, John laughed. 'Don't feel embarrassed about it. You are very much in love with your husband, you admit as much. And it is hard for you to snatch a moment's peace within the castle walls.'

'Won't it look rather odd for us to disappear together like that?' She could feel her cheeks growing hot. How many people knew what they had been doing up on the headland that day?

'I don't think anyone would begrudge the pair of you a short interlude alone, after being apart for so long, under such trying circumstances.'

She twisted her hands together, agonising over what to do for the best. She could hear Lady Lacey's voice urging her to behave with dignity. If she were here, she would insist that she ride out, properly escorted by the entire household staff, to greet her returning lord with all due pomp… She shook her head angrily. Lady Lacey was no longer in charge of her life. And her heart was urging her to run to the man she loved and tell him how much she loved him.

'I just want a few moments to tell him about the babe, you understand?' Gathering her skirts in her hands, she pulled herself to her full height, and swept past her brother with as much dignity as she could muster with her cheeks still flaming at the knowledge her love life had been a topic of castle gossip.

'I will send Christophe to your husband,' he said, his lips twitching a little in amusement at Maddy's futile attempt to look haughty. 'And escort you myself to your rendezvous.'

'There is no need—'

'But there is, Maddy, in your condition. You should not ride out alone, especially not on paths that are used so infrequently. Who knows what condition they may be in, particularly after the heavy rains we have had these past few weeks.'

Maddy relaxed immediately. She had been silly to behave in such a prickly fashion with her brother. He only wanted what was best for her, after all.

Joan was waiting for her in her chamber, the gown already laid out.

'I knew you would want to wear this.' She smiled, helping Maddy to unlace her workaday gown, when her fingers proved too shaky to achieve the task unaided.

'I have sent to the cook to warn of the imminent arrival of all those hungry heroes,' Joan twinkled as Maddy plunged a cloth into the ewer of warm water scented with roses. 'Once you have set out, I will make sure Sir Geraint's rooms are aired and fresh linen set upon the bed, although,' she added slyly, 'I dare say it will be this room you will both be sleeping in.'

Maddy was glad her head was hidden in the folds of the gown as she tugged it over her head. Her cheeks were hot with embarrassment that Joan should refer to the impending reunion in such a salacious tone. Really, did the woman have to speak so freely about what should be private between a husband and wife?

* * *

It took her no longer to undergo her hasty toilet than it had taken the groom to prepare her palfrey. As she strode into the stable yard, the man was just leading her horse up to the mounting block. Christophe, who had been on the point of riding out, wheeled his horse round, grinning as he saluted her.

John intercepted her as she made to take the reins of her palfrey from the groom's waiting hands and mount up. 'Let's take our horses out through the sally port,' he suggested.

'Of course,' she replied, wondering why she had not remembered that it would be far quicker to reach the headland by leaving from the little side entrance, crossing the stream, then cantering up the hill, although John's cob, and her own palfrey, were probably the only horses in the stables small enough to take this route. On horseback, she would have simply left through the main gate, crossed the drawbridge, then taken the main road until reaching the fork in the forest that swept round the outer defences. She would barely have reached the rendezvous before her husband, who could by now have reached the outer edges of the forest.

Before she knew it, they were up on the headland, her palfrey's hooves cushioned by the fragrant heather, the wind from the incoming tide whipping her hair from its restraining pins. With a laugh, she smoothed the errant strands from her face as John leant over to take the reins from her hands.

'Don't get too close to the edge, Maddy. There has been a rock fall, recently, and we don't want you going over by accident, do we?'

For the first time, she noticed roots sticking out at crazy angles from a patch of raw rock, where once there had been a soft cushion of heather. She was glad John had been with her to warn her. With a grateful smile, she slid from the saddle, and tangled the reins loosely around some strands of prickly gorse, well away from the crumbling edge of the cliffs.

She straightened, smoothing down her skirts as John dismounted and strode towards her. 'I am glad you came with me, John. I wouldn't wish my horse to have strayed into such danger.' He had not tethered his own mount, she noticed. He must have trained the beast to stand with its reins dropped to the ground. Of course, he often rode out on his own. He would not have a groom in attendance to hold his mount should he wish to go somewhere on foot, when there was no convenient place to hitch his mount.

'No. It is a sheer drop to the beach below. Over a hundred feet, I should say. Nobody would survive such a fall.'

And, without warning, he punched her in the face.

Chapter Seventeen

The next thing Maddy knew, a pain was arcing across her shoulders. Her hands were tied behind her back.

John had hit her! Gingerly, she pressed her tongue to the inside of her cheek, wincing as it connected with the bruised flesh. There was a tight band round her chest, which was making it hard to breathe. Her feet were icy cold—no, not just cold—wet.

She dragged her leaden eyelids upwards, trying to make sense of the hurts that were manifesting themselves in various parts of her body. The hard unyielding pressure at her back was a post; the band round her chest the rope by which she was bound to it.

And now she'd got her eyes open, she could see that, while she'd been unconscious, John had brought her down to the beach. He was kneeling at her feet now, in the waves that lapped round her ankles, busily securing more rope about her knees.

He was tying her to one of the ancient timbers that had once supported the jetty!

'Why?' she croaked through painfully split lips.

'You really are a stupid girl,' he replied, tugging the knots viciously tight and rising to his feet. 'It's hard to believe sometimes that we share the same father. I was quite prepared to do a deal with you, you know,' he continued, brushing damp sand from his hose. 'You are the only one of my family I ever liked much, and over the last few weeks I had begun to grow quite fond of you. It's a pity you let slip that you had fallen in love with your husband. If not for that…but then, there is your intractable attitude towards the theft of your jewels, too. You condemned yourself out of your own mouth, Maddy.'

'I don't understand.' She felt dizzy, and as she shook her head, to try to clear it, he sneered,

'You want a confession? Very well, but it must be brief. I don't want your husband to catch sight of me down here on the beach with you when he reaches the headland.'

When she only looked bewildered, he explained, 'By the time he reaches the headland, the tide will be at about the height of your knees. He knows how fast the tide comes in. He will see this post is cloaked in seaweed right to the top and that he will have to move fast if he doesn't want you to drown. He will dash down to the only safe access point to the beach he knows. From where he comes out of the dunes, he will think he can gallop straight up to rescue you…right across the mudflats. There's a particularly treacherous spot directly in the path from the dunes to this post at the moment. It will swallow him whole. Him and his horse.'

And there would be nobody to rescue her then. She would drown. Even if, by some remote chance, somebody else spotted her tied to this stake, it was not likely they would be able to reach her. Hardly anyone knew the safe route through the shifting sands. As the cold certainty of her fate swamped her, she began to tremble.

'Don't worry,' he said, giving one last tug on the knots to make sure they were secure. 'Once the tide ebbs, I will reclaim your body, and deposit it in the same grave that contains his remains. Your last resting place will be beside the one you love.' He brushed a strand of hair from her face, tucking it behind her ear in a gesture that was almost tender. 'Together, for eternity.'

How could he think that would be a comfort to her? 'You're m…mad!' she stuttered. Her whole body was shaking with fear and cold. 'What do you hope to gain from this? When our murder is discovered…'

'Ah, but nobody will discover your murder. Without a body…'

He grinned. 'The recent rock fall from the headland will make it look as though you both fell to your doom from there. In the first rapture of your reunion, you grew careless. Your bodies fell to the beach. Even if one or other of you survived, with the tide coming in, your bodies will be swept out to sea.'

And he would be the one to carry the explanation to the men who would later go out to search for them when they didn't return home by nightfall. She could see him, shaking his head in mock-sorrow as he pointed out the crumbling rock at the cliff edge. Indignantly, she cried, 'You won't get away with this!'

'Why not? I got away with almost exactly the same thing with that old fool Robbins.'

'You murdered my father's steward? Why?'

'Like you, Maddy, he was asking too many questions about what had become of your mother's jewels. We are alike, aren't we, in some ways? We will do anything to keep what is ours.' He laid his hands on her shoulders, leaning his face close to hers as he spoke in an urgent undertone. 'I understand that. I would even have shared Woolton with you…after all, you had no choice. The King forced you to marry that man, under threat of treason. Lady Lacey let everyone know how reluctant you were to marry that brute, how you fled the betrothal feast in tears, how scared you were on your wedding day. I felt sorry for you, I truly did. You hadn't deliberately come to push me aside. And so I forgave you. I could tolerate you here. You have some claim, though you are only a female. But what rights has Geraint the sheep farmer?' His face grew red. 'I may be a bastard, but at least my father was a lord. What was his? A merchant! If only our father had acknowledged me, Woolton would have been mine already. Other bastard sons inherit. Why not me?' He flung himself abruptly away from her. 'And why did you have to go and fall in love with your husband? Taking his side against me!'

'I didn't take his side against you! I made sure you were acknowledged as my brother. You sat at table with us. And in return, you plan to murder us both!'

He shrugged, but his features took on a sorrowful cast. 'True, you could have lived if only he'd fallen in battle. Even though the King would have sent someone to take his place, as you explained, he would have let you have a decent period of mourning before forcing you into another union. And during that time, we could have come to an…understanding. I would even have let you keep his brat, if it had been a girl. We could have outwitted the King somehow. You could have said you were too distraught over losing your husband to think of taking another. You could have even petitioned for me to be recognised as the rightful heir.'

Seeing the look of regret on his face as he contemplated her murder, Maddy began desperately to plead for her life. 'John, it is not too late…you don't need to do this wicked thing! I won't say anything about Robbins if that is what you fear.'

Though his expression of regret did not waver, he shook his head. 'But your husband is coming back. He will have me tried and hanged for the theft you say Lawless found the evidence for.' He sighed. 'And I thought I had silenced him in good time.'

'You k…killed Lawless? On purpose?'

'Didn't you even guess that? Who did you think it was, you little fool? Some random rebel, looking for a stray Lancastrian to use for target practice?' His mocking laugh sent a shudder right through her. How could he laugh when he had her tethered to a post, terrified of drowning! 'You really believed your husband was the target, then?'

He shook his head, his face suddenly growing hard and cold. For the first time, she felt as though she was seeing the real man.

'I will hang, for sure, and Joan along with me, if I let either you or your husband live now. I saw how angry you were about the jewels. I warned her you would not forgive the theft of your property, but she insisted you were different from your father and brothers until she saw I could barely keep you from tearing the castle apart to find their hiding place. But I heard you describing forgiveness as a weakness, don't forget. I saw you tear up the letter to your cousin in a fit of rage not many would guess the saintly little Lady Agnes capable of. You can't help yourself. You are your father's daughter, as I am his son.'

She gazed up at him in bewilderment. She just could not follow his train of thought at all. 'Where does Joan come into this?'

'She has the jewels. Oh, she didn't take them. She is not a thief. She…earned them.' His face contorted with disgust. 'He knew she was my woman, but that didn't stop him. That disgusting old man, and my Joan. He draped them over her naked body, after he'd finished with her, saying she was the only woman in the castle beautiful enough to do them justice.' His face was unrecognisable to her now, spittle flying from his lips as he finally vented out his boiling rage, so long suppressed. 'She crawled back to me, bruised and weeping, dreading the day he would return from battle, and force her to his bed again. Thank God he fell when he did, or I would have had to kill him myself.'

So that was what had finally tipped her poor wronged brother over the edge. The revelation of her father's base conduct pierced her to the core. He had raped his son's woman, then had the gall to toss jewels at her, as though she had been a willing whore. John, unable to exact revenge on the man who had defiled and degraded her, had begun to lash out at anyone who might threaten her further hurt. First Robbins, then Lawless, now Geraint and herself.

All this, she could understand.

But not his insistence he had any rights of inheritance over Woolton.

'You have taken leave of your senses!' she cried. 'The King will never permit a mere nobody, with no political affiliations, to hold such a strategic position in these turbulent times!'

A wave broke over Maddy's ankles, drenching her skirts to her calves. John glanced down, the shock of the cold water soaking his boots clearly bringing him back to the present.

'I am sorry it had to end like this,' he said, stepping back and shaking his head as though he really felt remorse.

Fear such as she had never known had her struggling against her bonds, though she knew she could never escape them.

'John!' she cried, terror robbing her of every last vestige of pride. 'You can't do this! Please untie me!'

'No. My mind is made up. I cannot let you live, for his spawn to inherit what should always have been mine.' His eyes flicked down to her stomach, growing implacable in the instant before he turned and began to walk away.

'But this babe is your kin!' she shouted after his retreating figure. 'I'm your sister! Your family!' He mounted his patiently waiting cob, and began to steer a zig-zagging course through the restless wavelets. Angry now, as well as frightened, she lifted her head, and screamed into the wind, 'I will haunt you, John! You will never know a peaceful night's sleep again!' She fought her bonds till the rough ropes began to saw through the satin of her gown, chafing her skin. At length, exhausted, she abandoned the futile struggle, sobbing in despair. There was nobody to hear. John had left her. He really meant her to die. He had killed before, without it touching his conscience. There was nothing she could do.

The sand beneath her feet was changing in consistency already. As the waves broke about her knees, the water churned the previously solid ground into a foaming broth of mud and grit. At this point, he had said, her husband might well arrive on the headland, and see her. She lifted her head, but tears blurred her vision. Even if she could see her husband, there was no way she could prevent him from galloping to her rescue, just as John had predicted. Her voice would never carry over the roaring of the waves.

She gasped as a huge roller broke just before her, swamping her to the waist with freezing cold spray. When it subsided, water swirled about her thighs. The speed at which the tide came in had never ceased to surprise her. How often she had stood on the headland, watching it devouring the land. And now it would devour her, too. And her babe. And then her husband.

How could John say he was fond of her, while condemning her to a death like this? How could he leave her to die unshriven?

'Oh, God!' she cried, her head dropping to her chest in an attitude of prayer. 'I commit my soul into your keeping. And my baby,' she sobbed. 'Oh, Lord, forgive my sins and receive us into your bosom…' But of course, without a priest to give the last rites, her soul must needs be purged of its sins in purgatory.

A surge of water rushed over her shoulders then, dragging her body slightly sideways as it lifted her from her feet. As it ebbed, and her feet again felt the shifting sand beneath them, she closed her eyes and began to babble out prayers of penitence.

For the first time in her life, she meant every word of the confession that poured straight from her terrified heart. She begged forgiveness for every uncharitable thought she'd ever harboured for her cousin Eleanor, who she now knew had nothing to do with the ambush. Standing on the brink of eternity, she was finally able to see that Lady Lacey was just a spoilt beauty, guilty of only petty female spite that stemmed from disappointment with her own love life. She could easily forgive such frailty.

But she could not find it in herself to forgive John. She could not pray, as her saviour had done from the cross, Father forgive him, for he knows not what he does. He knew exactly what he was doing! His plans were cold blooded and meticulously laid. Though it cost her an eon in purgatory, she could not pray for anything less than vengeance for her murder.

The ferocious roar of the incoming tide filled her ears. Glancing over her shoulder, she saw the white-capped rollers rising inexorably higher, like huge jaws gaping wide to devour her.

'Oh, God!' she cried, as the foam rose to her chest, lifting her from her feet for the second time, 'spare my husband! Let him survive this somehow, and bring my murderer to justice! And avenge my babe, my babe, that has not even had the chance to be born!' she wailed.

She moaned then, fearful of dying in her sins, yet completely incapable of letting go of her desire for vengeance or forgiving her killer.

'Lord have mercy on my soul!' she wept, in the certainty that there was nothing now that would keep her from meeting her Maker, and that right soon.

Sir Geraint raised his hand, signalling the cavalcade to come to a halt. A single rider was approaching from Castle Woolton. His face hardened as he noted that it was a man. Too much to hope his wife would have come herself, he sighed. She was probably up in her nice warm sitting room, calmly sewing, or reading, or whatever it was that women did with themselves all day when their husbands were away fighting for the things that really mattered.

Christophe pulled his rangy mare to a halt a few feet from him, grinning from ear to ear.

'My lord,' Christophe panted. 'I have a message from the Lady Maddy.' Blushing bright red, he corrected himself, 'I m…mean, the Lady Agnes…your lady wife.'

Sir Geraint's jaw hardened. It hadn't been until he left, and witnessed the fondness of their leave taking, that he had begun to suspect her of dallying with Captain Fritz. And now it seemed, while he had been absent, she had got on intimate terms with this scruffy foot soldier. For a second, he heartily wished he had succumbed to the lures her cousin had thrown out to him on their journey to York. Maybe then he would be able to face his wife's faithlessness with at least an appearance of nonchalance. In an arranged marriage, Lady Lacey had whispered, nobody expects either party to stay faithful. His blood had run cold at the inference that his wife could stray, as well as he. Convinced the woman must have known something, the temptation to commit adultery with the beauty in a fit of defiance had been strong. And yet he had held back. Foolishly, stubbornly, he felt he was not ready to sink to that level, yet. Maybe in the end, that was all their marriage would be about. A petty keeping of scores. But not so soon!

Until he had proof of his wife's infidelity, he was not prepared to abandon his dream of having a true marriage. Just as sad had been witnessing Captain Fritz's defection to Lady Lacey's bed. If Maddy had to choose another lover, couldn't she at least have picked a man who would appreciate the honour she'd bestowed on him? But the minute they'd set out, the man had begun a pursuit so relentless, it could only have one outcome.

'What is it, man?' he grated. 'Spit it out.'

Christophe's hue deepened by several shades. 'She requests a private meeting with you, on the headland, before you return, my lord. Most insistent she was.'

'Insistent?' His lips tightened. It seemed his attempts at disciplining her had not been harsh enough. Not only did she demonstrate her defiance by setting up a flirtation with Christophe, but the moment he set foot on her land, she made an attempt to manipulate him. The very place she had chosen for the meeting could not help reminding him of what a love-sick fool he had been. But if she thought he would dance to her tune, then it was as well she learnt how wrong she was!

He was done with waiting for a kind word from her, for any sign that she would put him first in her life, and give him the name of whoever it was who had attempted to kill him. She could have written to him at any time, during the month of his absence, confessing what she knew, and he would have forgiven her reticence to deliver someone she was clearly fond of to justice. But she had not written. Not even to express a wish he might come through battle unscathed.

Not that, in the end, there had been a battle.

Lovell's rebellion had petered out like a damp squib.

The rebels must have been as ill equipped as the King's own hastily assembled army. For when the Duke of Bedford had brazenly ridden into Lovell's camp, promising pardon to all who would surrender, the entire company had done so, without even a token fight. And Lovell had fled.

But she had not known that.

Cursing himself for a fool, he nodded grudgingly to Christophe, and wheeled away from the main body of men, taking the path through the forest that led to the headland. If there was any chance, any hope that her desire to see him privately, where once they had made love with such wild abandon, might mean she had a tender spot in her heart for him, he had to seize it!

Though he had not weakened sufficiently to write and beg her for a word, a crumb to see him through the battle he had believed he would have to fight, he had not wanted her to remain for ever ignorant of what was in his heart. Words that he had not been able to speak had flowed from his pen. He had sealed the letter, leaving instructions that it was only to be delivered to his wife on the event of his death. She would have known how much he had loved her; though it would have been too late to do him any good. Now, he patted the pocket where the letter still nestled, wondering if there would ever come a time when he felt sufficiently confident of her reaction to openly offer her his heart.

As the path wound through a rocky draw, Caligula shied. 'Steady there!' He leaned forward, patting the beast's great neck, his heart thundering as he saw for himself what a perfect place for an ambush this was. Was that why she had sent for him? The previous attempt on his life had failed, he had not fallen in battle, so she had decided to dispose of him by other means?

He groaned aloud. How had it come to this? He could not trust her with his life, never mind his heart.

But if she was so faithless, what was his life worth? The days he had spent apart from her had been the most miserable of his life.

Setting his jaw resolutely, he dug his heels into Caligula's flanks, determined to meet her and finally end the misery of not knowing how things stood between them.

Though he kept his visage stern, by the time he reached the rendezvous, his hands were trembling upon the reins. There had been no ambush, so at least it was not death she had in store for him. Had she summoned him here to confess her infidelities? Or to reveal, at last, what she knew of that abortive attempt on his life?

He made for Maddy's sorrel palfrey, which was standing sentinel on the windswept headland, its reins tangled in a clump of gorse. With a sigh, Sir Geraint dismounted, dropping the destrier's reins to the ground.

'Maddy!' he called, his gaze sweeping the headland for sight of her. He frowned. Why lure him up here, only to play some childish game of hide and seek with him?

'Maddy!' he roared, frustration with her evasive tactics finally getting the better of his temper. 'If you don't come out right now, I'm going home!'

Caligula jerked up his head and snorted in reaction to his master's mood. Sir Geraint patted the horse's neck. 'Women!' he growled, gentling his tone to soothe the animal. But Caligula skittered sideways, tossing his head irritably, causing him to have to leap aside to avoid being pushed into the gorse thicket. With a frown, he stooped to snag up the reins, freezing in horror as he first caught sight of the churned earth and exposed rocks where once had been an upsweep of heather that had shielded this whole area from the wind that now scoured unfettered across it.

'Maddy,' he whispered, ducking under Caligula's neck, and making his way to the cliff edge. Peering over, he could see where rocks had tumbled to the beach below, staining the pale sand with smears of crushed grass and heather. But there was no sign of her. Thank God! For one awful moment, he had pictured her body, lying at the foot of the cliff, shattered by the force of the fall. Though his eyes scoured the beach, he could see no sign of her. He whipped round. Her horse was here, so she must have been here. If she hadn't fallen, where was she? He leaned further out over the edge, hoping that she might have perhaps landed on a ledge, or clung to a tree root, or something.

It never occurred to him to look out to sea. He could only envision her lying injured, maybe crawling across the sand to get help. And the tide was coming in! If she was down there, unable to get herself to safety, she would drown!

Striding back down the incline, he mounted Caligula and urged him into motion. He had ridden every inch of the estate, and could vaguely remember that there was only one safe path that a man on horseback could take from here, that would get him down to the beach. Digging his heels into Caligula's flanks, he rode as fast as he dared along that path, until, his heart in his mouth, he emerged, as he had hoped, from the dunes on to a patch of shingle.

But as he wheeled the horse's head round, to ride to the spot where he was certain Maddy must have fallen to her fate, Caligula shied. When he dug in his heels, the horse turned in the opposite direction, raising his head and neighing, as he had only once heard him neigh before, on the battlefield, with the weight of King Richard's army charging down the hill on the attack.

'Not now, you obstinate nag!' Sir Geraint cursed, sawing at the reins. Trust Caligula to get all fired up at the worst possible moment. 'It's just the waves you can hear thundering, not an approaching army.'

But something drew his eyes out across the waves nevertheless. And the sight that met his eyes shocked him to the core. Bound to one of the half-buried jetty timbers was Maddy. He saw her clearly only for a moment, before a mighty roller broke over her shoulders, almost obliterating her from sight.

He knew there was not much time. Digging his heels into Caligula's flanks yet again, he urged the horse forward, into the breakers. But to his dismay, Caligula would only dance along the edges of the waves, refusing to so much as dip one hoof into the foaming water.

'You stupid beast!' he cursed. 'It's only water! It has never bothered you before!'

Dammit, he had to get to Maddy. To cut her free before the rising tide swallowed her! Muttering a string of curses, he kicked his feet free from the stirrups and went to swing himself out of the saddle. And Caligula chose that moment to rear up on his hind legs, causing him to grab at the destrier's flying mane, instinctively keeping himself from being flung to the ground. It would do Maddy no good if he was injured now. He had to stay whole, if he was going to effect a rescue.

In desperation he looked out across the heaving breakers again, to where she was tossing her head to and fro as though to clear the clinging tendrils of hair from her face. Her sweet mouth was open, as though gasping for breath, or releasing a scream for help. But he could not hear her voice above the roaring of the sea. All he could hear was the gulls crying overhead, as they wheeled crazily amongst the buffeting currents of air.

'Go baaack!' they seemed to be crying. 'Stay awaaaay!'

Absurd. He could not go back. Maddy needed him. If he didn't cut her free, and that right soon, she would drown.

And when he got his hands on the evil bastard that had tied her there… His heart skipped a beat. Why would anyone want to harm her? More specifically, why choose such a cruel death? She must be terrified, as each wave grew deeper than the one before it. Why put her through such an agonisingly slow torment? It was an act of such diabolical evil that it beggared belief.

And it hit him. It was to give him time to see her predicament. She was merely the bait in a trap set for him!

The sands beneath the waves Caligula had stubbornly refused to step into were treacherous when the tide turned. She had warned him herself to stay away from this beach.

Whoever had staked her out there knew that he must either watch her drown, or risk crossing the shifting sands to get to her.

If Caligula had not instinctively avoided the danger… Thrusting his feet back into the stirrups, he leant forward, and patted the great beast's neck.

'Well done, old fellow,' he murmured. 'You saved me from rushing headlong to my doom. And now I must rely on your strength again.' Wheeling away from the pitiless sea, he urged the horse back up the path leading inland. 'I know you have gone all day, but don't forget, you were bred to carry the weight of a man bigger than me, in full armour. And now I need you to ride like the wind. Run as you have never run before.'

Caligula snorted, as though accepting the challenge, tossed his head proudly, and lumbered into what passed for a gallop to the great warhorse.

Sir Geraint had remembered the nearby fisherman's cottage, and the peculiar craft leaning against the wall of the pigsty. A boat that was useful when the tide was coming in, the owner of it had said. At the time, those words had made no sense, but now he understood. In such a craft, he could skim over the shallowest waves, perhaps even get over patches of quicksand. It was a desperate gamble, but better than nothing. He could not stand by and watch Maddy drown. Whatever she felt about him, whatever she might be guilty of, his life would be empty without her in it.

He had gone. He had left her. For a moment Maddy stared at the spot on the shore where he had been with disbelief. And then she truly began to drown. In despair.

If she had meant anything to him at all, he would have plunged into the waves in an attempt to save her. Not that she wanted him to drown as well, but couldn't he at least have thought about it? It meant nothing now that she had screamed to him to go back, to stay away. He hadn't even tried to come to her.

It could only mean he had slept with Lady Lacey. Now he had tasted that golden flesh, the very sight of her left him cold. Once she was dead, he would be free to pursue her. Her cousin would have her revenge indeed. She would have not only her husband, but her castle, and her wealth to boot. As a distant relative, she had no doubt the King would agree she was exactly the wife Sir Geraint would need to keep the locals happy.

The water ebbed to just below her chest, and she knew this meant another roller was about to surge inland. She drew a deep breath and braced herself as it broke over her shoulders. She shut her eyes against the salt water that poured over her face, though she could do nothing to prevent gallons of it forcing its way into her ears and nostrils. Her feet could find no purchase. The sea bed had been churned to slurry. Her dress was torn to ribbons now, from the sharp shards of shingle stirred up by the power of the water. When this wave subsided, she sank until her bonds snagged on the knotted clumps of mussels growing on the timber. Her hair was plastered to her face as the water level sank, clogging her mouth and nose so that she had to spit it out, shaking her head to clear a passage through which she could breathe.

It seemed she only had a moment to fill her lungs with a few gasps of air before the next wave broke over her head. The world disappeared under a torrent of water for what seemed like eternity. Just when she began to think she could not hold her breath any longer, she felt cold air on her face, and the sensation of the water dragging her down against the restrictions of her bonds, and she drew in a shuddering gasp.

Her eyes stung from the salt. Her throat was raw with screaming. But nothing hurt so much as the pain in her heart.

Her husband had left her here to die.

A great wave of loneliness swamped her. Nobody had ever really wanted her, let alone loved her. Would it have been different if her mother had lived?

She thought of the babe in her womb. If Ger had known about it, would he have made an attempt to reach her? She should have swallowed her pride, put aside her fears, and told him he was to be a father. Men would take risks for their children, even if they did not love their wives. But it was too late now. She had not confided the one fact that might have saved her life.

She would die, as she had lived, alone. Her father had forgotten about her as soon as she was out of his sight, her cousin had regarded her as a nuisance thrust upon her, her brother had plotted to murder her, and now even her husband would be relieved to see the back of her.

Nothing had ever hurt so much as watching him ride away, leaving her to die.

The water swirled around her chin now, even at its lowest ebb. She could hear the roar of the next approaching breaker.

The water pouring into her lungs would end for ever the torment of her husband's desertion. The cold of the water had already numbed her to the extent she no longer felt the pain where the ropes had sawn at her flesh.

And the cold, cold water would take all pain from her, the next time it broke over her head.

Yet, when the moment came, when the sky was blotted out by a thundering wall of water, even the darkness of her despair could not stop her from fighting for her baby's survival. Squeezing her eyes shut, she held her breath until her lungs felt as though they were going to burst.

Her head swam. Dark spots danced before her eyes. And still the water did not recede.

It was the end. Opening her mouth, Maddy gave in to one last despairing cry as the sea forced its passage down into her lungs.

Chapter Eighteen

The sea swallowed acres more sand in the short time it took Sir Geraint to gallop to the fisherman's hut, slash the ropes that bound the coracle to the pig pen with his sword, strap the strange craft over his back, tuck the paddle under his arm, then guide Caligula back with his knees and a string of curses more than anything else. He'd dealt with the shouts of the wide-eyed woman who'd burst from the hut at the sound of her pig squealing, the stamping of horse's hooves and the cursing of her lord, by ignoring her.

His heart froze in his chest when he could see no sign of Maddy. Then, the tip of the post to which she was bound made a brief appearance in the trough behind one of the massive breakers that was rolling in from the ocean. The water receded only as far as her shoulders. She just had time to fling her head back as though gasping for breath, before the next roller blotted her from his view. Flinging the bowl-like boat to the ground, he jumped in, grabbed one of the paddles, and began to try and skim it over the wet sand towards her. As soon as the boat was able to float, it took on a life of its own, preferring to go round and round in circles, than in the direction he tried to steer it. It seemed to take for ever before he could persuade the skittish craft to head more or less in the direction he wanted it to go. And then his battle against the power of the incoming tide truly began. For every inch he progressed the waves seemed to drive him back three. Finally, a huge wave tossed him sideways, almost tipping him out of the boat as the frame rammed one of the posts. Fearing the flimsy craft might shatter if the waves drove him against it again, he used the stubby paddle to push himself off it. Amazingly, he found this method of propulsion worked more effectively than anything he had tried thus far. He shot forward several feet, and only spun round once before the next roller dragged him sideways and shoreward again, forcing him to fend off a collision with the next post. Leaning over, he thrust hard with the oar against the next post, then the next, and the next, shoving the coracle inexorably onward. By the time he reached the post to which Maddy was bound, sweat was pouring down his back and his chest heaved with the effort of paddling against the sea's relentless drive inland.

Just below the surface of the water, he could make out a dark patch, something like streamers of seaweed, swaying with the current.

It was her hair.

A sob of rage and despair ripped from his throat as a wave caught his craft, spinning it away from her, and back towards the land. Desperately he paddled back, and this time, instead of giving way to the fear that he might already be too late, he scrabbled in the bottom of the boat for the ends of the rope that had been used to fasten the craft to the pigsty. Wrapping it round the post and knotting it hastily, he reached down into the water. Her hair coiled round his questing fingers as it had done on so many nights when he had likened the feel of it running through his hands, and over his flesh, to liquid silk in which a man might happily drown.

'Maddy,' he sobbed, plunging into the water.

Immediately the force of the current tried to drag him away from her, towards the dry land, where the living belonged. Only the grip he had on her hair kept him from being torn from her. His feet stirred up thick sludge at the base of the post in his strenuous effort to gain purchase and make his way back to her. Keeping one hand fastened in her hair, he reached into his belt for the dagger he cursed himself for not having drawn before he leapt into the water, then, taking a deep breath, he dived under, and hacked at the rope that bound her.

His knife cut through it like butter, and long before he felt he needed to take another breath, the top half of her body abruptly swung free. Her torso swayed shoreward, her hair billowing in the current like the fronds of some underwater plant. In shock, he reeled from her lifeless form, bobbing to the surface where he drew another agonised breath, before diving lower, to feel through the thick mud for the bonds which kept her staked at the knees. Again, it took only one swift slash to part the strands asunder.

This time, it was her body that began to rise to the surface. Clasping her round the waist with one arm, he flailed wildly with his free hand for the boat. Miraculously, they broke the surface only a few feet away, although they had rolled over and over in the undertow, making him fear they had been carried well back towards land. Uttering a wild cry, Sir Geraint grabbed at a severed section of rope that was trailing from the craft, and with Maddy's dead weight clamped against his chest, he kicked and clawed his way to the side of the craft. It wasn't easy to manhandle her into the boat. It had shipped a great deal of water by the time he managed to tip her face forwards over the rim. Her hands, he saw with anguish, were tied tightly behind her back, the waxy white fingers arched like bird's claws. He couldn't bear it. It didn't occur to him that if he were to try to get into the boat with her, the whole craft might sink. He just scrambled in beside her, overwhelmed by the primal need to get as close to her as he possibly could. To his amazement, as he flopped into the waterlogged craft on top of her, he discovered that his own fingers were still welded to the haft of his dagger.

Tears poured from his eyes as he crushed her to his chest. 'Maddy,' he moaned, stroking strands of sopping hair aside so that he could look at her face. He knew she couldn't respond, but he kissed her grave cold lips anyway, with all the passion and love he knew he should have given her while she yet lived.

'Oh, forgive me my pride, my love,' he breathed against her

mouth. She lay limp and heedless across his lap, as he ran his hands over her face, down her back, clasping her up to his chest again, and rocking her in an agony of grief. Though he had been too late to save her, though it could make no difference to her now, he couldn't bear to think of her hands bound behind her back like that. Turning her over so that she now lay face down across his knees, he took the knife and gently began to work its tip between her wrists. He knew she was beyond pain, now, but he could not bear the prospect of nicking her, and leaving a mark on her flesh. He had to raise her arms slightly so that his knife had better access to the rope, and used his knees to brace her body as yet another wave swirled the boat around and slammed it into the piling.

He felt warm water gushing down his leg an instant before he heard a sound that was like music to his ears. The sound of Maddy coughing up seawater.

'You're alive!' he yelled, exultantly, catching her up and turning her to face him again. Frantically, he cleared her face, yet again, of the wet strands of hair that obscured her from him. There was water dribbling from the corner of her open mouth, though her eyes were still closed.

'Breathe, Maddy,' he cried, shaking her. 'You've got to breathe!'

She was so cold and still, lying sprawled across his lap. If she was breathing, it was too shallow a movement for him to detect.

'Hold on, sweeting, I'm going to get you back to dry land.' Half-blinded by the tears that were streaming down his face, he leaned out of the boat, and severed the rope that moored it to the jetty post. It was only when the craft began to spin that he thought about the paddle. He hadn't got a clue where it was. He couldn't remember what he had done with it.

But now the tide that had been his enemy came to his rescue. A long roller lifted the boat, and with Maddy clasped in his arms he was flying, soaring on the crest of the wave, back to safety.

As the boat grated on the mudflats, something splashed into the sludge next to him, jerking his attention away from his wife, who still lay inert and ghostly white, in his arms.

It was a length of rope. Bemused, he let his eyes follow the length of it, to where he saw the fisherman's widow standing on the shore, gesturing to him wildly for him to catch hold of the end of it.

Belatedly, he understood that they were still not out of danger. Struggling to sit up without letting go of Maddy, he fumbled for the rope, placing his hand through the loop the woman had fashioned in the end of it, then winding it round his wrist for good measure.

Thank God she had the sense to follow him, armed with a rope. If he had followed his instinct, to step out of the boat and wade to shore once the coracle ran aground, he could still have ended up drowning in quicksand.

She'd even tied her end of the rope to Caligula's reins, and, instead of trying to drag them to safety, was utilising the massive horse's strength by urging him backwards, up the dunes. Only when the coracle grated against a bank of shingle did she leave go of Caligula's reins, and come pelting back towards them.

Knowing it was safe at last to leave the craft, Sir Geraint tried to stand up. As his hold on Maddy tightened, a shudder shook her body, and she vomited again. Copious amounts of seawater flooded over his already soaked chest, but he didn't care. It was a sign she was alive!

'We'm best get the child to my cottage sir, and out of they wet clothes,' urged the woman.

Yes, that was right. Maddy lived, but barely, and he had to get her warm as quickly as possible. Staggering to his feet, he ploughed across the shingle to where Caligula stood, rolling his eyes and stamping his feet.

At that moment, he loved this temperamental horse. He would never have recovered his wife's body if it hadn't been for Caligula.

'One last ride, you magnificent beast,' he said, throwing Maddy up into the saddle, and mounting up behind, as he had done, he recalled with devastating poignancy, the very first time they had met, 'and then you will get more pampering than any horse has ever had in the course of history.'

Gripping the saddle with his knees, in true knightly style, he leaned down and slashed the mooring rope cleanly from Caligula's bridle.

Caligula trotted obligingly back to the fisherman's cottage with only minimal direction from his rider, who could not tear his eyes from his wife's limp form. He could see her chest rising and falling now as she breathed. But she hadn't opened her eyes and she was so white. So cold.

The cottage only held one room, but there was a fire lit, he noted with relief when he carried Maddy inside.

'Get her out of they clothes, me lord,' the woman panted. She had dashed up to the cottage behind him, and was proffering a rough-looking piece of linen. 'We need to get her dry or she'll never get warm.'

She was right. Maddy would never get warm while she was so wet. Dropping to the dirt floor beside the hearth, still holding Maddy on his lap, he began to tear away what looked like strands of seaweed clinging to every inch of her body. There was a leather girdle around her waist, but that was the only thing recognisable as an item of clothing. When he unbuckled it, green streamers slithered to the floor, exposing her pale limbs to the firelight. Her wrists, waist and knees were rubbed raw where she had been tied, her legs from the knees downward lacerated with dozens of little cuts where the sea-borne gravel had scoured her skin.

The woman sucked in a sharp breath at the sight, but insisted that she needed to rub Maddy dry before wrapping her in a blanket.

'No!' he growled, then, when she flinched away from his anger, repeated more gently, but firmly, 'No. I must do it myself.'

'But you are wet, too, my lord,' the woman remonstrated. 'She won't get warm with you dripping all over her, will she?'

Reluctantly he relinquished her body to the fisherwoman, while he hastily stripped off his own garments. And it was a further agony to him when Maddy's eyes flickered open while the woman was tenderly wrapping her in a blanket.

'Give her to me!' he said, pushing past the woman in spite of the fact that he was stark naked. Scooping his wife up into his arms, he cradled her to his chest.

'Into bed with you, then!' the woman prompted. When he could drag his eyes from the sight of his wife's wide, blank stare, he saw that she was indicating a low bed along one wall. 'Quickest way to get you both warm again,' she insisted, struggling not to let her gaze drop below the level of her lord's waist.

The fisherwoman had known what she was doing on the beach. He had to assume she knew what she was about now. Meekly, he lay down, holding Maddy close to his own body, while the widow began to pile all manner of bedclothes on top of them.

'Rub her limbs if you can,' she ordered him. 'Chafe some life back into them, while I stoke up the fire.'

The woman bustled about, throwing precious fuel on to the fire until the flames roared up the chimney. He would have enough logs delivered to her home, he vowed, to see her through every winter, for as long as she lived.

'G...Ger?'

His heart leapt in his chest. Maddy was coming to her senses!

'Oh, sweetheart, I thought I'd lost you,' he said, framing her little face between his hands.

'You c...came b...back for me,' she shivered, her eyes drifting shut.

'No, Maddy, don't go to sleep!' Panic seized him as she went limp in his arms again.

'Sleep is good, now,' the widow reassured him, handing him a bowl of steaming broth. 'You drink this up. 'Twill get you warm on the inside, so you can keep her warm, and then, when she wakes up, you can feed some to her.'

Bowing once more to the woman's wisdom, he pushed himself up to a sitting position, with Maddy curled under the blankets against his hip. When he'd finished every last drop of the broth, he slid down beside her again. There was no question of leaving her. It had been bad enough that she had opened her eyes while the woman had been ministering to her, rather than him. When she next wakened, his must be the first face that she saw.

* * *

It was not until well into the night that Maddy murmured his name in her sleep. 'I'm here, love,' he breathed into her ear. 'You're safe now.'

Her eyes opened. 'You came back.' She grasped his hand and clung tightly to it. 'I was so scared when you left me.'

'I only went to get a boat.'

'I thought I was going to die,' she whimpered. 'Oh, Ger, I was in hell!'

Her wide eyes reflected her terror as she shuddered in his arms.

'You would not have gone to hell, Maddy,' he crooned. 'The angels would have carried you straight to heaven, for you are one of their own.'

She shook her head, her eyes luminous with anguish. 'Hell was believing you had left me, Ger. Thinking you must have slept with Eleanor, and weren't going to come back for me.'

'I did not lie with Lady Lacey, though she invited me to her bed.' He stiffened at the sudden realisation that she seemed to know all about Lady Lacey's attempts to seduce him. Had the bitch told her what she planned to do? Had Maddy spent all this time alone, worrying that he had strayed? And he had unwittingly reinforced her fears by his stupid decision not to contact her before she made some gesture of repentance regarding their last quarrel. Be damned to his pride. He needed to tell her what was in his heart. 'I love you,' he confessed. 'I could no sooner lie with another woman than I could cut off my right hand.'

'But…' she frowned '…you must have been tempted. She is so beautiful, while I am…' Her face puckered.

'How could you think I would be tempted by a tawdry encounter with a whore after tasting paradise in your arms? Don't you know yet that, from the first moment I saw you, I wanted you as I have wanted no other woman? Even when I thought you were just a kitchen maid, I wanted to take you to bed. And now you are my wife, I count myself the most fortunate man on earth.'

'But I'm so plain!' she wailed. 'You can't possibly!'

'You are exquisite,' he countered, running his hands over her face, sifting her ebony hair through his fingers.

She tried to push his hand away. 'My hair is full of mud,' she protested. Her hair was thick with it, her scalp prickly with sand. 'I must look a sight! And I smell of seaweed.'

'You look and smell just like a mermaid, plucked straight from the ocean,' he murmured, lifting the soiled strands to his face, and kissing them gratefully.

And he was suddenly aware that they were both naked beneath the mound of blankets. And that every soft contour of hers was pressed close against the hard masculine planes of his.

But she was too weak for that, yet! What was he thinking! Guiltily, he sprang from the bed, and went to the fire to spoon a ladle of broth into a bowl for her. He could feel her watching him as he strode about, naked in the firelight. He heard her sigh, and knew she felt the same need he did. But she was too frail even to sit up without his aid. And eating even the few mouthfuls he fed her quickly exhausted her.

When he saw her eyes growing heavy, he laid the bowl on the floor beside the bed, and climbed under the covers with her again.

'Rest, now, little love,' he murmured. 'I won't leave you. You're safe now.'

Though she felt a niggling worry that there was something very important she had to say to him, she was too tired to think what it was just then. It just felt too good to snuggle down next to him, and feel his arm go about her, and know that he was hers. He hadn't left her to die.

And he hadn't slept with her cousin.

And he thought she was beautiful, even with her hair full of mud.

But when she next woke, and found the bed next to her empty, panic flooded her, driving all reason from her mind.

'Ger!' she screamed, sitting up and staring wildly round the shadowy room. 'Where are you? Don't leave me! Come back!'

Almost immediately, the door crashed open, and he strode in, his face creased with concern. 'I'm here, my love. I only went outside to…' he broke off, looking discomfited. Though her heart was still pounding with alarm, she subsided against the banked-up pillows. Even the most ardent of lovers must relieve other needs occasionally. But did he have to go outside? Couldn't he have used a pot? Feeling thoroughly betrayed by his foray into modesty, she burst into noisy tears.

'Don't cry, my love. There's no need…I will never leave you.' Kneeling at her side, he grasped her face in both hands, kissing her tenderly on the lips whilst brushing the tears away with his thumbs.

'Did I dream it—' she hiccupped '—or did you really say you love me?'

'Oh, I love you, my little mermaid. Never doubt it.'

'I love you too, Ger.'

He smiled the smug smile of a man who has made a conquest of the woman he loves. 'I know.'

'Did I tell you?' She frowned. The earlier events of the night were somewhat hazy in her mind.

'You didn't need to. You nearly drowned, and the only thing you wanted to speak about when you first opened your eyes was whether I had succumbed to Lady Lacey's charms. No questions about the rebellion, or whether we have a new King, or if I had been injured, or slain four hundred rebels and been made an Earl in recognition of my services to the crown…'

'Oh! Did we? Have you?'

'Nay.' Chuckling, he climbed in under the covers with her, pulling her close under the crook of his arm, so that she could rest her head on his chest. He had put his shirt back on now, filthy as it was. It had dried out in front of the fire, where the fisherman's widow had draped it, and he had not wanted to venture outside without some covering. After his first panic on Maddy's behalf had subsided, he had begun to remember all sorts of other things. Caligula's welfare, for one. He didn't think the woman would have had much success trying to unsaddle, or rub down, such a temperamental animal, and the beast deserved taking care of. But the redoubtable Caligula had already taken care of his most pressing needs himself, eating about half the thatched roof of the pig pen, before discovering the widow's vegetable plot.

'I was afraid you might have gone back to the castle,' she admitted, 'before I had a chance to warn you how dangerous it was.'

'I've been a fool!' He sat up suddenly, his blood running cold at just how stupid he'd been. Carried away by discovering she loved him, he had forgotten all about the murderer who was prowling their lands. 'I take it, after this, you are finally willing to confess all you know?' Even though she had said she loved him, her reluctance to confide in him about the traitor in their midst still rankled.

Maddy sat up too, leaning against the rough wattle of the cottage wall, so that she could look her husband in the face. In spite of his reassuring words of love, she could see that her reticence had displeased him. From the beginning, he had insisted he wanted complete honesty between them. And thus far, she had not given it to him.

'I am sorry,' she said, pulling the covers up so that her breasts were modestly covered, 'that I have kept my suspicions to myself. But it was as well I did not speak about them before you left, for they were entirely in the wrong quarter. You see, I thought Lady Lacey was the one who had organised that ambush. Because I was not certain, and because she seemed to want to leave anyway, I just asked Captain Fritz to make sure she had no opportunity to harm you.'

It had been concern for his welfare that had prompted that intense conversation they'd had in the bailey just before he'd left! They had never been lovers at all!

'But, in the end,' Maddy was continuing, 'I think all she wanted to do was humiliate me, by proving any man would prefer her to me. Even that first time, I don't think she had thought it through. I don't think she realised just how dangerous those dogs were…'

'Dogs?'

'Yes. She sent me out to walk where she knew those dogs were exercised. Out of sheer spite. You see, she was in love with Lord Hugo, though I only discovered that later the same day you rescued me. I found them together, plotting to trick me into marrying him so that they could divide up my wealth between them.'

'That was why you were crying, when I found you in the garden?' He felt poleaxed when she nodded.

'Did you love him very much?' He knew it should not matter who she had loved before she met him. She had told him she loved him now, and he believed it. But her response came as an immense relief.

'Love him!' she shuddered. 'That snake? Even if I could have overlooked his plan to keep my cousin on as his mistress after marrying me, I could never have forgiven the casual way he broke her heart. He told her to her face there was no point in marrying her, because she had no money of her own. And that right after he had taken her up against a tree!'

He had discovered she was a virgin in their marriage bed, but he had always, he now realised to his shame, feared she was hiding a flirtatious nature behind a cloak of modesty. Every time he had doubted her, he had wronged her.

'So when the Queen spoke to me of this mysterious man who the King wished to honour for his loyalty with my lands, I saw him as the means to escape from their plots. So long as the man I married was not Lord Hugo, I did not care much who it was. At least he was being honest about only wanting my land. Although I still couldn't quite believe in the wealth everyone suddenly started talking about. I had lived in such poverty for so long…'

She sighed, shaking her head. 'I suppose any funds that should have come to me got waylaid by Lady Lacey, who was acting as my guardian. She so loved pretty clothes, and I did not care overmuch… I suppose she thought it hardly mattered whether I had things or not since I am so plain.'

Though she was trying to understand why her cousin had

wronged her time and time again, the topic was clearly still painful. Wanting to ease as much of her distress as he could, he said, 'After your father died, you were a ward of the crown, Maddy. Any revenues collected during that time would have gone straight into the King's coffers.'

'Oh,' she said, looking somewhat relieved. Then, blushing, 'I…I am sorry I got cold feet about the wedding, once I realised you were going to be my husband. You see, when you kissed me, I finally understood how Lord Hugo had managed to wield such power over Lady Lacey. It was bad enough thinking I was going to marry a man who only wanted my land, but fearing I might fall in love with you, and yield absolute power over my very soul—' She broke off, her little face creased in consternation.

But he understood perfectly. Love was a terrifying thing to feel, when you could not fully trust the object of your affection.

'I too was full of suspicions of you at the time, Maddy, my love. I didn't understand what game you were playing, why you seemed to blow hot and cold.'

She knelt up, and hugged him. 'I wasn't playing any game at all. But I thought you were. Oh, the atmosphere at court was poisonous, wasn't it? Nobody did anything without some ulterior motive. I was so desperate to get away…and then when the steward was killed, I began to think I would never escape Lord Hugo's plotting!'

It took him a moment to realise her mind had jumped from their frustrating time of betrothal, to the day before he had ridden out to oppose Lovell's rebellion.

'You think this Lord Hugo was behind that ambush?'

'No, not any more. Though at first I truly did fear that Lady Lacey might have been in secret communication with him. I thought she might have put one of her admirers up to it. But it wasn't them at all! It was John.'

'Ah.'

'You don't seem all that surprised.'

'Well, I always wondered if that little reception committee he planned for us was only defused by your show of affection for him.'

She shook her head in dismay. 'And you have not heard the worst of it, yet.' She told him all about her final confrontation with her murderous half-brother.

'You are carrying my child?' he said, when she had finished, laying his hand over her stomach.

'Yes,' she replied, 'at least...' Fear suddenly clouded her features. 'Do you think it is all right, I mean, after nearly drowning? Joan said first babies often slip.' She looked up at him with growing horror in her eyes. He did not know how to answer her. He knew so little of women's matters.

'Don't fret, my lady,' came a woman's voice from the door. 'Life is in God's hands,' the fisherman's widow continued, venturing slightly into the room when they both turned towards her. 'Nothing will part the babe from your womb until its appointed time. Some girls, who find themselves in the family way when they shouldn't be, try everything to get rid of a babe, and just cannot—even being kicked in the belly by their angry father won't dislodge it. While plenty of married ladies can't seem to get one to stick no matter how much they want a child. It's as I said. All life is in God's hands.'

'It should be!' Ger roared, suddenly springing from the bed. 'How dare that cur try to take your life, because he discovered you were with child? My child!' He rounded on her then. 'You should have told me first, Maddy! I had a right to know first!'

'But I didn't know myself,' she protested, quailing before his anger. 'I am so ignorant of these things. If Joan hadn't explained the significance of missing my courses, I probably still would not suspect...'

The sight of her quaking before his angry outburst smote him to the core. Immediately contrite, he knelt beside the bed, scooping her into his arms again. He didn't doubt her words, and would not, ever again. Why, he only had to remember the fiasco that was their wedding night for confirmation of what she had just confessed.

She'd had no woman to tell her any of the things she should have known, except that malicious cousin of hers.

'I am not angry with you, sweetheart, but with him. For subjecting you, and our unborn child, to such cruelty. I cannot overlook this, Maddy. He must pay for his crimes.'

When he made as if he would have got up, Maddy clung to him. 'No!' she cried. 'Don't leave me, Ger, not yet!'

Seeing her very real fear, he capitulated. 'Not yet, no, my love, but you know I must bring him to justice don't you? Though he is your brother.'

'I am not the angel you think me, Ger,' she replied miserably. 'I threatened to haunt him, and with what I thought was my dying breath, I prayed for vengeance.'

Hearing again the horror she had been through put paid to any thoughts of leaving her side. He only wanted to hold her, comfort her, and, yes, to feel the beat of her pulse in her veins that proclaimed she was alive, and his. He climbed back into the rude bed, holding her close until she stopped trembling, and then until he felt her relax against his side, and then until she fell asleep. And then he carried on holding her, because he simply could not bear to let her go.

But when Maddy woke, to a hut flooded with the full light of day, the space in bed beside her was cold.

'Ger?' She sat up, feeling a little anxious, but not prey to the terrifying panic that had assailed her last time she found herself alone. The fisherwoman looked up from the pot she had been stirring over the fire.

'He has just gone down to the shore, my lady, to arrange the discovery of your body. I'll fetch him to you.'

Her perplexity at these ambiguous words was augmented by anxiety when he finally returned. She could tell from the very way he held himself that something troubled him.

'What is it? What has happened?'

He glanced over his shoulder, and even as he did so, she heard the noise of approaching hoofbeats, the mingled shouts of men's voices, coming from the beach.

'There is no time to explain it now, but for once I must insist you obey me absolutely and without question. You must stay in here, out of sight, no matter what you hear. Do you understand?'

Tears filled her eyes at the abrupt tone of his voice, but she nodded mutely in acquiescence. When he turned and left without another word, she subsided against the wall, feeling very aggrieved that he should accuse her of the slightest tendency to disobey him. From the moment they had wed, she had done all in her power to be the best wife she could be!

It wasn't fair. He said he loved her, and then took that tone.

It really wasn't fair to insist she stay here, she repeated to herself a few moments later, wriggling uncomfortably. She needed to relieve herself, and there didn't seem to be a chamber pot within doors. He had gone out when he needed to, she reflected mutinously, crawling shakily out of the bed. She couldn't even ask the fisherman's widow where she should go, since she had darted out of the door behind Ger, clearly determined not to miss whatever it was that was about to take place.

Clutching a sheet round her to cover her nakedness, Maddy got out of bed and made her way shakily to the doorway. She was only going to go a very little way outside, just far enough to locate the midden. It was hardly an act of rebellion.

But even as she straightened from her task, the brisk sea breeze carried the sound of Captain Fritz's voice, then John's, to her ears.

And indignation at the way her brother had treated her pushed all else from her mind. Hitching up the trailing ends of the sheet so that she would not trip over them, and flinging them over her shoulder, toga style, she marched up the side of the sand dune to confront the man who had attempted to murder her child.

Chapter Nineteen

'Well,' that was John's voice, 'have you found them?'

Cresting the dune, she saw a small crowd gathering around two bundles of rags, lying side by side at the high tide mark. Caligula was standing stoically over one of the bundles, exactly as a warhorse would stand over its master should he fall in battle.

'Oh, my lady, my poor, poor lady!' Joan half-fell from her horse, but before she could get more than a couple of paces towards what she assumed were two bodies, Christophe caught her, and held her fast.

John dismounted, his whole body betraying his anxiety. She grimaced. He must have been really worried when he went to the jetty at low tide, intending to dispose of her corpse exactly as he had threatened, and found her gone!

'But it's only clothes!' she heard him exclaim, straightening up and looking about him wildly. 'Where are their bodies?'

'Well, mine is right here, John.'

Everyone whirled to where Sir Geraint had stepped out from his place of concealment, behind the dune next to Maddy's.

Though John turned rather pale, all he said was, 'Where is Maddy?'

'Not here!' Sir Geraint advanced on him, his features fraught with suppressed rage. 'The tide comes in very quickly along this shore. By the time I reached her, all I could see was the ends of her hair, beneath about three inches of water. She had been tied to one of the old jetty posts and left to drown.'

The entire assembly expressed shock, but it was Joan who reacted the most strongly. Tearing herself from Christophe's hold, she flew at John, her hands clawed into talons.

'She was with child! You knew she was with child! How could you—?'

But before she could give him away, John silenced her with a sharp slap to the face. She collapsed to the sand at his feet, staring up at him in mute horror.

'Calm yourself, Joan. Tears won't bring her back.'

But her words had been enough to create suspicion in the minds of all who had heard them. John found himself looking at a sea of hostile faces.

'Would you mind telling me why no search was made for us when we did not return last night?' Sir Geraint coldly asked Captain Fritz, who was looking from John to Joan, his hand on his sword hilt.

'John, sir. He said you and your lady wanted time on your own.'

'So you simply took your orders from him?'

'Yes, sir. Sorry, sir. It won't happen again.'

'You are correct. It won't happen again, because, John, I am banishing you from my lands. Take Joan, and…'

'Your lands?' John's face twisted with fury. 'Your only claim on these lands was through her!' He gesticulated at the heap of sodden rags. 'Now that she's gone, you're nothing! Nothing! I have more claim here than you! Every last man on these estates would rather see me in my father's chair than you and your band of cutthroats!'

'You think so? You believe your claim takes precedence over that of a royal warrant?'

'Aye! Your so-called King is nothing more than a rogue with a band of mercenaries at his back, stealing what rightfully belongs to the heir, just like you! When my father's last whelp died, all this should have come to me!' John smote himself on the breast.

'You could never inherit.' Sir Geraint spoke in calm, though stern tones. 'You realised that when you learned Maddy was pregnant.

Your father was never married to your mother, and you knew the legitimate line would take precedence over a bastard.'

'Yes, and if your spawn had ever seen the light of day, I would have watched it grow, and had my face ground into the dirt yet again!'

Joan wailed, her hands reaching out to him in supplication. 'How could you, John? She was your sister!'

He rounded on her, his eyes wild. 'It was for you, Joan, don't you see?' He gripped her by her shoulders, and yanked her to her feet. 'I had to avenge what the old lecher did to you. It was his fault you lost our babe…'

Maddy's heart turned over. No wonder Joan knew so much about women losing their babies. It must have happened to her. After the assault her own father had committed.

'But our lady Maddy had nothing to do with that! She was innocent!'

'I wanted to spare her!' His eyes were beseeching her to understand, while all around him, Woolton men and mercenaries alike were drawing their swords, his confession spurring each man to avenge his beloved lady mistress. Still he seemed to see nothing but Joan. 'But she was searching for her mother's jewels. I couldn't let her hurt you. I couldn't let anyone else hurt you.'

'You freely confess to the theft, as well as attempted murder?' Sir Geraint interjected.

As though finally realising he had condemned himself out of his own mouth, John looked about at the assembled company in panic. Pushing Joan away from him, he lifted his chin and cried, 'Yes, I stole some jewels from my father's strongbox. What of it? He stole everything I ever loved from me!'

Then, before anyone had a chance to react, he turned and ran down the beach, towards the mud flats shimmering in the early morning light.

'Hold!' Sir Geraint cried, when his men moved, as one, to pursue him. 'Those sands can swallow a man whole! Only he knows the safe path through!'

In the confusion that followed, Joan broke free from the crowd, and darted out after her lover. Christophe set out after her, bringing her to a halt by grasping her round the waist, and swinging her off her feet, before she had gone more than a few yards.

'John!' she screamed, struggling against her captor. But he did not slow down. Grimly, Sir Geraint took a bow from Captain Fritz, and nocked an arrow to the string.

Tears were streaming down Maddy's cheeks. Even after all he had done, she could not help weeping for his pain. Her full brothers had taunted him, treating him worse than any of the other servants. She knew how her father's indifference must have wounded him, for she had suffered that herself. She could imagine the agony of knowing another had taken his lover. And she had felt rage at the attempted injury to her own unborn child. To have experienced all this was bad enough. But to suffer so at the hands of his own family! No wonder he had lost his sanity, for 'a house divided against itself cannot stand.'

'No!' she screamed, as Sir Geraint let the arrow fly from the bow. 'He is my brother!' The only family she had left.

At the sound of her voice, John swerved, half-turning, and the arrow caught him in the shoulder. He dropped to his knees, his face bleaching with horror as he saw her, standing on top of the dunes, her hair, stiffened with mud, standing out wildly from her head, the ragged sheet wrapped round her like a shroud.

Uttering a cry of terror, he staggered to his feet and backed away, his hands held up as though to ward off an evil apparition. Too late, she remembered screaming that she would come back from the grave to haunt him. Those few seconds of distraction were all that it took for him to lose his path.

'Someone must help him!' Joan screamed, kicking and clawing at Christophe as John's feet sank in the mire.

But it was already too late. His struggles to free himself from the quicksand only made him sink more swiftly. He managed to utter one terrified howl as he disappeared beneath the rippling mud. One eddy swirled round the pool that had swallowed him, and then it stilled, leaving no trace behind.

Maddy sank to her knees, a feeling of guilt crushing her, as Joan let out a keening wail. She saw Christophe gather her into his arms, rocking her as though she was a child, while she wept.

'It's over now, Maddy.' She looked up, to see her husband standing over her. 'It was better this way. Justice has been done. He met the fate he planned for you and me.'

Hunkering down beside her, he wrapped her in his arms. She laid her head upon his chest, so broken she had not even the strength for tears.

'I am glad we didn't catch him. There would have been a trial,' he said. 'And he would have hanged for his crimes. Maybe Joan too.' He took a deep breath, and grated, 'But I am glad he didn't escape, either. If he had got away, he would have been an outlaw, living like an animal.' Gently, he added, 'I think he had suffered enough, don't you?'

'Oh, Ger,' she breathed, looking up into his stern face with dawning comprehension, 'I do love you so.'

Maddy suffered nightmares for weeks. She kept seeing John's face, in the moments when he had realised he was drowning, hearing his cry of terror as his source of air was choked off. And she relived the moments she had endured when the waves had broken over her own head. When she woke in panic, her arms and legs thrashing wildly in the bed, her husband's strong arms would close about her, he would stroke her hair, and tell her over and over again that he would never let any man hurt her ever again. And she clung to him, needing to feel the strength and heat of his body next to hers. And though she believed his words, and received comfort from them, something of that cold feeling of isolation persisted through the hours of daylight. Even when their bodies joined during lovemaking, she had the sense of being alone within her own skin.

Joan disappeared shortly after John's death, along with Christophe. Captain Fritz was furious, demanding that they raise a hue and cry to apprehend them.

Wearily, Maddy begged her husband to let them go.

'But they might have those jewels John stole!' he protested.

John had lied about that, to protect Joan, with his dying breath. But only she knew of that. 'Let her have them, then,' was Maddy's response. As far as she was concerned, they were cursed. If she hadn't made such a fuss about them, maybe none of the ensuing tragedy would have happened! If Joan had them, maybe they could undo the harm her desire to find them had caused her. Mayhap Joan could sell them, and use the capital to set up a business somewhere. Christophe might marry her, and give her children, and help her to forget her ill-fated association with the DelaBoys family.

At any rate, she knew she never wanted to set eyes on the woman again, for she had only pretended friendship in order to get information she could pass on to John.

Anyway, she had the fisherman's widow, Maggie, to take her place. She had come up to the castle that first night, unable to rest, she'd said, until she knew the mistress and her babe were being properly nursed. She turned out to be very knowledgeable about all manner of herbal remedies, and since Ger had already ordered a place should be reserved for her at the staff table each day, to compensate for the depredations Caligula had wrought on her vegetable plot, she soon became a permanent fixture at the castle.

Then Sir Geraint's mother arrived. Maddy had told him she was grateful he'd arranged for a female to keep her company during her confinement, but, in truth, she'd dreaded meeting such a formidable-sounding woman. She was everything Maddy was not—competent, shrewd, a good judge of character, and a blessing to her husband in every way.

By contrast, Maddy felt such a failure. She had tried so hard to be the kind of wife he seemed to want, but when her birth pangs began, she gave up the struggle. She needed Ger, and she was past caring who knew how weak she was. She asked for him, she pleaded for him, and finally she wept for him to come. Seeing how distressed she was becoming, Ger's mother relented, though Maggie and the other female attendants protested that the birthing chamber was no place for a man.

The summons was so unusual that, on receiving it, Sir Geraint feared the worst. Women often died in childbirth. He could not let Maddy face the fear of eternity alone!

He crashed into her chamber, his face wild and white, shooing her attendants aside like so many fluttering doves.

'She will do very well now,' Ger's mother observed, as she saw the relief on Maddy's face, the smile she managed through her pain when he came to her side. And there he stayed, holding her hand, mopping her brow, until the moment their son gave his first lusty cry.

'I'm sorry,' Maddy whispered, gazing down into her son's face. 'I should have been braver, but I need you so much—' She broke off, tears welling in her eyes. 'You are the best thing that ever happened to me.'

'We have both been fools,' Ger admitted, remembering all the suspicions that had made him so harsh with her when they had first married. ''Tis as well we have such a wise King, and that we are both such loyal and dutiful subjects, or we might never have come to this happiness.' He smiled, wiping a strand of hair from her sweat soaked brow.

'I agree,' she sighed, tearing her eyes from her baby for a while to gaze up in adoration at her husband. 'King Henry must be one of the wisest men in Christendom.'

'The wisest, mayhap, but not the happiest. For I am that man, when you smile at me with love unfettered in your eyes.'

The baby chose that moment to remind his parents, at the top of his lungs, that he was someone pretty important too. Breaking apart, they grinned down at the indignant little mite who was the fruit of their mutual love. Over her husband's shoulder, Maddy could see her mother-in-law beaming down at her newest little grandson. And remembered how the woman had supported her wishes, against all convention.

'We are a family,' Maddy gasped in wonder. 'A real family, at last.' And this new family surrounding her was founded on love, not on duty, no matter what her husband had said in jest. He had wanted her before he knew about her land, when he had thought she was just a serving maid. And she had wanted him, believing he worked in the kennels. When his love had been tested, he had not failed her. He had truly plucked her from the depths, and restored her to life.

'I rather think,' Sir Geraint observed with a rueful smile as his little son promptly took his wife's attention firmly away from him, 'that little chap is going to rule over us both.'

Maddy gazed down in adoration as her son's questing mouth finally closed over her nipple.

'Then we'd better name him Henry, hadn't we?'

'Are you sure?'

'Oh, yes,' she sighed, as her little boy latched on, and she felt her milk come down to give him sustenance.

And it dawned on her that that terrible feeling of loneliness had gone. Ger's mother had told her all about his brothers and their wives. She had already planned to invite as many of them as could spare time from their business pursuits for a prolonged visit, for little Henry's christening. And after that, there would be Christmas. The castle would be full of children then, for Henry had a batch of cousins. There would be mummers, and feasting, and such merriment as would be the talk of the neighbourhood for years to come.

'I have no doubt, my love,' she sighed with contentment. 'No more doubts at all.'

* * * * *

HISTORICAL

Novels coming in January 2008

THE DANGEROUS MR RYDER
Louise Allen

Jack Ryder, spy and adventurer, knows that escorting the haughty Grand Duchess of Maubourg to England will not be an easy task, but he believes he is more than capable of managing Her Serene Highness. However, he's not prepared for her beauty, her youth, or the way her sensual warmth shines through her cold façade...

AN IMPROPER ARISTOCRAT
Deb Marlowe

The Earl of Treyford, scandalous son of a disgraced mother, has no time for the pretty niceties of the *Ton*. He has come back to England to aid an ageing spinster facing an undefined danger – but Miss Latimer's thick eyelashes and long ebony hair, her mix of knowledge and innocence, arouse far more than his protective instincts...

THE NOVICE BRIDE
Carol Townend

As she is a novice, Lady Cecily of Fulford's knowledge of men is non-existent. But when tragic news bids her home immediately, her only means of escape from the convent is to offer herself to the enemy as a bride! With her fate now in the hands of her husband, Sir Adam Wymark, she battles to protect her family...

MILLS & BOON
Pure reading pleasure

HIST1207 HB

HISTORICAL

Another exciting novel
available this month is:

A COMPROMISED LADY
Elizabeth Rolls

Something had wrought a change in Thea Winslow

As a girl she had been bubbling over with mischief.
As a woman she seemed half lost in shadow. But Richard
Blakehurst couldn't miss the flash of connection between
them when his hand touched hers. It was as if he had
awakened something deep inside her.

Seeing Richard again brought back the taunting memory of
their dance at her come-out ball. She *must* tame her
wayward thoughts, because Thea doubted even her
considerable fortune could buy Richard's good opinion of
her if ever he learnt the truth…

MILLS & BOON
Pure reading pleasure

HIST1107 HB ACL